How often have I said to you that when you have
eliminated the impossible, whatever remains,
however improbable, must be the truth?
—Arthur Conan Doyle

Savannah Secrets

Savannah Secrets

Patterns of Deception

RUTH LOGAN HERNE

Guideposts

Danbury, Connecticut

Patterns
of Deception

Chapter One

"Whoa." Wyatt Waverly didn't just look surprised by Meredith Bellefontaine's request the first week of March. He looked dumbfounded. He got up, shut his office door with a solid *click*, and retook his seat before he said another word. "Payroll Inc. has hired you two to do what? Look for some kind of money leak that professional auditors couldn't find?"

"I know it sounds unlikely," Julia Foley said. Wyatt's aunt Julia had partnered with her old friend Meredith to reopen Meredith's late husband's detective agency. She motioned to Meredith. "Meredith and the CEO are old friends."

Meredith cut in quickly. "Not like *real* friends," she told Wyatt, but that only made the furrow between his brows go deeper. She took a breath and sat forward in the chair. "Ron and I knew Carolanne and her husband, Rusty, from the early days. Decades ago," she added in explanation.

"Russell Van Valken was called Rusty?" That seemed to surprise Wyatt even more.

"Back then, yes, but as the payroll corporation grew everyone called him Russ or Russell," she went on. "Anyway, we were all young together. Ron had left the police department to open the detective agency and Rusty saw that companies were outsourcing all kinds of things via technology, so he thought, *Why not payroll? Why not us? Why not now?*"

"He created a mega start-up before start-ups were a common buzzword," noted Wyatt.

Meredith nodded eagerly. "Yes, and that's just the kind of people they were. He and Carolanne both had degrees in accounting and business, but Rusty had coupled his with technology skills. He programmed his own software, so when he launched the company, it climbed the ladders of success solidly until it became the multibillion-dollar corporation you see now." She made a face, acknowledging Wyatt's expression of disbelief. "Look, I know it's weird that they came to us."

"Not weird," he said flatly. "Frankly unbelievable. And that's not an insult to you or my wonderful aunt," he assured them with a look of affection toward Julia. "Payroll Inc. can have the best of the best of anything. Why would they come to a newly formed agency that only has a year of experience? And that doesn't have a skill set for investigating computer or financial crime, if that's what's occurred?"

"Because Carolanne and I both lost our husbands within weeks of each other, and we bonded," Meredith said. "Not like best friends bonding but bonded by loss. And by the changes in our lives. We even"—she sighed softly and gripped the handle of her spring-floral quilted purse more tightly—"went to the same grief counselor for a while. When she approached me earlier today, I asked the same questions you just did." Meredith met Wyatt's gaze firmly. "But she told me they've had big auditing companies come in and snoop around, and they saw nothing wrong, but she has a couple of inside people who believe there could be a leak. They just can't find it. If it exists, she has to do everything in her power to track it down. She's afraid if she doesn't, she'll have the board micromanaging her every move."

"So if the professional auditors can't find it, how does she figure we might stand a chance?" asked Julia. "I have to agree with Wyatt, that doesn't make a lot of sense."

Wyatt raised a hand. "I'm not saying it doesn't make sense," he said, and when Julia looked surprised, he continued. "It seems odd, but the reason forensic auditing differs from traditional auditing is that we go further. We begin with the suspicion that something is wrong. In a general audit, if the company's numbers fall within one percent of the total worth, it's considered clean."

"Which means that a two billion-dollar company can hide twenty million and be listed as clean?" Meredith's voice fairly squeaked on the question. "Seriously?"

"Theoretically, yes. It's more complicated than that," Wyatt explained, "but that's how the numbers roll. The more layers a company has, like major university hospitals and medical insurance billing and corporations running a full stable of other corporations under one massive umbrella, the more opportunities for criminal activity. About the only way you find a needle in that very big financial haystack is if you have a whistleblower."

"I had no idea." Julia stared at him, then Meredith. "But that brings us right back to the question of why would Carolanne bring us in?"

"Because people talk to us," said Meredith.

Julia looked skeptical, but Wyatt lifted a brow of interest.

"We don't go at things the way other places do," Meredith went on. "Carolanne thinks that if we listen to what people are saying and ask the right questions, we might figure things out before the next major quarterly meeting."

"When is that scheduled?" asked Wyatt.

"The first week of April in Miami. It's always off-site so they can talk more freely. But here's why we need you, if you have some time and don't mind helping us." She smiled at him. "Carolanne is correct. Julia and I have the people skills. At our age we've learned the art of listening. We read people well. But if we say yes to this, I want a numbers person on board. A person who's willing to look beyond the obvious—because I honestly don't know what that would be in a financial corporate setting. Give me a small-time swindler or someone stepping out on their spouse, and I can follow the rabbit trail. But I don't think your aunt and I can say yes to this without expert backup. And that means you."

He frowned.

Then he folded his hands together and stayed quiet for what seemed like a long time. After slow beats of the clock and Meredith's heart, he leaned forward. "I'm overseeing two cases right now, but fortunately they're in the discovery phase and that leaves me a little time. Not a lot," he told them, "but I have to say I'm intrigued by the idea of someone skimming off of a major corporation like this, a corporation that makes money by simply channeling funds where they're supposed to go. If we find it, I want to be able to use it as one of our firm's credits. Is that agreeable to both of you?"

Julia didn't waste a moment. "Absolutely. Give credit where credit is due."

Meredith nodded. "Of course. But I'd like to keep your involvement quiet initially. I think Carolanne is right, that people might slip and say something in front of us that they wouldn't say if they know you're on the job."

"Agreed," he replied. "And while you two make friends with the folks inside the walls, I'll do some quiet digging on Payroll Inc. A company is only as strong as its weakest link, and if that weak link has access to financial controls, then it should show up somewhere. But not always," he reminded them. "It's a huge operation after all."

"So you're in?" Julia stood up.

"I'm in."

She hugged him fiercely. Then she took a step back. "And you're sure we're not imposing?"

"If you were, I'd have said so, Aunt J. Promise."

Their look of sweet affection tugged at Meredith's heart. Julia had helped her parents raise Wyatt, and he bore more resemblance to his aunt than his former absentee mother. It was there in his looks but also his devotion to giving a job 100 percent. His two girls called Julia Nana, and she treated them like her own.

"Thank you, Wyatt." Meredith extended her hand. "I'm grateful."

He took it, but he didn't just shake it. He folded her hand between both of his and smiled down at her. "Walk in there and be yourselves. Pretend to chat while you're listening. Act more than your age. Or stand in a corner looking utterly bored. Any one of those ruses will keep people talking around you if not at you or to you, because you'll be invisible. Like faded wallpaper. With ears."

Meredith wasn't sure she loved being compared to old wallcoverings, but it was sound advice. She nodded as he loosed her hand. "I like how you think. We'll keep you posted, all right?"

"I can't wait to hear what y'all glean. But Aunt J?"

Julia paused at the door. So did Meredith. They both turned back.

"Don't forget that you're dealing with a multibillion-dollar corporation. Even a tiny percentage of that is more money than most of us see in a lifetime. And plenty enough to kill someone over."

Julia's mouth dropped open.

So did Meredith's. She swallowed hard. "I hadn't really thought about it that way."

He met her eye to eye with a firm expression. "You can't think about it any other way," he said. "Gather what you can, but don't put yourselves in harm's way. It's only money, and it's never worth endangering yourself over. Understood?"

Julia dipped her chin. "Understood. And Wyatt, thank you for the help and the reminder. It's easy to see the people side of things but tough to realize what some folks will do for money."

"Tale as old as time," he said. "Love you."

"I love you too."

They walked outside and climbed into Meredith's car. Then Julia let out a breath. "We're really doing this? Looking into a major corporation like this? And what kind of fee do we charge a monster-sized company, Mere?"

Meredith told her the amount she'd proposed to Carolanne.

Julia's eyes went wide. "That's a year's salary on the bench." Julia had served as a judge in the juvenile courts for over a decade.

"Then clearly our judges are underpaid," Meredith retorted. "We're working hourly, but I said that was the base rate, and Carolanne didn't blink. Not once."

"I'm not accustomed to working with ultrarich people," Julia said as she snugged her seat belt into place. "We saw some in juvenile court, but it wasn't the norm by any means. Beau and I have been blessed abundantly, but when we start talking millions and billions, my money-meter goes on high alert."

Meredith's phone interrupted their conversation. She hit the Bluetooth connection and answered smoothly as she pulled out of the parking lot outside Wyatt's building. "Hi, this is Meredith."

"Meredith." Carolanne's voice came through the car speakers in just above a whisper. "Come quick. Someone has hacked into our computer system, and they may have taken over everything. And I mean everything!" It was impossible to miss the panic in Carolanne's voice. "Hurry. Please. I honestly don't know what to do right now, but I know I need help. Serious, serious help."

The phone went dead.

Meredith looked at Julia.

Julia pointed straight ahead. "Take that next left. It will get us around the traffic, and we can be there in a few minutes. If we can park nearby."

Meredith darted across two lanes of traffic and took the left before the light had time to fully change. "Are you thinking what I'm thinking?"

"That Wyatt is right and people will do anything for money?"

"Well, that and"—Meredith accelerated to merge then slipped into the exit-only lane about two thousand feet up the expressway—

"this might be the most exciting job we've gotten yet. I'm totally psyched. I'm not sure what that says about me," she said as she signaled the exit and took the curve. "But I know exactly what it says about Magnolia Investigations, my friend. We've arrived. Literally." She signaled right, made the turn, and then made another hard right into Payroll Inc.'s corporate parking lot. "And figuratively. Now let's go inside and see what in the world is going on."

Chapter Two

CLOWNS.

Laughing clowns at that.

Once the front desk manager had sent them to the proper elevator, Julia and Meredith took it to the fourth floor, got off, and were surrounded by clowns.

From every computer monitor, the image of raucously laughing clowns glowed in bright spectral colors, making the garish faces more disturbing than anything should ever need to be.

"Mrs. Bellefontaine? Judge Foley? I'm Mary Murphy, Mrs. Van Valken's assistant," said a youngish woman who met them as the elevator door silently closed behind them, stifling Meredith's urge to jump back on and escape.

She faced Julia and Mary Murphy. "I hate clowns."

Mary cringed. "My dad was a clown, and he would visit the pediatric units over at Savannah Memorial. He'd make balloon characters and do jokes, and the kids loved him. There was nothing the least bit scary about him. This, however, is nothing like that." She indicated the obnoxious screens with a hook of her thumb. "Ms. Van Valken's office is right here."

She opened a door. The moment Carolanne spotted them, she moved forward. She'd gotten over panic and had gone straight to angry. "We can't get rid of them," she snapped. She led them to a nearby wing of office cubicles. "The whole system has been taken over, and I'm standing here waiting for the ransom call to arrive. The very thought of paying out money to retake control of what's ours is downright infuriating."

"Ransom?" Meredith frowned.

"Like what's happened in some cities and hospitals?" countered Julia. "Where outside hackers won't release their hold on a computer system until they've received a big payout?"

"What else could it be?" hissed Carolanne. "Unfortunately, it looks like this is going to become the new norm for major businesses around the world. I think eventually it'll get written off as office expense, but I can't even begin to tell you how angry I am. Because I don't know how to fight this."

Neither did Meredith, and that was a disconcerting feeling when she'd been hired to do a job. The idea of total computer systems takeover hadn't entered into the conversation. "Can't you turn them off so we don't have to deal with crazy clowns taunting everyone?"

"IT is trying, but they said—"

Silence interrupted her.

Blessed silence.

And then, almost in unison, all the screens went back to business as usual, as if they hadn't just been jeering at everyone on Payroll Inc.'s corporate staff.

"They fixed it," breathed Carolanne. "Without me paying a penny."

"Not exactly."

The three women turned. A handsome, scholarly-looking man came toward them. He was medium height, with brown hair that could use a trim and black-rimmed glasses. He thrust his chin toward the bank of cubicles to their left.

"Mick." Carolanne's mouth dropped open as she faced the man. She scowled. "You did this?"

"I *found* this, and I'll take the agreed-upon payment," he said smoothly, before turning to Meredith and Julia. He stuck out a hand. "Mick Cavendish," he said, and then his next words made Meredith swallow hard. Real hard, because maybe they had just gotten in way over their heads. "I'm a corporate hacker for hire. I freelance for multiple corporations to help plug holes that may exist in their systems."

"Businesses hire you to do that?"

"All the time," he told them. "I'm not cheap, but I'm cheaper than the alternative, which is a systems takeover by outside influences who then demand a hefty ransom to remove their holds. At that point businesses and governments really have no choice but to pay it because these worms propagate within a program. I've just shown Ms. Van Valken how easy it is to get into her newly updated system. Fortunately for all of us here today, it was me and not them." He indicated the bank of windows for effect. "This time," he added. "Shall we meet in your office before I see the folks in IT about plugging this newest hole? Or after?"

Carolanne seemed to have recovered somewhat. "Go fix it. Or make them fix it, however you guys work it out. And then come back up here, but Mick, if you ever do that again, without warning me, I swear—"

He put his hands up, palms out. "I don't make promises I won't keep, and sometimes people need to have reality sprung on them for full effect. If I'd sent you a corporate memo about this flaw, would it have gotten your attention the same way? Or would you have argued about the amount I charge like you did the last time?" he finished.

"No, but it wouldn't have given me a near heart attack either," she retorted.

"But it didn't." The hacker softened his voice. "And it drove home the point of vulnerability, and that's exactly why I get paid for what I do. To find the holes software designers miss and plug them."

Carolanne sighed. Meredith wasn't sure if it was relief or that her adrenaline levels were dropping. "And you do it well. Go see IT, and I'll have a check waiting for you when you come back."

"Always a pleasure." He pivoted and strode toward the elevator but then took the stairs instead.

Meredith and Julia exchanged looks. "So he did this on purpose?" Meredith asked.

"Follow me." Carolanne led the way into her office and shut the door. "Yes. And before you think I'm crazy, he's not the first hacker from hirehackers.com to show us a gap in our systems. When you're channeling tens of millions of dollars weekly, the thought of people hacking into the system is a constant worry." She sat down and indicated the chairs across from her. "Most hacks are fairly mundane, but this one Mick just pulled off was major. His fee is a cool twenty grand, but twenty thousand dollars is far less than the million we'd be paying out if a dark hacker took advantage of that hole."

"It's like an insurance payment," noted Julia.

Carolanne nodded. "Exactly like that. Every time there's an update to the computer system, you run the risk that a design flaw will let a nefarious person in. Software updates happen all the time, so it's a constant struggle to keep ahead of the game, especially now that we're so big. No one would have cared twelve or fifteen years ago, when we were a midsize firm working Georgia payrolls, but now we're all over. We have code from all fifty states and everything has to be written according to state and federal standards, which means a lot of openings."

"Like a major hotel with thousands of doors and keycards."

Carolanne's expression said she appreciated Julia's analogy. "Yes. Only instead of entrance into comfy hotel rooms, they gain entrance into financial systems that go through every imaginable money-moving or storing entity in the US. And that gets a little dicey."

"So this money leak you came to us about. Could this be a hacker?" asked Meredith. "Someone who's gotten into the system from outside?"

"IT doesn't see anything like that, but that doesn't mean it's not there," Carolanne said. "They think it's someone inside, maybe two working together...."

"Making it much harder to find," noted Julia.

Carolanne agreed. "Collusion is every accountant's nightmare. Honestly, ladies, I want the two of you on board because if it is an inside job, I want to know the why of the matter. Not because stealing is ever right, but because we're a company that deals with real people, every day. Families, working paycheck to paycheck. I'm not oblivious to that. If someone has fallen on hard times, I want to take that into consideration." She chuckled. "By the way, I can't believe how quickly you made it over here. You must have been nearby."

Meredith wasn't about to mention their meeting with Wyatt. She shrugged. "An appointment on this side of town."

"Lovely." Carolanne opened an appointment book on her desk. "I want to kick this off with a cozy get-together dinner at my place on Friday evening at seven."

"A dinner party?" That wasn't exactly how most investigations got started in Meredith's long years of experience with investigations.

"I find the best way to get folks to open up is to create a social environment that invites them to do just that. Not black tie, but not informal either. I'll have all of our main players there. Then if you could come to the annual Corporate Challenge Celebration on Saturday, that will give you an opportunity to meet a solid percentage of our workers. We host a stellar outdoor gathering for all employees and their families, honoring those who take part in the 5K, 10K, and half marathon races that raise money for the Homes for Veterans initiative. Russell didn't serve, but his father did, and his brother too, so we hold veterans' issues close to the heart."

"So Friday night at seven, and when does the celebration begin on Saturday?"

"Eleven," said Carolanne. "That way most of the racers have already come through the chutes. It will give you a chance to mingle with our everyday workers without being obvious about it. We use the veranda at White Stag so that everyone feels like a champion that day. Anyone who can run a half marathon is a champion in my book," she added.

White Stag Country Club on Skidaway Island was a serious expenditure, and this was prime wedding season in Savannah, but Meredith held back her thoughts on that. If Carolanne wanted to spend tens of thousands of dollars to treat her employees to a sumptuous midday banquet, she should be lauded, not criticized. But was it driven by kindness? Or to give a glimpse of how the other side lived? The side that didn't live paycheck to paycheck.

"It sounds lovely." Julia smiled as she stood. "My father served as well, and supporting our veterans is dear to my heart too."

"Wonderful. I'm sure you'll enjoy the celebration."

Meredith stood too. "We'll see you on Friday night then."

"Perfect." Carolanne came around the desk. She reached for the door, but before she opened it, she lowered her voice. "I know you both understand the need for absolute discretion in this matter."

"We do," Meredith said.

"Other than pertinent members of the board, I'll keep this between us," she went on in a very soft voice. "They'll be pleased to have private investigators on board and doubly pleased by the discreet manner in which things are handled. Corporate stockholders don't like whispers of scandal."

"Nor do we," Meredith assured her.

The assistant crossed the narrow hallway and motioned right. "I'll be happy to see you out."

"Thank you." Julia smiled at her, then paused. "Miss Murphy, you look familiar to me."

The young woman acknowledged that as they walked. "Mrs. Murphy, although I'm a single mom now. Please, call me Mary. Judge, you presided over a case against my cousin Daniel about eight years ago. He was a reckless kid back then, and you gave him a stern talking-to that helped turn his life around. I testified that Daniel had come to our house before his gang buddies robbed the old man who ran the liquor store off of Franklin. I've never forgotten your kindness to a boy who'd lost his mother, then his way. You even pulled strings to get him a job, and he's been on the straight and narrow ever since. My family is very grateful for your wisdom and intervention. His name is Daniel Jack Wick."

"He went on to get a degree in welding from Savannah Tech," Julia replied. "He sends me a Christmas card every year with an update."

"The entire family remembers your efforts and judgment. You engineered a turnaround for him and that made all the difference." Mary smiled at them. "It's nice to be able to thank you in person, and nice to meet you both."

She stepped back as the elevator door slid open.

"And a pleasure to meet you as well," said Meredith. When the doors closed she kept her voice light as she faced Julia. "I'm so excited about this party," she told her best friend, who knew that she never got excited about parties. "We'll have a wonderful time. I'm going to have to check my closet to see what to wear, which probably means what fits after a long, chilly winter."

She smiled brightly at Julia, then rolled her eyes up and to the left.

Julia got the message quickly and answered in kind. "I only wish Beau were able to come, but he'd be bored out of his mind. He's more at home in a rowboat than hobnobbing with corporate types. I, however, will be in my glory."

It wasn't until they got into Meredith's car and pulled away that Meredith wiped the pretend smile off her face. "Cameras in the elevators?"

"Can't be too careful, I suppose," said Julia. "But I need coffee and I need it now. I'm trying to wrap my head around paid hackers and those nefarious clown faces. And the thought of wasting all that money on a luncheon when you could just give it to the veterans' outreach you claim to be supporting doesn't make a lick of sense. But I grew up in middle-class circumstances, so maybe the ways of the rich and famous are just that much different."

Meredith had grown up with money, but the whole thing didn't quite compute with her either. "So we listen and learn, my friend. Because we'll be speaking two distinct languages on this case. Rich. And not rich." She merged back onto the expressway. "Did you jot down that hacker's name? I want to know more about hackers for hire. That's an odd-duck business if ever there was one."

"I did. I can't even imagine deciphering code, whatever that is," said Julia as she began a search on her phone. "Or even how it all works, so the idea of unraveling it and looking for holes doesn't compute." She searched for options on her small screen. "And yes, that pun was firmly intended. I've pulled up his name on the hackers for hire website and if the words 'now out of the deep web and into the light of everyday tech management' don't strike fear within you, then you're either way more knowledgeable or trusting than I am. But how can we go see him if we're being discreet?" she asked. Then she grinned. "We pretend we're looking to hire someone."

"Bingo." Meredith gave her a thumbs-up. "We play like we're examining our need for hacker insurance."

"Because we're two ladies of a certain age, floundering our way through a new business."

"And we take Wyatt's advice—"

"And act a touch befuddled—"

"Very Columbo and Sherlock friendly!" declared Meredith with a grin. "Because who better to be pilfering from the till than the one person trusted and hired to hack into the systems? He wouldn't be the first person who caves while floating in a mammoth sea of temptation, and he's clever enough to hide it. How do we contact him?"

"Just did." Julia set her phone on her lap. "Two things," she added as Meredith navigated across the clogged lanes of afternoon traffic, worse now that tourist season was ramping up. "I still need coffee, and I mean really good coffee."

"Well, there's no getting near the office, it seems." Meredith frowned as she came around a bend and spotted the congestion. "I forgot they've closed roads to do a film shoot here today, which means our access to our beloved and very frugal coffee service is blocked."

Julia's phone pinged a text. "'Can see you now. Home office. R U available?'"

"It seems we are," said Meredith as she made a face toward the nonmoving traffic tie-up ahead of them. "Ask him if there's a coffee shop nearby."

"He says there is and he can meet us there in twenty. And it gets us out of this traffic jam if you make a right in point three seconds."

"On it!" She swung a hard and rather quick right-hand turn back toward the expressway. "Right now I'm glad that Ron set the driving tone for the business years ago. Drive with purpose, and there's no purpose in traffic jams. Get out and get going."

"He was a get-going kind of guy, and that's a must for a business like this," agreed Julia. "For any business, actually. The GPS will guide us the rest of the way while I prepare to be befuddled." Julia pulled down the visor, and Meredith heard the resignation in her voice a few seconds later. "You might have to be befuddled enough for both of us, Mere. I seem to look more like a dried prune when I attempt befuddled. Now if you want embittered…" Julia shot Meredith a look at the next traffic light that made Meredith laugh out loud.

"You do the bad-cop face real well," Meredith told her. "So you pull that out as needed, I'll act a little overwhelmed, and let's see if Mick Cavendish is as clever at reading people as he is reading code. My vote would be no."

Chapter Three

MICK CAVENDISH WAS A COOL cucumber in every way.

Meredith wasn't sure if she liked that.

She took a seat at a corner table offering a triangulated view of the coffee shop. Ron used to do that all the time. He said it was the cop in him, and she realized there was no better view of what was going on around you than that corner perspective with a wall at your back. Large, lightly tinted windows compromised the safety of the wall because their booth nestled against a windowed corner, but she chose the seat deliberately, and maybe so that Mick Cavendish wouldn't lay claim to it.

Julia brought their coffees back.

Mick followed when his order came up. A super-hot caramel macchiato with an extra shot of espresso in a to-go cup with a lid. The extra shot brought her appreciation of him up a notch.

He took a seat to her right. Julia was on her left, and when he took his seat, he didn't target one specific lady. He included both of them as he opened the conversation. "You ladies have opened a detective agency?"

"Quite the lark for two retirees," Meredith replied brightly. "And it's not like we lack experience." She leaned in as she spoke. "My husband ran the agency for years—"

"Making you Watson to his Sherlock, I presume?"

Meredith couldn't deny it. She held a most sympathetic view of Sherlock Holmes's assistant. "A role I played well, but the driver's seat affords a very different view, which is exactly why having Julia on hand is crucial." She aimed a grateful look Julia's way. "Being a retired judge brings a different outlook to our work, but let me be frank, Mr. Cavendish." She aimed an imploring look his way. "Neither one of us is as technologically savvy as we'd like to be. Today's modern devices"—she held up her phone—"make everything pathetically easy. My late husband called these PhD devices, and it wasn't a compliment. It was an acronym for 'push here, dummy.' There's a grain of truth in that because everything is so user-friendly that we don't have to really think about what we do. After seeing your demonstration at Payroll Inc. today, we realized we could be vulnerable. The last thing I want to do is risk everything my husband worked for by leaving gaping holes for hackers to get through."

"You're wise to think that way," Mick began, but then he folded his hands. "Do you ladies work with sensitive information?"

Julia took that question. "At times, yes."

"Medical, financial, political?"

"Depending on the case, any one of the three could apply. Plus others of a more sensitive nature."

Meredith was anticipating his answer, so when he didn't offer to take them on as clients, he surprised her and gained another point or two on her estimation scale.

"Here's the thing," he said. "Do you need a hacker scan? Probably not, not if you've equipped your computers with the latest protective software."

"They have that protection," Meredith assured him. "It's dreadful what can slip into a system these days, so I always keep protections in place, but Payroll Inc. has mammoth fire screens." She used the inaccurate term intentionally. "And even with all of that, you got into theirs," she went on. "Our vulnerability became apparent the moment I realized you were able to infiltrate a big company like Payroll Inc., so Julia and I wanted to meet with you right away. Thank you for accommodating us, Mr. Cavendish."

"Mick, please, and it was my pleasure, but let me explain why you probably don't need to hire me," he continued in a frank but kind voice. "You're not a huge corporation."

"So we're not big enough to be on anyone's radar," said Julia.

"Right. Now if someone was avidly looking at a case you were working on and you left a footprint on your computer, could they see it? Possibly, but that's a targeted approach. In Payroll Inc.'s case, their nationwide sprawl means the attack doesn't have to be specific. If they have a general hole in any of their software applications, a hacker could gain access—"

"As in your display today," noted Julia.

"Exactly." He nodded in her direction. "I played up the hack deliberately to show Carolanne the susceptibility, but if you picture their channels being like a map of the national interstate system, and all the roads leading to an interstate, and then the two-lane roads leading to the smaller expressways, that's what Payroll Inc.'s profile looks like to a hacker. All those roads, with all of those intersections, and every one leads to cash." He shrugged. "I'd love to take your money, scan your work, and pronounce you clean, but it's probably unnecessary. I mean, I'll do it if you don't mind throwing away a few thousand dollars."

Meredith didn't have to pretend to choke on her coffee. "That much for a small company like ours?"

"You pay for the skill level and the time. I'm highly skilled." He said that without boasting. "And time is money."

"So you think we're all right?" Meredith breathed a full sigh of relief. "I can't tell you how absolutely good it is to hear that, Mick."

"But help me out here," said Julia. "You found what could have turned out to be a massive hole in Carolanne's corporate system. How does a mistake like that happen? Why wouldn't a hole like that be discovered?"

"Because it's actually far smaller than you're thinking," he said. "A blip in code, allowing backdoor access."

"So tell me, Mick." Julia gripped her coffee cup with both hands. "Could or would someone leave a back door entrance open purposely?"

"Of course. That's how the rebels found the flaw in the Death Star." When Julia's eyes lit up at the Star Wars reference, he grinned. "The simple answer is yes, they could, which is why people like me stay in business. Sometimes it's a simple logistical mistake of data intersects, like how a pull-off on the highway gives us extra ways to get on and off. But it could be deliberate. I run interference on several corporations each time they do a software update."

"I had no idea." Meredith didn't have to fake her wonder. "How do you know all this? How did you learn to do this? Tech school?"

"Self-taught," he said. "Back then we had dark web groups that would pinpoint possible problems, almost like game-playing. We built on one another's skills."

"And are they all like you? Upright and honest?" Julia asked directly, and when Mick cringed, Meredith knew the answer.

"No. That's part of why it's fun and more relaxing to be on the upside of the web. The dark web earns its name in multiple ways, but it's also been helpful to polish my skills. Now I only go back as needed. In a game like this, there is no reason to tempt fate or stir the pot."

"You lie low."

"Exactly. So, ladies." He glanced at his watch. "This has been a pleasure, but duty calls."

"Another business to hack?"

He grinned as he stood. "A two o'clock feeding for a very particular young lady. My wife has the evening shift at St. Joe's and that means I'm on a very different and much-appreciated duty tonight. Dad duty."

"Oh, that's wonderful." Meredith gave him a genuine smile now. "You go take care of that precious baby, and we'll get on with our day. I'm afraid we've let the excitement of your clown takeover muddle the original plans somewhat."

He paused. Eyed them both. Then he gave them a two-finger salute to the forehead. "I'm pretty sure that nothing you've done today is the least bit muddled, ladies, but I'm also glad to do my part. Rusty Van Valken was a friend of my father's and one of the people who inspired me to look deeper than everyone else. To look beyond what others see and gaze into the unseen. It was a lesson that made me financially comfortable at a fairly young age. And if there's anything else I can do for you"—he slid his chair back under the table, a gentlemanly thing to do—"don't hesitate to ask."

"We won't." Julia raised her cup in his direction. "Thank you. We appreciate your honesty."

"My pleasure."

He made a beeline toward the door, but just after he exited and turned left in front of the plateglass window, he withdrew his phone from his jacket pocket. He stared down.

And then his face changed.

Gone was the easygoing demeanor. Whatever Mick Cavendish saw on that phone drew his brows in and down. He didn't remain still for long, but long enough for him to use his right thumb to send some kind of message before he shoved through the door.

And then, chin down, he spun around and strode off in the opposite direction down the sidewalk.

Was he lying about going home to baby duty?

Or had someone waylaid him?

"Do you find that odd?" asked Julia softly.

Meredith nodded. "Very," she replied. "Can you still see him?" She spoke softly, barely moving her lips.

"Yes, he's just crossing the intersection. And—" Julia's eyebrows lifted slightly. "He's meeting someone. A woman. She's young and her hand movements suggest that she's unhappy. Well dressed. Almost too well."

"Welcome to March on the streets of Savannah," replied Meredith. "The parade of spring fashions begins the minute we hit seventy degrees." She batted her eyes to make her point. "We Southern girls like to put on the dog the moment we ditch the coats. Handshake or a hug?"

"Neither, and from this angle, she looks put out and he seems frustrated. He handed her something. Something small. Now he's coming back this way, the direction he was going when he left here."

"So what was his message?" Meredith tapped a finger to the polished tabletop while she watched him pass the coffee shop on the opposite side of the street. "Why did she call him out? And how did she know he was here? Did she follow him?"

Julia turned back to Meredith. "I don't know, but it was a different man getting into that car. He didn't just look upset, Meredith. He looked scared."

Chapter Four

MEREDITH AND JULIA GOT BACK to the office just in time to hear Maggie Lu King offering instruction to Carmen Lopez, their spunky assistant. The scent of something wonderful drifted from the recently updated kitchen at the rear of the agency's remodeled house on Whitaker Street. They hadn't gone all-in on the kitchen update, but new sterling-toned cabinets beneath a silver-grained white solid surface countertop brightened the room. The beveled edges gave the countertop the look of a much pricier option while staying budget-friendly, and the wrought-iron-look pendant lights over the island updated the old lighting that had been compromised in last year's fire.

"There are some who prefer their jambalaya without shellfish," said Maggie Lu in her soft, cultured drawl. "But I've had folks come quite undone by this combination, and I think it's one of those recipes that can become a family favorite."

"You gals made jambalaya?" Julia's excitement made Meredith smile as they hurried down the hall. "We never got to lunch, though we did manage coffee as we met with a new VIP—"

In Julia-speak, VIP meant *very interesting person*.

"But nothing akin to food, because you know I can't interview folks with food in my teeth. It's simply unsavory."

"Our Carmen has mastered a true Southern masterpiece. She's cooking for the shelter next week and wanted to make a real Southern dish," declared Maggie Lu. "Jambalaya today. And maybe pecan-topped sweet potato pie tomorrow. I hear it's one of your son's favorites," she said to Meredith. "Smart boy."

Meredith lifted both brows. "It is, and he just happens to be coming to town this weekend while the university is on spring break. What an amazing coincidence."

"Perfect timing," noted Julia. She winked from behind Carmen's back. "Although no great dessert should be offered as a new recipe without undergoing rigorous taste testing by the official house committee, correct? So you might want to make two pies, Carmen. Right now, I'd love to try that jambalaya. If it's up for taste testing?"

Carmen laughed. "It is, *mis amigas*," she told them. "And you two can stop with the winking and thinking and raising those eyebrows. If there's time to make the pie, it will be a nice thing to do for a friend."

"Still trying to make up for clonking him the first time you met?" asked Meredith as she kicked off her shoes. Chase had surprised Carmen the year before, and she'd whacked him with a rolling pin before discovering it was Meredith's son walking down the hall. Fortunately Chase's quick reaction time deflected the blow.

"Totally his fault for creeping into the house," declared Carmen. "The pie will be my way of saying congratulations," she went on. "While some folks have been buying their way into fancy colleges, four of Emory's hardworking students are heading to Switzerland. They're finalists in a contest that invites students to explore ideas to end poverty in small communities. Their proposal won the attention of the international judging team."

"And Chase was one of their advisors," noted Meredith.

"Exactly." Carmen set a hot pad on the island then placed the pot of jambalaya on the pad. "I just thought it was cool that these young adults came up with an idea to make a difference. And I knew it meant a lot to him that they finaled."

It sure did. He and two other professors had been the sounding board for the competitors' proposals.

"Buying your way into an institution of higher learning isn't a new thing, of course," noted Maggie Lu. She sipped a glass of sweet tea and sighed softly. "It's been done as long as there's been money and universities, but folks were more genteel about it back in the day by doin' legacy gifts. I've heard they'd give a hundred thousand for a library fund, or two million for a building and then they'd ask, by the way, can my child be part of this year's freshman class? What smart administrator would say no to that?" She looked at Meredith. "What a great example these Emory students are to tackle an antipoverty project like this. On top of their schoolwork," she added. "Because Emory isn't a place that cuts slack."

"True words," said Julia. She joined the conversation, but her gaze never strayed from the steaming dish of seasoned rice, veggies, meat, and shrimp.

"Having Chase back home for a few days will be nice," added Meredith. "He's always loved spring. Not because of the weather, but because it brings all kinds of people out and he likes to study people. Carter is the business-minded son. Chase studies personalities. They're as different as night and day." Meredith moved to where she could smell the fragrance from the soup pot. "Carter's kids are playing soccer right now, so maybe we can get to one of their games while Chase is here. The greening of the fountains is scheduled for Friday, which means parking and traffic will be back to tourist-season levels." Savannah took great pride in celebrating warming trends with a strong nod toward St. Patrick's Day celebrations throughout the month, and tinting fountain water kelly green was one of the first big gatherings.

"That means allowing more time to get anywhere away from here," added Julia as she withdrew a stack of four dishes. "Can we try this?" she asked as she set the dishes down. "Not too much, because it's late, but the smell—" She leaned forward and breathed deeply. "Intoxicating."

"Of course." Carmen settled the big spoon alongside the broad saucepan. "I was able to dig up some of that background information you all needed. Copies are on your desks, and you'll find some very interesting information on a key person with proximity and possible motive, if being broke, abandoned, and having a sick mother is considered a motive."

"Money is a temptation," noted Maggie Lu as she took a small serving of the Cajun dish. "Not just for those pulling themselves up from poverty, but also for those perched on the top. Why is enough never enough for some folks?"

"An age-old question," Julia replied. She sank onto a barstool along the edge of the broad island and gazed happily at her steaming bowl. "If I go for a second helping, stop me, please. Remind me we're meeting Rebecca for supper at the diner in three hours, and it would be foolish to stuff myself now."

"This is amazing." Meredith savored the combination of flavors on her tongue and waved her fork in Carmen's direction. "Honestly, Carmen, I've never had better."

She was pretty sure that Carmen blushed slightly, but her honey-toned skin made a nice cover.

"And I promise we won't touch tomorrow's pie until after you've had a chance to surprise Chase with it," added Julia as she finished her dish of deliciousness. "After that, all bets are off. Unless you have time to make two."

"I will hide the pie," Carmen warned her mentor. "It will poof! *Desaparecer!*" She waved a spoon like a magician's wand then shifted her attention to Meredith, "Of course, I'm not trying to contest your wonderful sweet potato pie. This was just something I saw online and it sounded amazing." She eyed Julia's hand reaching for the big spoon. "Um, Julia, didn't you just say you're eating at the diner in a few hours?"

"We are." Julia sighed and slid off the stool. "I need to get those backgrounds read, so you're right. But if you could put some in a storage container for Beau, I'll take it along to the diner later. He'll love it when he gets back from his trip."

"How about I drop it off later?" Carmen suggested. "I'm picking up Harmony for a romp in the park with the weather so nice, and then some ice cream by the water. It's the perfect night for it, unlike our first ice cream adventure, which melted in seconds. I learned a valuable kid lesson that day." She swiped a cloth across the counter-top. "I'm going to hang out here until six thirty rather than drive all the way back to my apartment then chase all the way back here to pick her up an hour later. If that's all right?"

"It's absolutely fine, you know that," Meredith said as Julia moved up the hall. "And thank you for the jambalaya. It almost makes me hope we never get so busy that you can't fire the stove up now and again. Maggie Lu, are you walking to the diner or do you want to wait and ride over with me?"

"On a day such as this a walk is essential, and as long as my health allows, these feet will take me where I need to go," declared Maggie Lu. "I've got a sweet great-grandbaby, and whatever I can do to stay healthy for little Jake, I'm doing."

"And that, dear friend, is a fine perspective." Meredith smiled at her friend. Maggie Lu had seen decades of hardship, then times of goodness as a local schoolteacher. She brought a world of wisdom wherever she went, including Magnolia Investigations, which was aptly named in honor of her. That great-grandson would be blessed to have her around for a long time.

"I came straight over here after my morning session at the library," Maggie Lu added as she reached for a lightweight sweater with pearl-like buttons, vintage and old-school, total Maggie Lu. "There was a ruckus there, let me tell you, because someone got into the library system and marked all the borrowed items as 'returned on time.'"

"Seriously?" asked Meredith.

"Oh, I'm quite serious," Maggie Lu returned in a firm teacher's voice. "Even books that were just taken out yesterday morning were marked returned. They will have to physically track each book, and no one has time to do that with shortened staff at every branch, so I told them I'd do the book tracking at Carnegie tomorrow, even though I wasn't scheduled to volunteer. It's a pickle, and if they got into the system once, they can get in again. Why would someone try to wreck a system that's already struggling? The last thing we want them to do is close branches, especially in a walking community like this one."

"Walking sure beats trying to find parking," agreed Meredith, but the timing amazed her, that someone had hacked the library system at the same time she was looking into computer hacks and possible misappropriated funds for Carolanne. "I wonder how prevalent this has become?" she mused.

"It's everywhere," said Carmen as she finished washing the bowls. "My credit card was hacked over the winter, but the bank caught it so all I had to do was activate my new card and then change five auto-payments, which, by the way, was a pain for two of them. So that's not fun. But you know how someone tapped into that big safety network two years ago? The one that was supposed to protect all of us?"

"I remember," said Meredith.

"Whoever did it got away with mega information. Then there was the ginormous medical insurance hack and then another one when they got into email servers. For most of us, our stuff is out there and there's not much we can do about it until our number comes up."

"So it's that easy?" That seemed so wrong to Meredith, because it shouldn't be easy, should it?

"I don't think it's easy at all," Carmen said. "But if you've got a hacker mindset, and you're all right studying miles of code for a break, or emailing people and hoping they'll click on your innocent-looking link, and using back-door access to grab on to their computer, well, then you've got the chance at a major payout because all of that information is now at your fingertips to use. Or sell."

"Even with protections in place."

"For some people, firewalls and virus killers are just the kind of challenge they love," Carmen replied as they moved out of the kitchen. "It's like modern-day piracy, only no one has to walk a plank. It's a power play with no loss of life."

She was right.

Carmen was young enough to have been raised in the digital age. She hadn't had to adapt. She'd been surrounded by it for the last twenty-five years, unlike Julia and Meredith. "So there's never enough real protection?" Meredith asked.

Carmen shrugged. "The privacy you knew is becoming a thing of the past," she said, "but that's not such a huge deal to people my age. Now, money is different." Her serious expression underscored her words. "Leave my bank accounts alone. But we don't care if you know our dating status, our likes. So that's different, because communication is different, but what I don't like is that people can know where I am. To me, that's a downer. If it's a good person, who cares?" she went on. "But if it's random stalker guy, I don't want him to zero in on my location. Maybe you shouldn't always tag stuff with 'checked into Leopold's for ice cream' or 'stopped at historic museum,' but if you turn off geographic settings to make yourself unfindable, you can't order a Lyft or an Uber, so it's another trade-off."

So much information, free for the taking.

"I still pay with cash," said Maggie Lu as they neared the front entrance. "But then I get nervous walking around with money in my purse, so I don't know if there's any right or wrong way anymore. Except to be kind and good and honest. There is never a thing wrong with that. And on that note, ladies…" She smiled at them as she secured an old-fashioned hat into place. "I shall see you soon. Have a blessed rest of the afternoon."

Carmen reached out and hugged Maggie Lu. "Thank you for sharing that recipe with me. It meant a lot."

"It was a joy to share in your kindness toward people, and if the crew at the homeless shelter likes it, now that's a wonderful thing." With typical purpose, Maggie Lu walked out the door and down the steps to the sun-filled sidewalk below. She crossed the street to the shaded park and headed east, toward the Downhome Diner, her daughter Charlene's business, while Carmen crossed over to her desk in the reception area.

Julia—*bless her!*—had brewed a half pot of fresh coffee.

Meredith filled her mug and took it into her office. She'd go over Carmen's notes about notable Payroll Inc. employees so that when she strolled into that Friday night party she'd be ready.

Right until she heard the scream that sounded like someone was facing imminent danger. And that someone was Julia.

Chapter Five

"A SNAKE!" JULIA SHRIEKED FROM her perch on the middle of her refurbished desk. "Right there! On my Aubusson!"

Julia was correct. There, in the middle of her very pretty rug, and blending in quite nicely, lay a coiled copperhead, head up, ready to strike. It had its beady little eyes trained on Meredith's best friend, and Meredith was 100 percent powerless to do anything because she hated snakes even more than she hated clowns. Especially poisonous snakes.

Julia, standing on top of the desk, was well out of reach, so safe for the moment.

"What on earth?" Carmen slid to a stop next to Meredith.

When the snake opened its jaw, Meredith was pretty sure that an old-fashioned Southern belle fainting was about to occur.

Hers.

"I'll be right back." Carmen raced down the hall, and the echo of her footsteps seemed to extend well beyond where she could have made a phone call for help from either her cell phone or the company landline. When she came back with a pair of Meredith's high-end hot dog tongs in her hand, Meredith was pretty sure her heart stopped beating. "You can't mean to catch it with those. Stop. Now. It's not worth the risk, Carmen, we can call for help, we can—"

Carmen didn't pause for conversation. She slipped into the room and said, "Meredith, get the front door." Then in a move that would have done a TV wildlife adventure show proud, she snagged the neck of that reptile like a pro. With the long body wriggling and jiggling to get free, Meredith cringed back, then hurried to the front door. She drew it open and flattened herself against the wall. A shiver traveled at light speed from her toes straight to the tiniest hair follicles on her head. She hurried to the pretty front steps as soon as the coast was clear and stared, amazed, as Carmen marched that elongated varmint across the road and into the park. And when she set it down in a thatch of small bushes and leaves, Meredith's mouth dropped open.

"Did you really just release a poisonous snake into the park right before the greening of the fountain when thousands of people are going to be trekking from square to square, kicking off the annual St. Patrick's Day month of festivities?"

Carmen had the nerve to look totally unaffected. "I think this is where you congratulate me, thank me, and offer a reward for using nothing more than my wits and hot dog tongs to dispatch our little friend."

"No friend to me," grumped Julia now that she was off the desk. "And what if there are more? What if we've become a viper's nest?"

"Not a viper," replied Carmen as she went to the kitchen. Julia and Meredith trailed after her, and she put those tongs—snake tongs!—into the dishwasher.

Meredith let out a squeak. "You can't possibly think we're going to use those again, can you? After they've touched a poisonous snake? Throw them away and order another pair online ASAP. That's an office expense I can get behind."

Carmen gave them both a look, rolled her eyes, and closed the dishwasher with the tongs firmly inside. "It wasn't poisonous."

"It was." Meredith had seen enough copperheads in her life— *well, four*—to know what they looked like, and she'd even kept a picture of one in her kitchen so the boys would never mistake one as they were growing up. Georgia rattlers had never been a problem in their area, but copperheads were more independent, and they weren't nearly as fearful of people as some other poisonous snakes were.

Carmen shook her head. "Corn snake," she said. "Depending on the coloring, they can look a lot alike, but this wasn't a copperhead. It was a corn snake."

"Are you sure?"

She nodded. "Harmony and I visited the Georgia Reptile Society over the winter, after they came to her school. They like kids to grow up understanding the creatures around them, and they had a whole session on look-alike snakes and how to tell them apart. That guy's markings didn't go all the way to the floor," she explained, but Julia jumped in.

"My rug. There was a snake on my rug. In my office. By my feet. And I had my shoes off."

Carmen winced in sympathy, but she smiled too. "I know it's creepy, and it's my fault. I propped the front door open to bring in some of that nice fresh air earlier, and it probably warmed itself on the concrete stairs and just slipped right in. I never even gave it a thought, Julia."

"Well, who would?" Julia grabbed a hoodie from the hall tree and pulled it on. "You're sure it wasn't poisonous?"

"One hundred percent."

"And that we don't have a nest in the lower level that's going to take over the house?" pressed Meredith. "I've heard of that happening."

"I'm sure it was just the combination of circumstances and my timing. I wanted fresh air, and that little guy wanted to be inside. From now on, I'll only open the windows—the ones with screens. I promise." Carmen crossed her heart.

"You saved me." Julia reached out and hugged Carmen. "It doesn't matter that you let him in, it only matters that you took your life into your hands to get him out and save my life."

"*¡Por favor!*" Carmen lifted both brows. "Nonpoisonous, friendly little creature, and fairly young, judging by the size. What do you do if you get a genuine nasty snake over at your house?" she asked. "That close to the water, you've got an even bigger selection, right?"

"I call Beau." Julia's tone left no doubt about her course of action. "Or if he's not around, I hide until he is. I will defend both actions because I've survived over sixty years as a Georgia woman so far. And intend to make it for many more."

"Well if you ever want company while you're hiding indoors, call me," Carmen told her.

"Or me," said Meredith. She turned toward Carmen. "Are you going to think I'm too much of a princess if I throw those tongs away?"

Carmen didn't have to say anything. Her expression said enough. Meredith sighed. "All right. I'll leave them to get washed, but let's make sure we at least use the high-heat setting. All right?"

"I concur." The office phone rang. Carmen hurried up front.

Julia met Meredith's gaze. "Are you really going to leave them in there to be washed?"

A part of Meredith wanted to cross the room, yank the dishwasher open, grab those tongs, and throw them away, but the thought of what her forebears endured to help settle the swamplands of the South kept her right where she was. "I am. If a young woman like Carmen can take charge and run her life so ably, an experienced woman like myself should do no less."

"Agreed." Julia linked her arm through Meredith's as they moved back toward their offices. "Although if another look-alike manages to come through that door"—she indicated the beautiful wooden front door with a thrust of her chin—"or any other, I'm back on my desk. Just so you know."

Meredith might approve washing the tongs, but she couldn't disagree with Julia. A coiled snake, ready to strike?

Reason enough to stand on a desk, right there.

***

"I am so ready for real food," Julia announced about ninety minutes later. "I'm glad we're walking to the diner because it's about the only exercise I'm getting today, other than desk-climbing."

"What did you think of the information Carmen got for us?" asked Meredith as they went down Whitaker Street. The fresh new leaves had all the youthful nuance of spring, and the air smelled of hope. "I've forgotten how intimidating a board of directors can be."

"There are a lot of powerful names on that list," noted Julia. "But unlike some directors, they seem to be really invested in the firm's success. They're not just figureheads. But I sensed some unrest in a few of those published comments." Carmen's research had uncovered a few short interviews with Payroll Inc. overseers both before and after Russ's death, and the difference in opinions was notable.

They'd reached the Downhome Diner. They were a few minutes early for supper with Maggie Lu and Rebecca Thompson, one of the librarians at their local branch of the Live Oak Library System. Charlene Jackson, Maggie Lu's daughter, spotted them from the kitchen and waved, then she joined them once they chose a table as far from the door as they could get. Fewer interruptions that way. "I've got just a moment," she told them, "but Mama wanted you to know that she's on her way. She got sidetracked by Eugenia Olson's little Caraway."

"A grandchild?" asked Meredith.

"A potbellied pig that might as well be a grandbaby, for all the spoiling that goes on," said Charlene. "Myself, being a cook, I'm more inclined to *dine* on pork, not make it a pet, but Mrs. Olson is quite in love with her little critter. Ah, there's Mama now. I'm dashing back to the kitchen," she added quickly. Charlene did everything quickly. She was an action-minded person, but then you had to be to run a busy diner. "Hey, Mama."

"My girlie." Maggie Lu's smile said more than the sweet words. She gave Charlene a quick hug then moved their way at her more measured pace.

"This must have been the afternoon for animal adventures," Julia said when Maggie Lu slipped into the hard-bottomed seat on the aisle side of the table. Maggie Lu often remarked that soft seats and aging hips weren't meant to be an item, so they always made sure there was a firm seat waiting for her. "You had a run-in with a pig. Ours was a snake."

"And that's the way of springtime, isn't it?" said Maggie Lu as if Julia's words weren't really a surprise. "The good Lord's creatures start feeling like themselves again, warming up, stretching toward the sun, looking for adventure. Or in Caraway the pig's case, misadventure that resulted in some rooting up of priceless hostas in Beatrice Enterline's yard."

"There's no such thing as a priceless hosta," noted Meredith. "I've got dozens. I like them well enough, particularly in the shade, but there's nothing that amazing about them. Is there?"

"The lady in question would beg to differ," replied Maggie Lu as Rebecca came through the diner door. "Hers being of a new hybridized sort that can supposedly withstand even the hottest of Georgia summers and was just now firmly taking root after a long, cold winter."

"Sounds like the Queen Bee to me," muttered Julia, using the nickname they'd come up with for Beatrice. Beatrice had her good qualities, but a pretentious nature obscured them too often. "In her defense, I wouldn't be happy if someone's critter took to digging up my yard either, so I'll cut her some slack. I could give her a cutting of my hosta if she'd like." She unfolded her napkin and put it in her lap. "Was hers damaged completely?"

"Well, let's say the leaves provided Ms. Caraway with a healthy salad-based lunch and the roots may have been considered dessert. Eugenia Olson loves this little pig, but I'm afraid that the pig realizes her owner isn't as spry as she once was and is bent on creating havoc. Very much like a toddler who realizes Grandma can't keep up the pace."

"Oh dear." Meredith frowned, because Eugenia was eccentric but a dear woman in many ways. "Can Caraway be fenced?"

"Could be, for certain." Maggie Lu arched one smooth brow as Rebecca joined them. "But being as kindhearted and besotted as she is with this creature, I don't think Eugenia has a notion of penning her anytime soon. She'll have to, of course, once Beatrice files a complaint."

Meredith frowned. "A complaint? With whom?"

"Savannah's finest."

Julia's mouth dropped open as her brows shot up. "She's calling the police on a pet pig?"

"A rather small one, at that, but yes. She claims that's what responsible neighbors do to keep things in check. Eugenia told me she's doing it for spite. When I asked her why Beatrice would be spiteful, Eugenia said it had to do with something that happened long, long ago between their families. Her family's moved on, but some of the Enterlines still hold a grudge, and Eugenia said that Jubal Early Jones is still one of their targets."

"Jubal? Really?" Jubal and his elderly aunt Miss Dicey Oglethorpe had been part of an earlier case involving River View, Miss Dicey's family estate. Julia smiled up at Justine as she stopped by their table to take their drink orders. "Hold that thought," she told Maggie Lu then faced the waitress who'd grown to know them quite well the past nine months. "Justine, I am on the verge of possible starvation, so if you could bring me the Cajun shrimp with cheesy grits special and a side salad, I would be most grateful. And my usual drink, of course."

"Diet Dr Pepper, coming up." Justine smiled at her. "Do the rest of you want a moment?"

Rebecca held up a finger. "In the interest of my friend's hunger, I'm the last one in and I'm ready, so let's save you a trip." She, Maggie

Lu, and Meredith all ordered, and when Justine hurried away, Meredith turned the conversation back around quickly.

"What has Jubal got to do with Beatrice? He lives over by Julia and is the sweetest old thing. He wasn't thrilled that Miss Dicey was leaving the Oglethorpe home to a music society, but he does stand to inherit the furnishings, so there's that. And I heard the music society is rethinking everything because they're not sure if they can handle the renovations that River View requires, so it's a conundrum right now. They don't want Miss Dicey to leave it to them just to be sold, but they're between a rock and a hard place if they accept it."

"His mama and old Mr. Enterline got into some sort of thing back in the war—" began Rebecca.

"Which war?" Julia asked.

"World War II," Rebecca said.

"That war has been over for seventy-five years, and the families are still at odds?" asked Meredith. She didn't hide her exasperation. "I can quote you chapter and verse that tell the evils of grudge-holding. And why would anyone bother Miss Dicey?" Laodicea Oglethorpe was over a hundred years old. "A sweet piano teacher with a flair for fashion."

Rebecca almost choked on her water. When she stopped sputtering, she leaned forward and held their collective attention by lowering her voice to just above a whisper. "That sweet little old lady helped bring down Hitler, Mussolini, and the Japanese Empire," she told them. She seemed to enjoy Julia's and Meredith's surprised reactions. "Miss Dicey was a codebreaker."

"A what?" Julia's brows lifted again but not quite so high this time. "You mean like the book that came out? About the women who broke codes for the military?"

"I mean exactly that. Miss Dicey and eleven other ladies who'd gone to Charleston College with her were codebreakers during the war. And absolutely no one knew anything about it, because they were sworn to secrecy and then not given one bit of credit for the work they did, work that helped save lives and end the war," declared Rebecca. "It's been one of the best-kept secrets around."

"Why would something so amazing be kept secret?" wondered Meredith.

It was Maggie Lu that answered. "Codebreakers were told that despite the war's ending, there could still be people targeting them if their identities became known. They were advised to keep their silence and maintain the integrity of a covert operation in case it needed to be used again."

"Which made it very convenient for J. Edgar Hoover to take all the credit," fumed Rebecca.

"I read that," said Julia as Justine dropped off a round of drinks. "But I had no idea Miss Dicey was involved."

"The woman was a puzzle solver," stated Rebecca frankly. "It came as naturally to her as did playing the piano. My husband is still incensed that she's never been given the acknowledgments she so richly deserves. Most of her coworkers have passed on, but here she is, tucked away in a home for the aged where no one knows or appreciates what she was able to do. If you ask her about it, she doesn't say much, because in her mind she's still under the instruction to keep it all hushed up. My Kelvin calls her the original hacker, and he's not wrong."

Julia and Meredith exchanged looks. "I wouldn't have thought of that, but I see the similarities now that you bring it up, Rebecca,"

Meredith said. "How deciphering code for the military is like running code for computers."

"Simply a different kind of puzzle," said Maggie Lu as Justine settled a tray onto the adjacent table. "Some just have a knack for enigmas. I think folks who make it big in the computer world have a different eye for that sort of thing. Like Miss Dicey in the war."

The thought of that sweet old woman's talents and gifts going unrecognized put a burr beneath Meredith's collar. Why wouldn't the men in power give credit where credit was due back then?

For the same reason people stole credit now. Their own selfish purposes.

Julia tapped Meredith's arm. "I want to go see her," she said. "I know she's old, but if she's got insight into puzzle-breaking or decoding, I'd like to hear it. If it doesn't help us currently, it could help us at another time."

"I think that's a great idea," Meredith agreed.

"I'd have Jubal come along or meet you there," Rebecca advised as she cut her salad into bite-sized pieces. "Miss Dicey is still sharp, but there's a lot of old detail involved, and Jubal knows the stories. He kept notes back in the day. I know this because he tried to get someone to publish them and got rejected. He was at a booklovers conference a dozen years back and we got to talking and he told me about his manuscript and his aunt's history. That's how I found out about it. Of course it was Kelvin who probed deeper."

Rebecca's husband was affectionately referred to as "the Voice of Savannah." He narrated river cruises during the visitor season, and his resonant voice was a favorite draw for river and history enthusiasts. "And let me just thank y'all for including me tonight because now that it's March, the river cruise season will be on the increase for the next seven months and I'll be an evening widow for the duration."

"Much like my Beau and the fishing season," Julia agreed. "But you know, after over forty years of being together, we're all right giving each other a little space in retirement. Just as long as it's not too much space."

"I concur."

Meredith couldn't concur. She and Ron never had a chance to retire. He was taken so quickly that she never had a chance to really say goodbye, much less relax into that no-work phase. Ron probably wouldn't have retired easily, anyway. He was a born worker. Also a puzzle solver. She'd learned so much from him.

Maggie Lu set her soft hand on Meredith's arm. "Retirement is different for you and me," she said softly. "On the one hand that's a sadness, but on the other it's a door flung open for us to shine our light on others." She got a twinkle in her eye. "The book of Titus tells us older women to train up the younger ones. We're the ones with the time to do it."

Such wonderful words of wisdom. Meredith smiled at Maggie Lu. "Different, but still all right."

"Absolutely all right."

"Maggie Lu, you never remarried." Rebecca didn't say it in a prying manner. More like a simple observation.

"Oh, I thought about it now and again," Maggie Lu said as she smoothed the folds of her napkin on her lap. "But the good Lord had given me two beautiful children. Wonderful young folks, a true blessing, my Jacob and Charlene, and I used to say to myself, 'Magnolia?'" She arched her left brow. "'What if you go fallin' in love with someone who turns out to be not what you thought? What if he turns nasty? What if he's not fatherly loving on your children? What is your first task, woman?'" She shrugged and sipped her lemon water. "To those children, of course. Two gifts from God who already had enough to contend with, things being what they were back then. So, no." She faced Rebecca. "I decided I would take the time and opportunities God gave me and use them for my children."

"Sacrificial love." Rebecca reached over and hugged Maggie Lu. "You are such a blessing to so many, Maggie Lu." And when Maggie Lu demurred, Rebecca raised her hands. "You are. To your children. Charlene, doing such a fine job here, and Jacob, who made the ultimate sacrifice in Iraq." She reached over and covered Maggie Lu's hand with hers. "And not to mention the hundreds of children you taught at Spencer Elementary. Our whole community is blessed to have you here."

"Oh, now."

Rebecca's praise made Maggie Lu uncomfortable. She didn't like the limelight, but Rebecca was correct. Maggie Lu had set an amazing example for so many others.

"So, shall we go see Miss Dicey tomorrow? If Jubal's available?" Julia asked.

Meredith nodded. "Yes. Because who better than an old code-breaker to give us insight into a codebreaker's mindset?"

"My thoughts exactly." Julia hurried outside, called Jubal, and returned. "He's happy to talk with us and her, so tomorrow morning, ten o'clock, after her physical therapy."

A hundred and one years old and still doing physical therapy...

Meredith just found one more thing to love about this elderly woman.

Chapter Six

NOWHERE TO RUN. NOWHERE TO HIDE.

Dicey Oglethorpe slipped the tersely written note into her leather bag as if it was of little importance.

The missive's very presence seemed to sully the satchel, even though the bag was lightly scarred after four years of hard-fought education in Charleston and a stint in the nation's capital.

A dream come true.

That's what Aleah Oglethorpe had called this chance for her oldest daughter, and it was. The chance to leave Savannah and garner a Bachelor of Science degree. The chance to become something other than a Southern gem in search of a good match. The opportunity to serve her country by deciphering enemy code.

Now the dream was a nightmare. Her nightmare. There was nothing she could do to alleviate the threat or the foreboding, except stay silent. Hide. Disappear.

She didn't clutch the bag to her side. That would indicate fear, and Dicey didn't cotton to fear, even when it threatened to consume her.

She stuck out her chin and headed for the bus stop that would take her back to the hastily built women's quarters. The codebreakers had been dismissed and would now begin their march toward new lives.

Or death.

There was no way to know which it would be.

Her palm grew damp along the bag's wooden handle.

Her mama had given her that bag when she'd come away from River View. Oh, Mama knew her girl, all right. Aleah might play the part of a traditional Southern belle as well as any Hollywood actress, but she understood the hunger in a smart heart to go further. See more. Do more. Learn more. And although Aleah had never been allowed to explore farther than Savannah's shores, she'd quietly encouraged her daughter's quest for knowledge.

That was because she'd never considered the consequences of a smart girl, a heinous war, and the recruitment of a keen mind.

She hadn't sent Dicey off to die as retribution for her government designation, but if the note Dicey held in her bag meant something, death was a possibility. One she didn't intend to have happen.

She got off the bus and hurried toward her second-floor apartment. Usually she'd exchange greetings with others. Or smile at groups of soldiers and sailors who always seemed to be nearby. *Those courageous young fellows had provided many a quick meal and conversation with the girls tucked here in northern Virginia. If nothing else, it gave the girls someone to write to. Keeping spirits high on the front lines might be just as important as breaking Japanese code.*

As Dicey rounded the bend of the stairway to the second-floor rooms, Theresa Becket was coming down the other side. She didn't say a word, but when she spotted Dicey, she spun around and followed her right back up the stairs to their shared rooms.

Dicey let them both in.

She shut the door snugly. Locked it. Then she turned back to Theresa. And when Theresa withdrew a similar-looking note, done on lined yellow paper, just like Dicey's, Dicey knew she wasn't alone.

Whoever was threatening them hadn't limited his or her intimidation to Dicey. Theresa's expression said she'd been threatened too. Now the question was, who was threatening them and what could they do about it?

Chapter Seven

MEREDITH SPOTTED JUBAL EARLY JONES coming their way from the assisted living center's bank of elevators the next morning. He was pushing Miss Dicey in a wheelchair, and the little woman sat quite prim and proper, in keeping with her Oglethorpe heritage.

"Miss Dicey." Meredith bent low and offered her hand.

Miss Dicey drew her brows down. "Now, that's very pleasant of you, Mrs. Bellefontaine, but it is still cold and flu season down here and I'm resisting all the human contact I can. With no insult intended," she added firmly.

"And none taken." Meredith took a seat opposite Miss Dicey. Julia settled into the seat next to Meredith, and after Jubal set the brake on the wheelchair, he took a seat on Miss Dicey's right. Meredith withdrew her notepad. "Is it all right if I take notes, Miss Dicey?"

The elderly woman hesitated before bestowing permission. "It is, if you will promise full discretion and secrecy. This is government policy we're talking about. I know some women have written books about codebreaking, but"—she hunched forward slightly—"you never know who might be listening. These days especially. They've got listening and talking things all over the place now, just like in one of those sci-fi movies. I hear they're recording everything we say." She lowered her voice to a whisper. "Just in case."

"We will keep this in the utmost confidence," Meredith assured her. "We talked to Jubal last evening."

Miss Dicey nodded.

"He told us about your group back in World War II and how amazing you women were at breaking code."

"It's all about seeing things different, you know," Miss Dicey explained. "We see things as we expect to see them, but in order to break code you need to see things from a different perspective. You need to study letter combinations, the most common couplings, and the most common endings. Series of three letters, or four. It's not unlike a word scramble in the Sunday paper. Some are just better than others at scrambles."

"They are," agreed Julia. "I have no patience for them, but my husband is quite amazing at putting them right."

"But what happened after the war?" asked Meredith. She hated to press, but Miss Dicey tired quickly and Meredith didn't want to lose this opportunity. "Jubal said you were threatened."

Miss Dicey cringed.

This patriotic woman cringed at the thought of those old threats, and that made Meredith angry. "Can you tell us about that, Miss Dicey? It must have been dreadfully hard for you."

Miss Dicey tugged a lace shawl more firmly around her shoulders. She looked left, then right, then sighed. "Jubal knows most of it. I told him a while back, when I was thinking the worst was over. No one can possibly be seeking retribution seventy-five years later. Can they?"

"One would hope not," Julia said. "Retribution for what, Miss Dicey?"

"For talking."

She motioned to Jubal, and he withdrew three faded pages of old steno paper and handed them to Meredith. They all contained the same warning.

You will maintain your military vow of silence and secrecy once home. Talk of your service will be viewed as an act of treason and will be treated accordingly. Be silent. Or you will be silenced. Take heed.

Once she'd read them, she shared them with Julia.

"We all got a note," Miss Dicey whispered, chin down. "As each of us from Charleston was released from duty, we were slipped a note warning us not to speak about what we'd done."

"These aren't just notes," said Julia. "They're threats."

Miss Dicey acknowledged that with a nod.

"What did you think when you received this?" asked Meredith.

"I thought it was downright cheeky but also believable because there were so many things going on in an underhanded fashion back then. Government secrets, government spies, people who were power hungry and money hungry. We'd already been advised not to talk about our roles, but this was like sealing the deal. To make sure we understood the repercussions of talking."

Meredith and Julia examined the notes, then Julia faced Miss Dicey. "May I keep these to copy them?"

"You won't lose them, will you?" The aged woman seemed downright scared that they might misplace the threatening missives.

"No, of course not. I'll get them straight back to Jubal. Jubal, you said you wrote a manuscript about all of this?"

He tapped a small accordion-style portfolio on his lap. "All right here."

"May I borrow that too?" asked Julia. "To read?"

Jubal looked cautious then nodded. "Yes, but I don't want Miss Dicey in any danger, you know."

"You think there could still be danger about this?" Meredith asked. That was about the furthest thought from her mind. Seventy-five years was a very long time.

Miss Dicey frowned. "Three of my Charleston coworkers died within a few years of our dismissal. It's not normal for young women in the prime of life to just die, is it?"

Meredith shook her head. "That is unusual."

"One never rightly knows about these things, do they?" said Miss Dicey, as if searching for reasons that had evaded her for so long. "Was it a temporary threat that kept a crew of women silent so that men in power could have their day, or were those early deaths a result of these threats? How is one to know?"

"And no one went to the police?"

She shook her head. "We were all going our own way. Most simply went on with their lives, but when we lost Ginny, then Theresa, then Pansy, I won't pretend I wasn't shaken to the core. These were my friends. My colleagues. When I heard that Pansy's death did not happen as reported, that she likely took her own life, it crushed my spirit because I should have helped her. Talked with her. I knew how sensitive she was, and how caring, but I was too timid to reach out. I stayed quiet, like the good Southern woman I was brought up to be."

Sorrow laced her words.

She was disappointed in herself, in her choices.

Meredith hitched herself a little closer. "Now, Miss Dicey," she said in a gentle, comforting tone. "Here's what I think. You worked hard to crack code, you graduated magna cum laude, and you helped at USO functions. You have nothing to be ashamed of, and I'm sorry that loose threats left such a grievous effect on your life."

"That's just it." Miss Dicey gripped one hand with the other, clinging, like a small child. "I don't think they were loose threats, but I never had the strength to find out. I should have," she finished in a whisper as one lonely tear worked its way down her cheek.

"There, there." Jubal patted his aunt's arm gently. He turned toward Julia and Meredith. "That might be enough for today, ladies."

"I agree." Julia stood and accepted the manuscript from Jubal. "Jubal, I'll get this back to you once we've read through it, and Miss Dicey, I want to thank you for seeing us today. It's an absolute pleasure to see you again."

Miss Dicey's hands still gripped one another. Then, with concerted effort, she relaxed them and settled them in her lap. "I'd like to know," she said in a more normal tone. "Whatever you find out, I'd like to know. I can tell you more about coding, about patterns, all the things that we learned, but in the end, I want to know why someone threatened a group of women willing to work hard for their country. Although I expect it's too late now."

"We'll see." Meredith spoke firmly. She'd helped Ron with the historical side of several cases, and she knew that sometimes the key to the past helped shed light on the future. "We will absolutely keep you informed. And thank you for that information about letter patterns. I've never really thought of things that way."

"You're welcome."

Jubal wheeled her back up the hall, and when they went around the corner, Julia turned to Meredith. "I know we don't have time to solve this for her—"

"We don't," Meredith agreed.

"But I want to, so we simply must fit it in," Julia insisted. "To think she's lived this long beneath that shadow—"

"And too refined to confront the situation."

"The threat of being silenced *is* daunting," Julia said as they moved toward the door.

"It is. I don't know that I would have pursued it."

Julia rolled her eyes, and Meredith conceded. "All right, I would have done something. But it might not have been the smart move, and I think sometimes we have to make the smart move when facing the unknown."

"Shall we order in and read up on this before Carolanne's dinner tonight?"

"Let's. And we can have Carmen run a check on the women who died young."

Julia put the manuscript onto the back seat and slipped into the car. "Let's go."

Chapter Eight

Julia paused by Meredith's office on her way home a few hours later. "There are way too many coincidences to make me think those early deaths are unrelated," she stated firmly. "Three good friends, Ginny, Theresa, and Pansy. All gone within a couple of years. Natural causes, tragic accident, and suicide." She ticked off her fingers. "What's the likelihood of that?"

"Odd things do happen, but I don't disagree." Meredith had been highlighting pertinent pages of her copy. "There's no way law enforcement would see any connection when no one had the courage to point out the women's relationship. Or question the deaths." She worked her jaw as she considered the place, stage, and time, then sighed. "That enforced silence put an effective lid on things, didn't it?"

She propped her elbows on the polished top of Ron's old desk and folded her hands. "And yet murder is a drastic means of silencing someone who's done nothing more than talk about a group endeavor. And those notes." She indicated her copies of the notes they'd borrowed from Jubal. "They don't seem military enough to me."

"Unstructured," said Julia.

Meredith nodded. "That, and they seem almost personal. As if the person making the threat has some sort of connection to the women we don't see."

"If it's not military-based, it makes no sense to threaten these women," said Julia. "So was someone trying to sound regimented and failed?"

"Perhaps," said Meredith. "They used steno paper—"

"Unusual now, but available everywhere then, and most likely a standard issue in military offices. Now that I've read Jubal's pages, I'll mull things over. But right now I'm going home to dress up for this dinner party."

"Do you want to come to my house and we'll drive to the island together?" asked Meredith. "That'll give us time to talk afterward. We can table one problem while we investigate another."

"Exactly my thoughts." Julia moved toward the back door where her car was parked. "I'll come back around six thirty, all right?"

"I'll be wearing my pearls," Meredith answered. Her mother's pearls were a running assessment on any event. It was either pearl-worthy or not. Tonight's fancy dinner party with the upper echelon of Payroll Inc. was definitely a pearl-wearing event.

***

Meredith did not wear her pearls.

She decided to have a slightly different strategy this evening, and when Julia arrived looking positively elegant, she knew she'd done the right thing. "I'm happily playing the wallflower tonight while you play the hothouse orchid," she told Julia when Julia alighted from her car.

When Julia looked at Meredith's plainer attire, she grinned approval. "You aren't afraid to do whatever needs to be done, my friend, and I love that about you." She climbed into the passenger seat, and while Meredith drove, she studied an online list of board members and execs from Payroll Inc. Twenty minutes later Meredith drove around the last curve on Wilmington Island Road and was stopped as she put her signal on to turn into the Van Valkens' long drive.

A middle-aged man wearing a valet suit jacket waved a flashlight their way. When she rolled down her window, he indicated the drive. "There's valet parking at the house, ma'am. With rain coming we didn't want folks parking themselves."

It was a thoughtful way of letting folks know what to expect when they got to the grandiose manor. She thanked him and proceeded up the driveway.

Although a fairly recent build, the Van Valken mansion was Old Southern pretty, modeled in the antebellum style. The long, curving drive took Meredith beneath an arch of moss-draped live oaks and into a park-like area, dotted with more oaks and willows. Azaleas, just shy of bloom, lay in a thick carpet beneath the trees lining the drives, then split off to line walkways leading to the house and shadowed gardens beyond.

Dusk was settling in, and Meredith couldn't see much beyond the front lights until she stepped out of the car to allow the valet access.

Floodlights opened up along the back of the majestic home, bathing the areas stretching away from the house with pale yellow light. Nothing stark or bluish would be acceptable here.

Instead, in keeping with the antiquated look and modern conveniences, yellow light offered the warmth Carolanne loved.

Meredith paused then wandered around the back when the valets were distracted. The house was lavish but not ostentatious. Just visually impressive, as if it understood its value and carried it well.

But it was a monster-sized house for four people, and even more so now that it was just Carolanne living here.

"Meredith?"

Julia's soft tone made her turn. "Right here."

Julia moved toward her. "Poking around other folks' bushes seems to be a habit of ours, doesn't it?"

"Sure does," Meredith replied in a hushed voice, then she sighed. "Julia Foley, you look divine in that sheath. First, I'm envious that anyone our age can wear a sheath."

"You could too—it's just not your style, Mere. You tend toward more flowy fashions. Usually."

Meredith acknowledged Julia's glance at her denim jumper with a wink. "You have to have a certain panache to carry off that level of sophistication. You move with such regal composure. I feel quite underdone next to you."

"Except I do believe that's deliberate on your part," whispered Julia. She gave Meredith's arm a tiny pinch to show she knew what Meredith was up to. "This is not the aqua chiffon you'd picked out, dear one. Although denim and calico is nice too." She rolled her eyes to show she was kidding.

"Our new friend told us to blend in. You're blending one way." Meredith pulled out a pair of fake glasses and slipped them into place, knowing they made her look like everyone's former schoolteacher. "I'm blending in in quite a different manner."

"And you do it well."

Exactly what she wanted to do. She wanted to be the almost-bumbling older woman who fumbled her champagne flute and licked her fingers.

That would distract every bit of attention away from her, and that's just what she wanted.

She turned and walked quietly with Julia through the massive double front door.

***

Julia was being courted by several influential-looking people and one of Carolanne's beautiful daughters on the far side of the huge designer-friendly living room.

Contrarily, Meredith was being left completely alone, exactly as she'd hoped.

She didn't bumble anything, although she came close, just fumbling enough to get three very elitist women to snub her.

But they didn't move far enough away to dull their conversation, and when they got into a slightly heated discussion about quarterly bonuses, the voice level pitched up.

"If Russ were still here, we wouldn't be treading water," sniped one. "He had a head for business."

"Carolanne does fine," argued another. The woman had really bad red hair, almost puce-colored, but it was nice to hear her defend Carolanne.

"There's more competition now," returned the third woman. "When they started Payroll Inc., we were some of their first employees. When they went public, we got stock packages that have done quite well."

That woman spoke total truth.

Payroll Inc.'s stock had split several times in twenty years, and the valuation had increased more than fourfold, so those original stock packages had shot way up in value.

"I think we need to hold together in hard times," the third woman finished. "No bonuses isn't the end of the world. None of us are hurting for money, Gwyneth. And you know that last year put a serious hurting on stocks. Sometimes we just have to be patient and let things rebound."

The first woman humphed before they moved away, but Meredith had gotten a nice earful. She crossed the room with a too-big smile on her face.

That was generally enough to clear a path, and it did. For some reason, corporate types tended to avoid overly happy people. She paused by a sumptuous table filled with an abundance of steaming hors d'oeuvres and did a really good job of studying one after the other, as if a great deal rested on her food decisions.

She came to stop alongside a very dignified gentleman. "It's always so hard to make these choices, isn't it?" She glanced from him to the food selections and back then sighed, but it was a happy sigh. "I'm quite delighted to be working with my old friend Carolanne again. We'll have a marvelous time sorting through things together, but right now the primary choice is figs with bacon and chile or caviar and crème fraîche tartlets? And of course those bite-sized lobster rolls are absolutely calling my name."

The man hesitated as if unsure how to react then lifted one shoulder just enough for Meredith to realize the quality of his jacket was way beyond her mere mortal budget. "I'd suggest the lobster rolls first. One's palate should always be properly prepared for lobster, and the maple glaze on the fig will oversweeten your tongue."

Oh dear heavens.

She stayed in character and did not roll her eyes. Instead she leaned slightly closer as if inviting more advice. "You understand these things, Mr....?"

"Bruce Kayhill. Corporate investments."

She widened her eyes. "What a pleasure to meet you. I'm Meredith Bellefontaine. My husband did some work for the Van Valkens during the early years."

"Not any longer?" asked Bruce.

"We lost him over two years ago," said Meredith softly.

"I'm so sorry." He drew his brows together. "It's always a shock, isn't it?"

Meredith nodded.

"I lost my wife when our kids were young," Bruce went on. He reached for a sampling of skewered barbecued shrimp. "I was a one-man band for years. It was hard. Nannies and chauffeurs and household help isn't the same as having two parents on hand to fix things. Talk about things. Figure things out."

"I agree." She tried one of the shrimp skewers and decided then and there that she'd procure this recipe from Carolanne's cook or die trying. "My boys were grown, but still. They miss their dad. We all do."

"Of course."

A woman came their way. She surprised Meredith when she grabbed Bruce by the lapels, kissed him soundly on the mouth, and laughed up at him. "Are you enjoying yourself by avoiding as much conversation as possible, darling?"

Meredith tuned into this new dynamic instantly. The well-dressed, shapely woman sounded like a caricature cartoon stepmother, and the ruby red lipstick added to the look.

"I was enjoying my conversation with Mrs. Bellefontaine here," he replied. He kept his voice dignified but there was no hiding his delight in the kiss. "But yes, Dahlia, I'm staying out of the fray." He turned back to Meredith. "I deal with most of these folks at every board meeting," he said. "Partying with them isn't tedious, but it's not what I'd call a rollicking good time either."

"Yankee or Brit?" Meredith asked.

Bruce beamed. "Good ear! Brit. I came over as a boy and lost most of it, but I'm still known for spewing the odd UK term now and again. Although most folks tell me my drawl has progressed some these last sixty-five years."

"It's a perfect drawl, and purely a lucky guess on my part based on word choice."

"You can tell a lot about a person by the words they choose. And sometimes…" He frowned slightly as his wife hurried off to throw her arms around some up-and-coming young executive much closer to her age. "By what they don't say."

"True words."

He excused himself to cross the room and station himself behind his young and very vibrant wife.

Meredith watched without appearing to watch.

Would the young executive take the hint and back away from the director's wife?

Did he realize who she was?

A pair of men paused by the laden table. "Carolanne knows how to throw a party," said one as he popped back-to-back hors d'oeuvres into his mouth with amazing alacrity. "But I'm wondering if she's got the self-disciplined rigor to run a company this size, Xavier. I can't deny I'm concerned. This place ran like a well-oiled machine until we lost Russ, and I'm sensing some rust in the cogs lately."

The second man, slightly older, kept his answers sparse. "Russ ran a tight ship."

"The markets loved him. So did the board. But now—"

The other man winced but didn't disagree.

"When Carolanne restructured corporate," the first man continued, as if Meredith wasn't standing less than three feet away, "I think it left a few people too free and easy. Including several in this room. A corporation that shuffles money should never be free and easy. That's an open invitation to mischief."

The other man waved that off. "The checks and balances are all in place. It's a multilayered system. There are corporate minds examining things all the time. Useless worry is just that, Jack—useless."

Carolanne laughed right then, a light, airy laugh, the kind that drew attention. Including the attention of the two men near Meredith. Jack considered Carolanne from his vantage point across the vast room. "No one can be that happy if there's trouble afoot. Can they?"

The second man—Xavier—frowned. "You're assuming she'd know. I'm presuming she wouldn't have a clue. And that's what worries me."

"That's why you're a CFO and I'm not," Jack replied. He took a long drink from a crystal goblet. "You look around this room and immediately start adding up costs."

"A solid bottom line is essential to growth."

"I look around," Jack went on, "and see a great party, great food, some good folks, and some wretched boors. The boors are why my phone will chime at exactly eight thirty-seven to tell me I need to get home straightaway."

"I wish I could take this that easily," countered Xavier. He glowered, then bit back a sigh.

"I wish you could too, but that's what makes a good money man, Xavier. You understand that leaching funds can start easily, and like the financial bloodhound you are, you know how to watch out for it. I just get to lower the boom."

The man named Jack walked away. True to his word, six minutes later his phone chimed. He pulled it out, made a face of regret mixed with concern, offered his apologies, and slipped out through one of the gorgeous, multipaned glass doors and into the yard beyond.

Meredith watched him leave. Immediately, four doors down, a woman appeared from beyond a gorgeous tree. And not a fake tree either. A real one.

Who keeps real trees inside? Carolanne, now, she realized. In the old days Carolanne would have been happy to have a struggling philodendron. Now she had a stunning live tree rooting through the floor, stretching toward the magnificent skylight above. A lot had changed in the last twenty years.

The woman who'd slipped past the tree had closed the door behind her softer than a stealthy ninja.

Meredith moved across the room, pretty sure that the woman was Bruce Kayhill's gorgeous young wife.

She surveyed the attendees as she pretended to hunt down a fresh drink. Bruce Kayhill was chatting with a couple of older gentlemen while his sassy little wife was nowhere to be found, which meant that she was probably the one who had slipped outside after the younger executive.

Meredith went through a nearby door on the opposite side of the glass-walled room. Gorgeous bushes blocked views from some windows, but not all, and she had to proceed with caution. The floodlights pointed outward, pouring golden light across the greening yard, leaving smaller lights to brighten the shadowed walls.

Then...

As she came to the second turn of the walk...

A soft laugh and a sigh made her draw up short.

She paused.

A man's breathing wafted along a light breeze. A cool breeze, not cold. And then he groaned. "We can't do this, Dal. We don't dare."

"Jack, my love. We already are."

A door opened behind Meredith. Perhaps the very one she'd used, but the concrete walk offered no sound of footsteps.

Did she dare turn back?

She sure didn't want to be here, listening to whatever was going on around that corner, but what if she ducked behind the pyramidal yew and let things play out?

She glanced through the window and there was Julia, stunningly gorgeous and quite in control of her situation inside while Meredith was skulking in bushes and wood chips. Making a decision, she slipped behind the yew just before Bruce Kayhill came along.

She held her breath, knowing what he was about to find, and wishing—

His footsteps kept going, fading softly in the darkness, and a few moments later she saw him reenter the room through the far door. The same door Jack had used to get outside.

How had he missed them?

Silence bloomed around her.

No laughing. No sighing. Nothing.

Had they disappeared?

She bent low then slipped out from behind the bush, confused.

And there, right there, stood Dahlia and Jack, arms folded, staring straight at her.

And she had moxie enough to stare right back.

***

"Who are you?" Jack demanded. It wasn't a gruff tone, but it was plenty firm, and Meredith wasn't a big fan of men who used that kind of masterful voice. She drew herself up to her full five feet six inches, folded her arms, and tapped her toe against the stone pavers.

"Meredith Bellefontaine."

"Why are you here?" he demanded. "Why are you snooping around?" He stayed in that same tough-guy vein, although she had to hand it to him. If she wanted a bulldog at the door, this guy would do the trick. He was way cuter than any bulldog she'd ever seen. And he didn't slobber.

She could go low-key.

Or she could tell him the truth and check his response.

Truth won. "I run a detective agency with my partner."

He looked singularly unimpressed and that spiked her ire further, but she owed him nothing, and so she waited.

So did he.

Dahlia looked from one to the other and made a face. "So, this is it? You two have a standoff out here while there's a cozy room filled with food and drink just beyond our reach? Where, pray tell, is the sense in that?"

"If you'd like to slip back in, I'd understand," Meredith told her. "I do believe your husband was wondering where you'd gone off to."

Dahlia laughed, and it was still that wicked stepmother-type cackle, but then she surprised Meredith completely. "He knows exactly where I am. Playing a role for my brother here, because Jack wanted to lure you out and see if you were really spying on us. Which, by the way"—her expression indicated the obvious answer—"you were."

"Not spying." Being compared to a common trench coat didn't sit well with Meredith. "I'm learning my way around an unfamiliar corporate entity. In doing so it doesn't hurt to figure out who's who and what's what. And to meet the players."

The man extended his hand. "Jack Rietzinger, Director of Security."

"And Dahlia Rietzinger Kayhill, Jack's sister and Bruce's wife. Bruce thinks he made a pretty nice catch, so I'd appreciate you not hinting that wasn't the case," she scolded Meredith, teasing, as Bruce came out the near door. "We outed ourselves, darling." She stepped over to Bruce's side and tucked her arm through his. "Purposely. I think she's one of the good guys."

"We can always use more corporate good guys," said Bruce, but he paused when he got a phone alert. He frowned at his phone, punched a button, and put it away. "Doesn't anyone work nine-to-five anymore?"

"No." Jack sounded almost cheerful. "But that's why a mute button comes in real handy." He grinned and winked at his more mature brother-in-law.

Bruce didn't say anything.

He didn't look troubled, but he didn't look content either.

But just about no one at this sumptuous party seemed content, except maybe Dahlia, her brother, and Julia.

Was that because of the lack of bonuses?

Surely folks understood that the market downturn last year had left a lot of businesses reeling financially. People had made spur-of-the-moment decisions, good and bad, and now they'd had time to see the results. They'd need patience and time for things to improve.

Or was there more going on?

Not for the first time, Meredith wondered why Carolanne had brought her and Julia on board. What did she expect them to find? What was her endgame? The fact that Meredith was noticed so quickly made her even more leery, but Wyatt had made a good point too.

She and Julia were people-oriented, and from what she saw of Payroll Inc.'s executives, the company could use a splash of people orientation.

"Bruce, you told me you oversee corporate investing."

Bruce seemed to choose his words carefully. "I am the director, but I don't do the actual investing. Most of that is done via a very sophisticated computerized network put together with Haging-Symms to react to market moves and keep our investments solvent. Of course, everyone took a major hit with the stock market a few months ago, so there's still a recovery factor in place."

Haging-Symms was a national investment firm. "Did Payroll Inc. take a major hit?" she asked.

Jack whistled lightly between his teeth. Dahlia hugged her arms around herself as the night air grew cooler.

"I don't have clearance from the board to discuss anything with you," Bruce told her. "It's up to Carolanne to procure that, and she needs to do it quickly, because having investigators snooping around a formal dinner is unacceptable behavior. She's putting the board and all of her execs up for inspection without their knowledge, and that sends up a lot of red flags. None of which are good."

Meredith couldn't argue, because he was right. At the same time, to have everyone know they were checking things out could put the wrong person on guard, so she understood reticence.

"Everyone took a hit last year," said Jack, to answer her question. "It's public record, Mrs. Bellefontaine."

"Meredith. Please."

He pressed his lips together then sighed. "Like Bruce said, we're not free to talk to you, but if you're here because something is going on, then good. At least Carolanne is taking positive steps to lead the company back to prominence. And that's all I'm going to say about that."

It was time to back off.

They'd given her tidbits. For now, that was enough. "I understand. I hope you won't mind me being around the office over the coming days. I want to get as much done as I can before the first quarter wrap-up."

"I'd like that too." Bruce shrugged an arm around Dahlia. "Russ had vision. Rare vision. He was a guy who saw three moves up the chess board, and he planned for that occasion. He built an amazing company, and if it continues to slide, the board will have to move. We're a publicly traded entity now. We answer to investors. It's crucial that everyone sees that. If we all hang together, we can recover the losses we suffered last year when the market crashed and zero percent interest trashed a major part of our portfolio. But we need that vision, Meredith."

He didn't name names, but his meaning was clear. The board was concerned that Carolanne wasn't leading them back to a position of solvency. Did they need to be?

That was Wyatt's assignment. He was the expert on forensic accounting.

In the meantime, she and Julia would check out things on a more personal level.

Chapter Nine

"YOUR FRIEND'S BOARD OF DIRECTORS has a sleaze factor," Julia informed Meredith when the valet brought Meredith's car around about an hour later. Julia climbed into the passenger side and let out a groan she'd probably been holding in for a while. "I was asked out by three different men tonight, despite my wedding ring, even once I announced that I was married. Ugh."

"Seriously?" exclaimed Meredith. "I had no such problem," she noted wryly. Her glance down indicated her frumpier attire.

Julia tugged her seat belt into place and locked it with a very decided *snap*. "But I did garner some very interesting information about Xavier Rahm, the current CFO. I'll have to check further to see if my memory is serving me correctly, but I'm pretty sure there was some real shady stuff in Xavier's distant past, a dark spot on his record. I'll have to dig, because he was much younger then and I only know of it because my neighbor was familiar with the family and talked about it when Xavier got this appointment a few years ago. Xavier, however, was an absolute gentleman and did not flirt with me, and mentioned his wife several times. With affection, so that was really nice."

"And the others?"

"Sharks." Julia blew out a breath. "They've been watching too many TV shows. The rest of the crew tonight seemed okay, but this group of VPs was the kind I watch out for. Slick. Too slick, if you know what I mean. After so much time in a courtroom, you read through that facade real fast. I did meet Carolanne's daughter Hadley. Lovely young woman. Almost too sweet, if there is such a thing. How about you?" she asked. "Did you blend into the woodwork as planned?"

Meredith heard the amusement in Julia's voice and confessed. "I thought so, and then the VP in charge of security set a trap for me and caught me out, so I told him who I was and what I was doing. It was absurdly embarrassing, but I stood my ground."

"He set a trap?"

Meredith merged onto the expressway then explained what Jack had done. When Julia finally stopped laughing, she sighed. "The good thing about this is knowing that he's actually on the job, watching. So why is the board worried about the company's performance if the director of security is okay with everything? Are we sensing a vote of no confidence coming up? A couple of things I overheard seemed to lean that way, and I'm not sure that's a fair assessment. A lot of companies are struggling to regain lost ground after the economic downturn. So why point the finger at Carolanne?" she mused. "You said she started the company with her husband."

"Yes," said Meredith as she headed toward the Islands Expressway. "But Russ was center stage. Larger than life, a force to be reckoned with, and a great guy. He was a born leader. Carolanne worked alongside him but she let him take the helm, so maybe that's the downfall. Maybe someone thinks she's weak and is trying to capitalize on that. Or maybe someone's just trying to make her look bad and force her out."

"I hadn't thought of that." Julia turned toward Meredith as Meredith parked the car behind the agency. "When things are teetering it's the perfect time to set her up for a fall. It's easier to wreak havoc with it being a publicly held corporation now."

"And yet the company is still a strong, marketable commodity."

"Exactly. Someone can win power and control a huge corporation that doesn't manufacture or build anything. It's a financial processing center that's grown enormous."

"Which means it's less susceptible to customary problems, retail setbacks, recessions. Because people will always want their paychecks."

"You might be onto something, Mere." Julia opened her door and climbed out. "But I'm too tired to think right now. We'll talk tomorrow at the race. I'll meet you there, okay?"

"Okay. Let's see what the rest of the company thinks of their current leadership. And we'll see who actually comes to this thing."

Chase's car pulled up just then.

Julia waved, backed her car out of the drive, and Chase drove in. He climbed out, rounded Meredith's car, and gave her a swooping hug. "Please tell me you ladies were out having fun and not working on a beautiful Friday night like this."

"We were working, but it was a pretty upscale party, so not exactly a hardship. Welcome home! Did you just get here?" she asked when he slung an arm around her shoulders.

He shook his head. "I got in a few hours ago and took Carmen and Harmony around the green fountains and some of the fun stuff getting ready for St. Patrick's Day. You know how I love the crazy upswing of people when tourist season starts." He was right. Chase was a people person. Carter liked a greater degree of privacy. "We had pie," he told her, and she didn't miss the amusement in his voice. "It was really good pie, Mom, but it wasn't quite as good as yours."

She had to bite back a laugh. "Carmen told me she was making a pie with Maggie Lu, and it sounded amazing, but I'm going to let your compliment stand. Oh, it's good to have you home for a few days," she said again. "I love driving up to Emory, but it's nice to have you on home turf now and again."

A hint of wistfulness deepened his voice as they went through the back door. "I miss Savannah. I love my job, but I love this city. Maybe even more than I love my position there. If I don't get tenure next year, I may look closer to home. I'm good at what I do," he added. "I can teach anywhere. But I miss being home."

He'd been on the tenure track at Emory since he finished his doctorate. He'd worked hard on his dissertation, and was now on his first book, a necessary part of tenure at many major universities. But tonight she sensed a longing in him. A feeling she understood too well. She looped her arm through his and moved toward the stairs. "I'm putting that at the top of my prayer list, Chase. Mothers love to see their kids feel successful, but mostly we want you happy. To have a joy-filled life. I couldn't ask for anything more. And wherever you end up, there or here, I'll make the drive to see you. Because"—she leaned up and planted a big old kiss on his cheek— "your mom loves you. See you in the morning."

He grinned and hugged her tight. "Love you back."

Chapter Ten

"Well…" Julia stretched out the word as she and Meredith approached the Payroll Inc. party tent outside the posh country club the next day. They'd come early to get a sense of the setup and watch as racers and nonracers from the company filtered in. The huge tent had been erected in the shade of one of the country club's live oak groves. Patriotic balloons and streamers decked the tent, the tables, and adjacent trees. Large cooking areas had been brought in, occupied by a diverse group of chefs. And that was it. A beautiful, sumptuous setting of social grazing for grown-ups.

"This is the family event?" Julia's question smacked of doubt. "No bounce houses, slides, not even a playground? There's nothing here for families except food, is there? Not a kid-friendly thing in sight," she continued under her breath. "I can't believe that's not deliberate."

"It has to be." The whole thing smacked of catering to adults. In a separate patriotic-themed tent was a Veterans' Outreach area where people could get information from several organizations that supported veterans' affairs. Above the tent was a huge banner touting the Van Valken family's support of the military.

"It looks more like an advertisement for Van Valken largesse and less like something intended to bring a work force together."

"I can't disagree, Julia." Meredith whispered the words as Carolanne came their way.

"Good, you're here. I'm so glad you could make it!" she exclaimed in her bright voice. "We should start getting busy as the first corporate racers come across the finish line. We always do well in this corporate challenge. You know how important fitness is to employees' well-being."

"For all of us, actually," agreed Julia. "And the food smells amazing."

"A bonus reward for the people who come. I've spared no expense," Carolanne gushed. "The shrimp bar, the steak stockade, and Billy Bob's BBQ, of course, because what Savannah feast would be complete without Billy Bob's?"

"One of our favorites," said Meredith. "And how nice that you set up a tent for the veterans' organizations."

"Our focal point!" Carolanne's enthusiasm fit her over-the-top persona but not the setup. The food in excess was clearly the main attraction. "We do all of this for them," she asserted with a wave toward the veterans working the tables in their tent.

They waved back, acknowledging her gesture. "Of course, corporate does its own thing for charities, numerous ones, but this is the one we like to give full exposure to. It was always something dear to Russ's heart. Ladies, help yourself to anything you'd like, and thank you for keeping an ear out for me. When I meet with the directors this week I'll explain I brought you on board. They'll be so relieved."

"Wonderful!" Meredith replied. Before Carolanne slipped away, she added, "Our forensic accountant will be in contact with your accounting and auditing departments first thing Monday to check things out from his end."

"I'm sorry?" Carolanne had been moving away, but she swung back quickly. She raised her brows, surprised. "You gals have a forensic accountant? How wonderful!"

"Consultant," Julia explained briskly. "We bring him in to make sure our lack of accounting background doesn't undermine our investigations. Simple prudence, you know."

"It makes perfect sense," agreed Carolanne. "I was impressed with your venture before. Now, even more so. Starting a business at our age isn't something one sees all that often. It's quite refreshing."

"Thank you." Meredith smiled at Carolanne. "We wanted to go all-in when we restarted the agency, and I know you can understand how important that is. For me, keeping up the legacy that began with Ron is very important. Just like you're doing for Russ."

Carolanne's smile dimmed. "There are days when I realize I can't hold a candle to my husband's business acumen, but he left me a well-oiled machine, and only a fool wouldn't be able to step in and operate such a perfectly constructed corporation." Her expression darkened. "I answer to a board now, but I still own sixteen percent of the company, and no one else comes close. But the weight of that does get heavy at times. I'd be lying if I said otherwise."

A sliver of sympathy prodded Meredith. "You're doing a great job, Carolanne. And look, we've got groups coming this way. I'm sure they're all anxious for your welcome."

Carolanne hurried off.

Julia groaned, and Meredith batted her softly on the arm. "Pretend you like her."

"It's a pretense, all right." Julia pursed her lips then continued. "It's not her, exactly. It's her simpering, like a page out of a 1930s Southern women magazine that sends us roller-coasting back a couple of generations. The level of fancy, just overdone enough to be annoying. Maybe because I didn't grow up with money, we worked for everything we got, and I married a man who lived the same way. But then I look at her, running a major corporation and I have to applaud her, because I couldn't do that."

"Me neither." Meredith started moving toward the fresh fruit bowls table, where most of the arrivals seemed to be congregating. She changed the subject as she moved. "Tropical fruit medley with custard. And fresh fruit cups with mango, one of my favorites."

Julia followed her lead, and soon they were congratulating runners, meeting people, and when asked, introducing themselves as consultants.

Ten minutes later, a sweaty but familiar face came their way. "Hey, ladies." Mick Cavendish swiped a towel to the back of his neck, slung it around his shoulders, then mopped his face with one long end of it. "That humidity climbed quickly, but I finished, and that's all I'm going to say about that."

"Did you run representing Payroll Inc.?" asked Meredith.

Mick shook his head. "No, just on my own to get a weekend run in at a good pace. But Carolanne always invites her consultants to come by and have food on race day."

"Exactly why we're here," noted Julia. "How's the baby?"

"Cutest thing ever," he declared proudly. "She's got her days and nights confused still, but not as much as two months ago. And just about everything makes her smile now, so that's amazing, right? To make someone that happy just by being you? By taking care of them?"

"Isn't that a marvelous feeling?"

He grinned at Meredith once he'd tipped back a bottle of water and slugged it. "Yes. I know that'll change, but I'm soaking it up right now. I'm going for a cool-down run." He slung his bag and towel over a chair. "See you later."

He ran off just as two women began buzzing about the growing crowd and the laden buffets. "Do you think people like Carolanne know there are homeless in Savannah?" whispered one. It wasn't all that soft a whisper.

"Heidi, shh. Someone will hear you." The other woman pressed a bottle of water to her sweating face then took a drink. "I try to tell myself that it's a nice thing she does for us."

"It's a photo op for a woman whose whole life has been a photo op. And those girls of hers are the same way. Petted and primped to be Mama's little darlings, a matched set. Like high-priced bookends."

"Except never did I see identical twins who were more opposite," said the second woman. "Maybe they're mirror-image, or whatever they call that. They look alike, but it's hard to believe they hatched from the same egg, if you know what I mean."

The naysayers moved off toward the barbecue setup.

Mirror image.

Carolanne had used that term for Hadley and Holly when they were little girls. Their hair parted on opposite sides. One was right-handed while the other favored her left hand. And they'd changed schools several times because nothing exactly suited the twins, not in their mother's opinion anyway.

Julia opened her mouth to say something when the screech of a microphone pierced her ears. Everyone turned toward the far side, where Carolanne was fussing with an amplified mic. "Testing? Testing?" She sang it out in a musical voice, and when it didn't bark back at her, she flashed a smile as more people approached the tented area. "Good morning, everyone, and welcome to our Fifth Annual Payroll Incorporated Corporate Challenge Luncheon Buffet! We're so excited to be here again, to have all of you here." She stepped aside and clapped for the runners and their families then went on. "Mostly we're delighted to be supporting all of our friends and family from the armed services, the brave men and women of the military. So let's give them and you a big round of applause!"

While everyone was clapping, Meredith tipped her chin down and said, "Now, that was nice. Wasn't it?"

Julia kept her face serene, but when Carolanne went immediately into a spiel about the food and drinks, she slanted a look toward Meredith. "That's it?"

Meredith frowned.

"That's the sum of her address about the military that they love to support? No real recognition or personalized thoughts? That was it?"

It was. Once Carolanne was done explaining about the amazing entrees, she was off, directing servers to refill things that really didn't need refilling yet.

But they did it.

Julia watched as they took half-full trays of food back to the big roll-in trucks. "That's a crime. Unless they take it over to the City Mission to feed the poor. I bet they don't."

It did seem like a grievous waste, as if Carolanne was more concerned with making every dish appear overladen than in simply feeding folks. But then, that fit her persona too. Maybe it always had.

"So what about these kids of hers?" asked Julia softly as they moseyed toward another group of people. "Are they normal?"

"As normal as any, I suppose." Julia rolled her eyes, and Meredith shrugged. "I really have no idea. Carolanne and I weren't super-close friends, and the girls were about four or five years younger than Chase, so we never did stuff together on a regular basis and I don't know them personally. Now and again there's a picture of them in the *Morning News* and they're beautiful. Why?"

"Wyatt's always said that whenever you look for missing money, look at the ones closest to the money first. So next to Carolanne, that would be her daughters. And the direct accounting overseers. Wyatt says the more degrees of separation, the harder it is for someone to siphon funds without being noticed."

"Makes sense." Meredith introduced herself and Julia to a group of runners after she congratulated them, and after they chatted with them for another twenty minutes, she high-signed Julia.

Julia nodded, and five minutes later they slipped behind the food trucks to make a path to their cars. "Well, it wasn't a waste," Julia said. "Not entirely, anyway."

"We got a feel for the people."

"And their boss," muttered Julia.

Meredith grimaced. "You know, you could be right. When you've always had an overflowing plate and pocketbook, maybe you can't really get a feel for middle class 'normal.' My family had its share of money, and inheriting my house makes me look kind of opulent, but I know how hard Ron worked to build his business. I hope I've never lost that rooted, be-there-for-the-people mindset. I'd be ashamed of myself if I did."

"You haven't. No big head here," Julia assured her, giving her a shoulder nudge. "I didn't see Mary Murphy at this shindig. Now there's a dedicated employee that probably could have used a relaxing lunch, but from Carmen's notes, she's got her hands full."

"Which, unfortunately, makes her a possible suspect," said Meredith. "Close to Carolanne, probable proximity to passwords, and in dire need."

"Except we don't even know if there is missing money. It's like proving murder without a body, a very difficult task."

"That's where Wyatt's expertise comes in," said Meredith. "His job is to find the body, so to speak. What if there isn't one?" She met Julia's gaze. "What if there's nothing to be found?"

"Well, then we have to figure out why there's any suspicion at all," Julia replied. "Generally where there's smoke, there's fire. But if it's only a smoke bomb, we have to figure out why it was thrown. I'm going to do a little checking up on Carolanne's daughters. I don't want you to jeopardize your relationship with her at this point, so let me do a little investigating. What are their names again?"

"Hadley and Holly."

"Cute." Julia typed a few notes into her phone. "I'll let you know if I find anything significant."

"And I'll go home and enjoy some time with my son. When's Beau due home?" she asked.

Julia's quick smile made her want to sigh, but she didn't. "Tonight. I've got that jambalaya that Maggie Lu and Carmen made

Thursday. He'll love it. He's only home for a week before he does a quick jaunt with his brother Max and a couple of old college friends for their annual golfing trip. He missed it last year because he came down with the flu." She swung open her car door. "Give my love to Chase. I'll check in with you later on today or tomorrow."

Meredith stopped by the market and stocked up on some of Chase's favorites.

He'd be heading back to school tomorrow afternoon. He wanted to use the spring break to work on his book, but for now he was home and they were going to see Carter's two kids play in a soccer tournament later today. It would be about the best weekend ever.

Chapter Eleven

"THAT'S EXACTLY THE KIND OF family day I needed," observed Chase as he pulled around the back of the house to park his car on Saturday evening. "Shooting the breeze, drinking sweet tea with you and Carter and Sherri Lynn, and watching the kids run around—just perfect."

"And I loved having supper with all of you," Meredith said. "That made my day." Carter, her oldest son, was a wonderful man with a great job and a busy life, so she made sure to get up to Charleston regularly to be part of her grandchildren's lives.

"I did notice that Carter is still encouraging you to get on with your life." Chase sent her a somewhat wry look of sympathy as they approached the back steps. "For a quiet guy, my big brother isn't all that subtle. Maybe he should read up on the process of grieving a little more thoroughly."

Meredith half laughed, half sighed. "He's pretty sure that finding a new love will solve everything, while I'm unaware of anything that needs solving, except for a current case. If the good Lord puts the right person in my path, I expect I'll know it. Right?" Quin's image came to mind, but she kept that to herself as Chase made a funny face.

"You're asking your single son for romance advice?"

"Not asking, really. Let's make it a simple observation."

Chase unlocked the door and held it open for her. "I think you're right," he said. "You taught us to rely on God's timing, although I don't always do that. Sometimes I'm too busy pushing my own agenda. I need to start paying attention to God more, and less to my self-absorbed mindset."

He waited until they got inside to continue. "Take this weekend, for instance." He closed the door quickly because bugs were already populating the spring night air. "I could've stayed at Emory and worked on the book, but I knew Harmony had never seen this city the way I see it, and I wanted her to. And hanging out with Carmen is fun," he added. "She's down-to-earth and funny, and I don't meet many women like that around the school. I like getting to know her. She's different."

The landline jangled just then. "You are probably one of fifty people who still has a house phone," he teased.

Meredith pretended to scold him with a look and picked up the phone. "Florence, how are you?"

Her eighty-year-old neighbor didn't answer the question. "I've got a package for you. It was delivered to your front step, and you know the problem we've been having with porch pirates these days. Not like it's a surprise, with everyone and their brother getting piles of things shipped in and set on open porches." Disapproval laced her tone, but that wasn't uncommon. Meredith's elderly neighbor looked askance at a lot of things. "I snagged it and brought it over here for safekeeping."

"Florence, thank you. I'll have Chase come right over for it. How very kind of you."

"Neighbors look out for neighbors, and that's all there is to that." She kind of humphed at the end of the statement, as if imparting a life lesson—something she did quite often.

"He'll be right there." Meredith sent Chase out the front door. He trotted to Florence's house and came back several minutes later with a white rectangular box trimmed in green ribbon, the signature color for March in Savannah.

"Flowers?" he asked as he set it down.

"I can't imagine from whom," she said. She cut the ribbon with her kitchen shears. The box cover was tight, but when she finally managed to pull off the lid, layers of green florist tissue covered the gift.

Had Quin sent her flowers?

He was a nice man in many ways, but—

She lifted the tissue and stared.

So did Chase.

A bouquet of dead camellias lay in the box.

The contrast of the perky tissue and bright white box against the very dead flowers and the black satin ribbon sent her skin crawling. Goose bumps traveled from the back of her neck down her arms.

"Well, that's special," noted Chase in a tone that said it wasn't special at all. "Someone is sending you a message, Mom. A pretty stark one."

"It's probably a package that got misdirected and the flowers died in transit," she said. "In this growing heat, that kind of thing can happen." After grabbing a butter knife from a drawer, she eased the paper back until she saw a typical business-sized card tucked into the black satin ribbon tying the wretched-looking bouquet.

She lifted it up by its edges and read the message out loud. "'Nothing to fear but fear itself is a bad quote. There is, in fact, much to fear.'"

"Whoa." Chase stared at the card, then her. "Is someone really threatening you, Mom?"

She raised her gaze to his. "So it would seem."

"Does this happen often?" he asked. The look of surprise on his face almost made her smile.

She shook her head. "Not very."

"'Not very' means sometimes, and that's too often, except that this is crazy intriguing, isn't it?" He eyed the card and the flowers with one brow raised. "Who have you riled up this week?"

"I can't imagine. We've been doing nothing more than information gathering, but we struck a nerve with someone, it seems."

"Do you think they're dangerous?" Chase asked quietly. His sober tone heightened the question.

"Usually not. It's someone trying to scare us off, but why would they? Who did we talk to that even has a clue what we're doing?" she wondered out loud as her cell phone rang.

Chase picked it up from the counter and handed it to her. "Aunt Julia."

"Hey, Julia. We just got in, and—"

"We did too," Julia interrupted. "And we found a very interesting and somewhat disturbing package on the front porch."

"Dead flowers?"

"You too?" Julia's voice pitched up, and Meredith switched her to speaker phone so Chase could hear.

"Yes. Pretty box. Ugly contents."

"Bingo. So, we've stirred someone's pot, that's for certain," Julia announced. "Beau is not happy about this, but I assured him that most people use empty threats to throw us off the trail, and that we must be rattling the right cage, although we haven't actually rattled anybody's anything. So who could this be?"

Meredith was equally stumped. "I have no idea. Let's get together later tomorrow and compare notes if Beau doesn't mind."

"Come over for supper after Chase heads back to Emory, and we'll put our heads together. Beau says he'll grill some steaks."

"Best offer I've had," said Meredith. "I'll see you around five, okay? I'll bring dessert."

"Peach or pecan?" called Beau from somewhere in the room with Julia, and Meredith laughed.

"Pecan this time. Too early to pretend that peaches are good. See you tomorrow."

She hung up and faced Chase.

He motioned toward the box. "I expect you want to keep that for evidence?"

She nodded. "But it's not exactly what I want to see before services tomorrow morning. Can you set it downstairs?"

He took the box downstairs then came back up two at a time, total Chase. "Little did I know that your investigations could take such a macabre twist."

"Most don't," she assured him. "But every now and again we stumble into something that goes deeper than we expect. This could be one of those times. I'm not going to mention this to Carolanne."

"How's Mrs. Van Valken doing?" Chase asked.

"Mostly okay, I think," Meredith told him, then fought a yawn. "She thinks there's something going on in the company, and she's determined to find out what it is. I think someone may be trying to take advantage of the fact that Russ is gone and she's a woman, and that's a pretty despicable thing to do."

"To undermine a widow?" Chase's expression agreed. "Pretty low. What time do you want to leave for church in the morning?"

She didn't want to tell him that this was sometimes the hardest part of the week. To face Sundays alone. Services alone. It was good to hear well-wishes from some, but Sundays somehow seemed to exacerbate that ache that had started over two years before. And while it had lessened, it wasn't gone, and she'd be wrong to say it was. "Oh, around nine, I suppose. Sometimes I dread going to church because I've almost never gone to that church alone in my whole life. First my mom and dad. And Grandpa. Then your dad, and you boys, and then me and your dad again. Even though it's been over two years, it feels wrong to walk into church alone, Chase."

"There's no official timeline for grieving someone, Mom." He reached out and gave her a big hug. "You do you. And don't let anyone pressure you into anything." He drew back and met her gaze. "I have faith in you. Just the way you are."

She hugged him back.

His words bolstered her. She hadn't wanted to put her dread of Sundays and church into words, but once she did, it felt better. As if she wasn't abnormal.

He smiled down at her then headed for the living room. "I'm going to catch a March Madness update before I go to bed. I'll see you in the morning, okay?"

It was more than okay. She nodded. "Sounds good."

And it did.

Church with Chase. Fellowship with a lot of very nice people, time with Chase, and then dinner with friends. That didn't sound like a bad Sunday at all. And then to figure out who had the gall to send her and Julia a box full of really dead flowers.

Chapter Twelve

"Harlowe!" Meredith spotted her one-hundred-and-four-year-old neighbor clomping down the sidewalk as she and Chase left for services the next morning. Harlowe wasn't the only one out. The beautiful spring morning seemed to have stirred a lot of Troup Square folks.

"Hallooo!" Tay Tay Pomeroy caroled to Meredith from across the street. "A perfect morning to be out, isn't it? And doesn't that sun feel so good?"

"It does," Meredith called back. "Good to see you, Tay Tay!"

"And equally good to be seen," the hairdresser agreed as she hurried up the street.

There was no hurrying Harlowe. He and his walker had one speed, but Chase slowed his pace to fall into step beside the aged man. "Mr. Green, how are you? You look well, sir."

"I am well. That's a surprise to just about everyone who sees me, and I can't deny a spark of pleasure when I see that quick look of astonishment in their eyes," he said, and Chase laughed. "You home for the weekend?"

"I am."

"No better way to stir up the spring air than folks gettin' out and doin'. Cars are well and good as needed," the old man expounded, "but the point of a walking neighborhood is for people to walk. We've gotten a touch soft when fifty degrees is considered too cold for a stroll."

"That wind and rain may have curtailed some of that, Harlowe," Meredith reminded him. "When the wind's strong enough to whip the umbrellas inside out, that's not my kind of strolling weather. But this"—she drew a deep breath to make her point—"now, this is marvelous. Are you coming to service?"

Harlowe shook his head. "I went to a twilight preaching with an old friend last night. Down by the river. It was right nice, and it put me in mind of how blessed we are, so no. Just out for my first daily constitutional. And you, young man." He tipped his gaze up to Chase. Harlowe's diminished size was in stark contrast to Chase's six-foot height. "Thank you for taking care of your mother. She's good people."

Chase grinned down at the old fellow. "I concur. Have a good day, Mr. Green."

"At my age, every day I open my eyes is a good day," Harlowe quipped. His hearing loss made him punch up his somewhat raspy voice. "Best get on. The new reverend at Wesley Chapel is a bit of a tyrant if you're late. And don't try to duck out early. He's got a steely glare, if you know what I mean."

"We'll be quick," Meredith promised. When they got farther away, Chase posed the question.

"Is the new pastor really like that?"

Meredith hedged her response. "Let's just say his tolerance level is pretty low."

"That's quite a contrast to Reverend Keely."

Reverend Keely had been their spiritual leader for over twenty years. He knew everyone by name and joined in neighborhood gatherings wholeheartedly. He wasn't a Sunday pastor. He'd been a seven-days-a-week kind of neighborhood mentor. "He was a sweetheart, wasn't he? With such a heart for the downtrodden. That was a man who lived his life being the eyes and hands of Christ."

"Making him a hard act to follow."

"I know. And that's not exactly fair to the new minister." Chase's words reflected her feelings. "I want to be fair, but it's not just the church that's different, Chase. I'm different. And so is the congregation. I think it's important to recognize that. Don't you?"

Chase's look of sympathy almost drove her to tears, but she paused them with a deep breath. "So many of the older members have moved away or gone to Jesus, and we don't get busy like we used to. It feels kind of empty when I'm not surrounded by people I know and people who know me. Except that sounds vain, and I don't mean it to."

"It's not vain." Chase shrugged an arm around her shoulders and hugged her. "It's normal. You're a people person. Me too. There's nothing wrong with wanting to be around good people. You taught me that as a boy, to choose my friends wisely. I think the same holds true in church. Something to pray about, anyway. And you know that Aunt Julia would love to have you at her church," he reminded her. "She's talked about New Beginnings for years, and it's happy talk. That makes it something to consider. Also, there's that saying about God closing doors and opening windows. You always told us if a door closes, look for a window. Isn't that what Aunt Julia did?"

It was. And it was good advice. Except— "There's this part of me that feels like God should be the one to adapt to what I want."

Chase burst out laughing. "Well, I've felt that way a time or two myself. Then I usually find out I'm wrong and have to fix things."

"A trait you get from me."

"Stubborn. Yep. No denying that. But we're not so bad, Mom. I know you'll figure this out. You always do."

"Out of the mouths of babes," she said then hugged his arm. "I will do exactly that because you're right. Maybe going someplace where everybody doesn't know my name is a way to not only make new friends but find that peace that's been eluding me. It's topping my prayer list because I always looked forward to Wednesday night studies and Sunday morning services. I want that feeling back again."

"Atta girl."

She spent the next few hours with Chase, but once he headed back toward Emory, she made two lists. One, a list of area churches, including Julia's.

And two, a list of who might be threatening her and Julia. That list was much harder to compile.

Chapter Thirteen

"Dicey." Theresa drew the shade down over the window and kept her voice low. "I'm scared. I've never been so scared. I don't know how something so good and noble became something to fear."

"Do you think everyone from Charleston got these notes?" Dicey whispered. "And if so, why? That makes no sense."

It didn't, but with their mission complete, would querying the other women look suspicious? And did they dare look like anything other than young professionals, ready to go into the post-World War II world?

"We can phone them," suggested Theresa.

Dicey shook her head. "And have an operator overhear our conversation? No. And to gather together might draw attention our way, now that our lab sessions are over."

Theresa scowled. "How can something so vital become something nefarious in the blink of an eye?"

"Threats are usually spurred by someone who feels threatened themselves, but how could we be a threat to anyone?" Dicey mused. "I can't even fathom a reason."

"Twelve women who passed screening and were trained to decode enemy messages? That's not exactly an everyday skill in the job market. Although I heard some others are seeking work in the NSA," said Theresa.

Theresa was right. None of the twelve were likely destined to be codebreakers in real life, and all were honored to have passed the selection criteria put forth by the dean of students three years before. For over thirty months this select group of single, bright young women gathered in "labs" to decipher enemy codes gathered by the US military.

"And the war is over," Dicey continued softly. "So why the huge secrecy?"

"Maybe it's not really over?" Theresa posed a question that had been on Dicey's mind too. "Maybe there are components of the war that are ongoing but no one wants it to get out?"

"Covert actions?" Dicey wondered out loud. "A conspiracy?" She'd read enough history to know that could be a real premise. For a moment, she almost regretted her hunger for information, because dull minds wouldn't be bothered by thoughts like this. "May I see your note?"

Theresa slipped it out of her pocket and handed it over. Hers was slightly different but appeared to be in the same hand. "'Your silence isn't only advised,'" Dicey read softly. "'It is demanded under Top Secret regulatory directives. No word or words, allegations, or implications of your patriotic duties should be spoken to anyone, at any time. To do so would entail quick reckoning. If the ban on talking is broken, it will be traced. You will be watched. You will be found. You will be silenced. Take heed.'"

The note was written on the same paper as Dicey's, steno paper that could be found anywhere. "We already knew this was top secret, that we weren't to talk of it after the war, that we didn't want the next Hitler or Mussolini to know how we garnered their communications and broke the codes. Why threaten us? And why in this manner?" mused Dicey. "A handwritten missive on stenographer paper? Is this some random captain trying to maintain a sense of control on civilians who were brought in? We know that some personnel found our mission disturbing because we weren't registered military, but when you're scarce on people, you expand your horizons. Did we manage to bend some decorated nose out of joint, I wonder?"

"I'll tell you what fumes me," said Theresa boldly. "The thought that we're not smart enough to understand keeping quiet, as if we're a gaggle of schoolgirls going out to gossip about how we helped win the war."

"We did our part," said Dicey.

"And out of patriotic duty, nothing more," Theresa continued.

Dicey agreed. Their group had been honored to be asked, to be interviewed, to be tested, and to be chosen to work in the cipher lab.

It had been offered as an act of patriotism to give support to the men and women fighting overseas, and that was exactly how Dicey had gone into the prospect.

But this—

The threatening notes changed things.

"How can we meet with the other women and not be obvious about it?"

"We can't." Theresa was straightforward, as always. "But we can divide and conquer." She jotted down five names for Dicey and five for herself. "We've all been excused from duty this week, so everyone is heading south. Let's see who we can talk to before they go. The gals in this complex will be easier to reach. The others…" She grimaced. "I'm not sure, unless we actively seek them out, and is that breaking the vow of silence? To even talk amongst ourselves?"

"I'm pretty sure it is."

Theresa's gaze narrowed as she gripped the note.

"You know what angers me, Theresa?" asked Dicey.

"Being threatened for doing a great job for God and country?" The insult of that deepened Theresa's voice.

"The ruination of a wonderful personal accomplishment," Dicey replied. "I'm the first woman in my mother's family to achieve a BS degree, the first woman to attend college. This was as much for my mama as it was for me. And an example to my little sister, to work hard and learn to care for one's self. Now it's besmirched because of someone's jealousy or meddling or insecurities. Or lust for power."

"Lording it over a dozen women is a pretty lame power play," said Theresa. "But you're right, it messes up what should be a wonderful weekend of celebration and new beginnings."

"Although if one of your beaus happens to be your 'one and only,' your new beginning awaits you," said Dicey with a smile. "If you're okay with a shadow being thrown over your family. I can't deny the worry that brings to me."

Theresa frowned. "You can't possibly think this will have a long-term effect, can you? I foresee my future as being a darling of Atlanta's upper-crust society, just as it's destined to be, with an amazingly good-looking husband by my side, the likes of which will make other women swoon with envy. Such are my simple goals now that I'm heading home, a good match being the kind of thing that makes my daddy proud. Daddy does like to brag."

Dicey didn't mince words. "Someone is threatening to watch us and silence us. I take it very seriously. But logistics should spread the onus because we will all go our own ways, back to our own towns and lives. No single person can keep track of all of us."

"Unless—"

Dicey had been moving toward the door to check with the other Charleston College codebreakers. She paused. Turned.

"Unless it's not a single person." Theresa had dropped her voice again, and she gave a furtive glance around, as if the very room was listening to their conversation. "Unless they have enough people, enough means to keep watch on all of us."

A cold shiver shot down Dicey's spine. "To serve what end?" she whispered.

Theresa's expression darkened considerably. "I have no idea, my friend."

"Then it looks like we have one last puzzle to solve," Dicey said. "And this one may be the most important one of all."

Chapter Fourteen

"SO, WHOSE FEATHERS HAVE WE ruffled?" Meredith asked Julia while the scent of wood-fired steaks filled the shaded backyard.

"No one's, which makes this even more interesting, doesn't it?" declared Julia. "I went over the people we've met, the ones we overheard, the people closest to the money via family and corporate, and I'm flat-footed. Except." She dragged her chair closer to Meredith's. "That executive I told you about, Xavier Rahm? There's a rough history going back about thirty-seven years, long before my time on the juvenile bench. His records are sealed, but I did some newspaper research and I contacted an old neighbor, and it seems that the Rahm family had close friends living near their place upriver. Two of those friends were part of an embezzlement scheme that rocked the local offices of Schleigh Investing. Not as deeply entrenched as Madoff in Manhattan, but enough to serve a long stretch of federal prison time. Xavier Rahm and his brother, both young at the time, knew what was going on and kept quiet about it until they were caught doing some double dealing on another wealthy neighbor. The feds used that pressure to make the young men serve as witnesses for the prosecution, and the neighbors were proven guilty. They've served their time and are out of prison, and Xavier Rahm seems nervous. As if he's concerned about something."

"He seemed that way to me too," admitted Meredith. "When he was talking to another executive, I could hear the consternation in his voice. But if nothing is wrong, or obviously wrong, why would he be worried?"

"Exactly. Unless he knows something is wrong and it's eating at him. Maybe Wyatt's arrival will tip Xavier's hand. But that doesn't explain our surprise packages, because he doesn't seem like a 'send dead flowers' kind of guy."

"Agreed. But then how does one categorize a 'dead flowers' person?" drawled Meredith.

"Woman," Julia declared. "Not just the flowers, but the black bow inside. A cryptic but floral touch."

"Unless it's a man wanting to make it look like a woman did it," said Meredith as Julia stood up to get the salads. Meredith followed to help her. "That's what I'd do to throw shade. I'd make it look like the opposite gender right off. When I played 'Guess Who' with the boys, I'd always go for gender first. A targeted eliminator."

"I played that with Wyatt when he was little." Julia inhaled appreciatively as Beau lifted the smoky-smelling steaks off the grill. "You could be right. I'm hoping Wyatt uncovers something more solid in these next few days. With so many businesses still in recovery mode after last year's market slide, I hate to see this kind of thing happen. Carolanne employs a lot of people. Not just here but across the country. If corporations get wind of financial problems at Payroll Inc., other payroll firms will snatch up those clients in a heartbeat. I might not be a big fan of Carolanne personally, but I like seeing a woman take the reins successfully. So I'd hate to see rumors of misappropriation take the company down. But for now"—she gave Beau a thumbs-up—"dinner is served."

***

Beau got called to a neighbor's for a rogue possum that had wandered into their living room, leaving Meredith and Julia on their own after dinner. He hadn't even gotten around the corner of the sidewalk when Julia hurried to Meredith's side. "I have an idea."

"About Rahm? The flowers? What?"

Julia shook her head. "Miss Dicey."

Meredith patted the seat on the glider next to her. "Let's hear it, because I came up with very little direction. Of course, with Chase home, there wasn't a lot of time."

"I got to thinking about what happened to her as I was considering what's going on with Carolanne," Julia explained. "Something that Mick Cavendish said, about making one thing look like another. What if someone was using their government alliance to make it look like all the women were being threatened? But we know that most threats are of a personal nature, right?"

"Yes," Meredith agreed as she sipped her sweet tea. "You mean like someone was threatening all of them to mask targeting one of them."

"Exactly. I read a couple of those codebreaker books on my Kindle, and it made me wonder about Miss Dicey's story. Why would the government do this?" Julia asked. "Most of the women were sworn to secrecy, but why this threat? I didn't see anything about threats of silence in either book I read, so that's odd, right? If this was a 'thing,' it wouldn't have just been their group from Charleston."

"That's a valid point. But J. Edgar Hoover did take credit for the work, that's established," said Meredith.

"He sure did, but this is different, right?"

It was. This wasn't just taking credit, it was threatening well-being. And then three women died. "So maybe whoever this was had ties to one or more of the dead women, and they included Dicey and the others in the threat to disguise their relationship to the victims."

"Yes. They had decent communication back then but not private like now. Phones could be openly overheard and letters could be confiscated or shared, so talking itself was a danger. But what a clever way to shroud something, by masking it as a clear and present danger to the whole group."

"We've got to go see Miss Dicey again," said Meredith. "Later tomorrow, okay? Not late enough that she'll be tired, but maybe without Jubal this time. He means well, but he tends to take over a conversation. We really need Miss Dicey's recall straight on."

"Unfiltered," agreed Julia. "I'll call and set it up for after we get Wyatt into Payroll Inc. I know Miss Dicey and Jubal weren't think-ing of us actually getting involved in this, but the thought of some-one living afraid for decades saddens me. It's unacceptable. Think of what her life could have been."

The thought of a genteel woman like Laodicea Oglethorpe living under a mantle of fear for all that time goaded Meredith too. "You're absolutely right. If we can come up with anything that gives her a bit of peace, I'd be happy with that. Can you imagine, hiding a secret like this for all this time?"

Julia's expression went pensive. "I think a great many women were forced to do that for a variety of reasons," she said softly. "It's different now in a lot of ways but not so much in others, so if we can bring her some peace, I say we do it. Right alongside finding out who has absolutely dreadful taste in floral arranging." She indicated the white box sitting near the french doors leading to the deck. "Because that person is going to get a piece of my mind. I promise you that."

She made that promise right before Meredith's phone rang. Carolanne's name flashed in her display. She swiped the phone quickly. "Hey, Carolanne. What's up?"

"Me, for one, and I'm never up past nine on a Sunday because I like to hit the exercise room before work on Mondays. It invigorates me, and staying fit is so important, isn't it?"

Meredith eyed the slice of lemon pound cake with sour cherry pie filling that Julia just set before her. "Absolutely clutch," she agreed, and she did agree. In theory. But she wasn't foolish enough to say no to lemon pound cake.

"I got a note."

"A note?" Meredith lifted a brow in Julia's direction. She didn't want to put Carolanne on speaker, so she held the phone away from her ear for Julia to hear. "From whom?"

"I don't know, but whoever it is doesn't like the way I'm doing things. They warned me that I better get things in order ASAP or be looking for work elsewhere. And it wasn't worded that politely."

"Oh, Carolanne, I'm so sorry. An employee? An investor? Was it a local postmark?"

"No postmark. None. It was in the mail yesterday, I guess. Holly brought the mail in and tossed it on my desk, but there wasn't time to even breathe yesterday with the race luncheon and all."

The catered, all-she-had-to-do-was-show-up luncheon on country club grounds. Meredith didn't dare make eye contact with Julia.

"I just found it."

"Bring it to work in the morning."

"You don't want to see it now?" Carolanne didn't hide her exasperation. "What if someone means me harm? My daughter's here."

"Did they threaten you?"

"Well, it certainly sounds like they're threatening my job. As if they know something I don't. But my guess is that there's nothing wrong except bruised male egos."

Meredith looked at the cake. Then her watch. Then she swallowed a sigh. "I'll be right there."

"Oh, that's a relief." Carolanne did sound genuinely relieved, so at least she wasn't dragging Meredith out on a wild goose chase. "I just know I'll be unable to catch a wink of sleep if I don't have some comfort over this whole thing. I'm okay with straight-line accounting and so on, but this left-field nonsense is out of my comfort zone."

"Tell her that running around at nine o'clock on Sunday nights is out of ours," muttered Julia. But she grabbed a light jacket while she spoke, and Meredith knew she wasn't going to let her handle this alone.

"Let's drive separately so you don't have to come back here for the car. Beau!" Julia called his name across the neighbor's yard. "Gotta go! I'll text you and explain!"

Meredith didn't have time to read Beau's expression.

First dead flowers.

And now his sixty-five-year-old wife running off at night, for who knew what reason?

Meredith pulled out of the driveway quickly.

Julia followed.

It wouldn't take long to get to the Wilmington Island estate at this time on a Sunday night, but what would they find when they got there?

Meredith had no idea.

Chapter Fifteen

A FLASH OF PALE BLUE caught Meredith's eye as she waited for Julia to park her car. She turned quickly and scanned the Van Valken woods with a practiced eye.

Nothing.

And yet she was sure she saw it, and there wasn't a plethora of bluebirds flitting around Savannah at nine fifteen on a March night. She waited for Julia before moving forward.

"Did you see something moving through the woods there?"

Julia shook her head. "I was texting Beau and not looking. What would be out and around at this time of night? In March?"

Meredith shrugged. "I don't know."

Carolanne opened the door before they had a chance to ring the bell. "Holly's sleeping. I didn't want the doorbell to disturb her."

"Are the twins living at home?" asked Meredith. She didn't mean anything by the question. It was polite conversation because Hadley had been on hand Friday night, but Carolanne's expression changed instantly.

"Holly is. For now. A lot of young adults are living at home these days," she continued defensively. "It's costly to go out on your own, and it's not like the world is flush with jobs, is it?"

Meredith pretended nonchalance. "There's a lot of uncertainty in the air, isn't there? And it's nice not to be in a big house on your own."

"With only the cook and the maid," added Julia. She didn't sound condemning, but she didn't sound all that complimentary either.

"Except they go home at night, of course, and it's just me, rattling around a big old house that probably needs to go on the market. But selling a family home is like selling your memories," Carolanne said. Then she sighed. "There's so much finality to that, isn't there, Meredith? As if we're admitting they're really gone and everything we took for granted has changed."

Her words struck a chord with Meredith.

Carter had already suggested selling the house and buying something smaller and cozier.

She didn't want to sell a home that had been in the Hall family for several generations. She'd inherited it from her great-grandfather when she and Ron were newlyweds.

Oh yeah, she could see the pluses and minuses of reducing the square footage and of a littler place in the suburbs, but that wasn't her normal, and she'd already been thrust out of her normal, thank you very much.

But she understood the emotion. "I've taken the advice of other folks who've gone through this, and deliberately stayed put," she told Carolanne. When Carolanne nodded, Meredith knew they were on the same page. "I love my house, I'm used to it, and it suits me. It's been in the family for nearly a hundred years, and that makes moving a major consideration. But my house is a fraction of this place, and I can't imagine how you keep up with it all. I expect the gardens are beautiful."

"Other than work, my gardens are my pride and joy," said Carolanne. She crossed the grand entry to a small table and lifted a folded piece of coarse paper. "Here it is."

Meredith and Julia read the note. Julia spoke first. "The wording suggests this is business-related, and it's disguised on bad paper to make it look low-end. As if it's a low-end employee, not an angry, rich investor."

"You can tell that from looking at it?" Disbelief colored Carolanne's tone.

"Not for certain, but the wording suggests that the person has a high stake in Payroll Inc.'s future and that he or she is concerned that you're not taking that seriously enough. Of course, after last year's stock plunge, everyone's more reactionary than they used to be."

She was throwing Carolanne a deliberate lifeline with that last sentence, because clearly there were directors who didn't approve of Carolanne's efforts. Meredith wasn't surprised when Carolanne grabbed hold of the idea. It was always easier to blame outside forces than take personal responsibility. Sometimes outside forces were to blame, but Meredith wasn't 100 percent sure in this case.

"A major stock market decline scares everyone," Carolanne agreed. "But why go on the attack now?" she wondered.

"That's what we need to find out." Meredith kept her tone crisp. "And that's why we're here. May we take this with us for the file? That way we have it if the police need to be involved."

"Police?" Carolanne gaped at her. "No, that's quite impossible. We can't breathe a word of this to anyone. I would lose my job. There are a few board members who would love to see me fail. They didn't want me to step into Russell's shoes when he passed away, and their noses are still out of joint. They would take great delight in seeing something like this topple me. In fact, it could be one of them," she said with a glance toward the note. "There's always a power struggle at the top of a big corporation like this, unfortunately."

Meredith directed a look of sympathy to Carolanne but wondered if Carolanne's assessment was justified. Was this the norm for major companies? To vie for power at the top? Or were investors and the board justifiably concerned? She hoped Wyatt's part of the investigation would give them a better understanding of that side of things.

"Mom? Who are you talking to?"

"Holly. Oh darling, I'm sorry we woke you." Carolanne moved toward the beautiful staircase and peered up. "I had a couple of friends stop by."

A sleepy-looking blond tipped her pretty face over the railing. She gave them a faint smile and a wave. "All right, it was just weird is all. I'm going back to bed."

"Good night, honey." Carolanne gazed up the stairs for a few long seconds after Holly disappeared. When Julia cleared her throat, Carolanne turned quickly. "I'm so glad you came. I know we haven't solved anything, but at least I don't feel so alone."

Another emotion Meredith understood. "Glad to do it. We'll see you tomorrow morning at the office as planned. Thanks for bringing us in on this, Carolanne."

"I had to," she admitted softly. "Otherwise I wouldn't catch a wink of sleep. That's exactly what some people are looking for, waiting for me to go off my game. I refuse to give them that satisfaction." She led the way toward the massive hardwood door and swung it open. "Thank you, ladies. I'm more grateful than you can ever imagine."

"Happy to help." Julia said it, and Meredith was pretty sure she almost meant it. Almost. But there would be no standing at their cars and talking about this tonight. Not with Carolanne watching.

She climbed into her car and started the engine then waited until Julia had taken the curve of the long, semicircle drive before she followed.

She scanned the woods as she left and saw nothing, but she was certain she'd seen a flash of something on their arrival even though the distance between neighbors made that unlikely. She drove down the driveway, turned right, and saw a middle-aged man walking a dog. A smallish dog, wearing a light blue doggie vest as it pranced along.

A dog.

She made a face at herself in the mirror when she rolled to a stop at a light.

She'd let her imagination get the better of her, and she wasn't prone to do that. Something about money with six-plus zeroes before the decimal point messed with her head.

Wyatt was right. People had killed for a lot less than what they were talking about. And that wasn't something she faced every day. Ron had run a few major cases like that, but they weren't the norm then, and they sure weren't her norm now. But at least with Wyatt on board they stood a chance at finding the truth. She could only hope the truth was worth the possible danger involved.

Julia waved as she turned onto the Islands Expressway.

Meredith waved back and drove on home. When she got there, a shiver shot down her spine as she approached the house. It wasn't the dead flowers. Those were pure theater.

And it wasn't even the note she was about to put into Carolanne's folder.

It was that feeling of being alone after a great weekend with Chase, of seeing Carolanne's tired daughter looking out for her mother's welfare, and then coming back to a big, lonely house.

The outside lights were on.

She let herself in, locked the door, and went up the stairs.

A soft mew greeted her. GK, who rarely disturbed himself enough to be petted much less act as a greeter, padded her way as if he knew she needed a friend. That she didn't want to be alone tonight.

She bent low to pet him, and he let her. And then he wound himself along the palm of her hand and her leg, a rare moment of cat-bonding, because GK liked his own agenda. But tonight he made her feel welcomed. More than that...

He made her feel less alone.

Chapter Sixteen

"So this is our accounting genius?" Carolanne moved forward as Mary Murphy directed Meredith, Julia, and Wyatt into her office the next morning. "Nice to meet you, Mr. Waverly. I'm Carolanne Van Valken, and this is my company."

Wyatt couldn't see Mary Murphy's reaction to that statement, but Meredith could, and it wasn't pretty. But when the younger woman turned back, her face was professionally serene. Mission accomplished, she quietly backed toward the door until Carolanne stopped her. "Mary, can you see if anyone wants coffee, please? Or tea?" She turned to her guests. "We have our sweet tea made at the restaurant on the street level of the building, and nobody does it better."

"Nothing for me, thanks," said Wyatt.

Meredith waved it off. "Me neither. We're just here to get Wyatt settled."

"I'm a Diet Dr Pepper kind of gal," added Julia.

"Now that's a rule-break if ever I heard one, but fortunately that's available at every convenience store across the country," gushed Carolanne. The mass market availability didn't sound like a good thing even though she laughed.

Julia laughed with her, but Meredith was sure it was for a very different reason. "I've been known to break a few rules in my time,"

Julia asserted. "I think that's what helps me discern that trait in others."

"Where I am generally far too trusting of my fellow man to believe the worst." Carolanne put on an utterly sincere expression. "That can be a downfall when one is running a major corporation, can't it, Mr. Waverly?"

Wyatt didn't disagree. "It could be, but the long history of successful ventures for Payroll Inc. makes me think you're always on top of your game, Mrs. Van Valken."

"Carolanne. Please. And now if I can get you set up, I have some underused office space right over there." She indicated an office just beyond hers.

Wyatt shook his head. "I want to be downstairs with the auditors and accountants. That's where I'm most at home. If I can have a computer and the appropriate log-ins, I can get started right away. I understand you had both Byron-Pierson and Kenner Reed Accounting come in to look things over?"

"As I explained to Meredith, yes, and they found nothing, but I have a couple of eager beavers downstairs who raised a few questions. We know those two firms are the best of the best, but—"

Wyatt was quick to agree. "None better."

"I wanted Meredith and Julia on board to make sure we haven't overlooked something basic. You must know that professional audits don't necessarily get to the bones of the matter."

"That's my wheelhouse," Wyatt said mildly. He turned to Julia and Meredith. "I know you two have work to do. Feel free to go on with your day, and I'll get to work here."

That was their cue. Julia nodded briskly. "So true. We'll conference call in a day or two, all right?"

That was clearly for Carolanne's benefit, because Julia and Meredith had every intention of chatting with Wyatt as soon as he had some answers.

"Sounds good."

Meredith and Julia moved toward the elevator, Mary Murphy accompanying them. When they got there, Julia reached out and laid a hand on Mary's shoulder. "Are you doing all right, Mary? Are you okay?"

Mary's chin quivered slightly, but then she took a breath and planted a smile on her face. A smile that probably fooled most people, including her boss, but Meredith understood Mary's current circumstances. She didn't know they'd done a background check on her. "I'm fine." She started to back away, but Julia kept the conversation going.

"How's your mother? I remember she was a true champion for your cousin."

Mary tried to hide a grimace, then she pulled in a deep breath. "Older and needing some help, but that's what family's for, isn't it? To take care of one another, no matter the cost."

"Is there anything I can do to help?" Julia asked softly as Carolanne and Wyatt approached the other elevator.

Mary extended her hand to both ladies who took it, in turn. "A pleasure to see you both again," she said brightly. "I think the special downstairs is grilled chicken on salad with mandarin orange wedges and caramelized dressing. It's a company favorite."

"Thanks for sharing that." Julia went along, as if agreeing their conversation was food based. When she and Meredith got to Julia's car, she drummed her fingers on the steering wheel. "She can't be herself in front of her boss," she said.

"Who, Mary?"

"Yes." Julia put the key into the ignition. "So why is that? Is Carolanne a jerk to her? Is she coldhearted? Is Mary dipping into funds to help pay for elder care and/or child care?"

"I wondered the same thing." Meredith frowned. "I'd hate for that to be true, but it's got to be hard to have Carolanne put on airs, throw money around, and treat you like a counter girl at the local diner while you're struggling to make ends meet."

"It would drive me crazy," said Julia as she started the car. "That's a lot of pressure to be under, and to have all that money flowing through your fingers has got to be the very worst of temptations."

"Wyatt advised us to look at who's closest to the money first because they're often the most tempted."

"I might come to hate this particular assignment if it turns out to be Mary Murphy." Julia took the turn onto the expressway as they headed toward Miss Dicey's assisted-living complex. "I can't even fathom it, but then, I've never been in a situation like that either. My mom is in good health and ridiculously independent, and Beau and I have no financial worries. But being on your own with kids and a sick mom and an egocentric boss..." Her voice trailed off.

Meredith couldn't deny it. "Carolanne always wanted to be a princess. Or a debutante. That stuff meant something to her. Not to Rusty, not ever, but the younger Carolanne loved every step of their success. I pretty much lost track of her about fifteen years ago. Our paths didn't cross until we both lost our husbands. I daresay she's gone from princess to queen and may have a bona fide case of the Big Head, and you know that's bad."

"It's felled many a Southern aristocrat," agreed Julia. "With all that being said, I still don't want Mary to be our perp. If there even *is* someone pilfering funds. I still come up short when I envision two mega firms doing an audit and finding nothing."

"Which could bring us back to Wyatt's other assertion of it being two people. If one is layering beneath the other, he said no one would find it without a whistleblower."

"And that reality might let Mary off the hook, because she seems to be a loner there."

Meredith agreed as Julia parked the car in one of the somewhat small parking spaces adjacent to the assisted-living center. "I noticed that too." She took a small pad from her quilted purse. "I brought my notebook along. I know she might not be able to tell us much, but I didn't want to forget a thing."

"And I'll record her answers," said Julia as they went through the door and approached the front desk. A friendly woman waved them over.

"You're here again, how nice! To see Miss Dicey?" When they nodded, she pointed to her right. "In the solarium overlooking the sun garden. It's bingo time in the upstairs gathering room, and Miss Dicey likes her solitude. She only meanders down here when it's quiet. She's mobile today, no wheelchair, so that's always a reason to celebrate." She leaned slightly closer. "We only tend to see her on this floor during church services, bingo games, or parties in the gathering room. She likes the warmth of the windows but likes her privacy even more."

"An introvert?" Meredith whispered the question to Julia, knowing there wasn't time for an answer as they approached the sun-soaked room. "Or a woman who's lived her life scared?"

They walked in.

Miss Dicey looked up as if alarmed, but when she recognized them, the look softened. "You've come back. To find out more, I expect."

Julia slipped into a chair across from Miss Dicey. "Yes. Your story intrigued us, Miss Dicey, and we can't stop thinking about it."

"I know the feeling," the old woman muttered. "It's been with me night and day for seventy-five years. Sometimes I look back and wonder if I'm a fool for letting it govern so many of my choices." She peered from Meredith to Julia. "Maybe my imagination got the better of me. Maybe I let the coincidence of untimely deaths paint a picture that didn't exist. Because try as I might, I can't see the sense in anyone threatening us to keep silent, although it seemed quite ominous back then. But everything seemed upside down for a while after the war. Men needing jobs, women giving up their jobs for men who might not do them as well, women being paid half what a man got for doing the same job. You were labeled unpatriotic if you complained. Some did all right, just going on and marrying and having families, but there were a lot of questions raised about a lot of things. And few answers."

"Does it bother you that we're asking more questions?" asked Meredith kindly. Miss Dicey hadn't been nervous when they'd met together months before. She had, in fact, been quite delightful. So maybe bringing up old wrongs wasn't fair to an elderly woman. "Because we don't want to trouble you, Miss Dicey. We'd like to look into this, but not at the expense of your peace of mind."

"Well, that flew out the window a good while back, don't you know?" Miss Dicey quipped. She gave them a frank look. "The problem of having a slowed-down body and a quick mind is that I have way too much time to think and little opportunity to do, so if you gals are willing to look deeper, I'm willing to tell you anything I know. It's not a lot," she cautioned. "But who knows what nugget of truth might clear things up?"

"And that's why we do what we do," Julia said. She went through a list of simple questions, then got a little more personal. "So Miss Dicey, the codebreakers weren't supposed to be married or engaged, correct?"

"Correct," she said crisply. "It was thought that women simply couldn't get through the day without pillow-talking to their fiancés or husbands about their jobs. Which is ridiculous," she humphed. "If you examine history, it's generally men who brought down kingdoms and governments by their loose talk."

Meredith winced. "Did the double standard bother you? Any of you?"

Miss Dicey weighed the question for a moment. "Yes and no. We found it absurd, but we also believed in what we were doing, and that outweighed everything else. And Dean Withers, the woman who recruited us after we'd left Charleston, was an amazing woman who believed that women were on the brink of liberation because Georgia stopped dragging its heels and gave women control over their earned wages in 1943."

"Twenty-three years after we got the right to vote?" Julia didn't try to mask her astonishment.

"Well, our fair state waited as long as it could on that one too, and it took the national amendment to secure our voting rights," declared Miss Dicey. "My mama cheered it quietly and voted, but she didn't have the stomach for upheaval. Dean Withers was so different." Miss Dicey smiled fondly. "A born inspiration. Her mother was part of the Georgia Woman Suffrage Association back in the nineteenth century. They took up a cause before it was popular in the South. Just hearing the dean speak of such things lit a fire inside me," Miss Dicey said. "Being a high school teacher wasn't anything like being a teacher now," she explained. "I was required to teach algebra, geometry, chemistry, and world history, and when the biology teacher walked out, they asked me to take that on too." She leveled them another frank look. "The only thing I was good at was English, and that was the one thing they didn't have me teach. Across the nation there were a lot of unqualified teachers making very little money. Things are quite different now."

Meredith nodded. Miss Dicey seemed revved today. Her left hand shook until she stopped it with her other hand. "When Dean Withers looked for help and contacted women to train as decoders, I was thrilled. And to go to Washington?" That memory lit her faded eyes with excitement. "It was noble and good and exciting in its own way. We were given an opportunity to help, to work for the government, under cover. To aid a noble cause. And meet some really cute military men," she added, smiling. Then her face changed, and her voice softened. "But then we got those notes just as we were dispatched home. We wanted to discuss them with each other, but timing was against us even with our own group. We kind of assumed everyone got them as part of the nation's push for secrecy, but when I heard about Ginny's death, I wasn't so sure. There was no reason a newlywed should go to sleep and not wake up again."

"We can stop." Julia put her hand over Miss Dicey's. "We don't have to go further right now, Miss Dicey."

Miss Dicey looked tempted, but then she raised her chin. "When you've hit triple digits, you don't wake up in the morning thinking you've got a lot of time left, so if you can stay a few more minutes, I can tell you a little more. Once the bingo crowd comes this way, I'm heading back upstairs."

"I'm in." Meredith flipped the page of notes she was taking.

"As I said, Virginia was first." Miss Dicey glanced around as if afraid to be overheard. "So sweet, funny, and lovely, and so excited to be marrying Ben Converse."

Julia sat a little straighter. "The former state supreme court justice?"

"Yes." Miss Dicey took a sip of her tea then set the glass down with shaky hands. "He was a young lawyer then, a law clerk for some bigwig and the kind of man that worked his way up after his service, step by step. Losing Ginny was a huge blow to him. Their wedding had been planned for years, and it was an absolute heartbreak to hear of her funeral not long afterwards."

"Hear of it?" Meredith frowned. "You didn't know she'd died until after her funeral?"

"None of us did. I don't know if they just didn't think to contact us or what happened, exactly. If they'd told just one of us, that one would have made sure to tell us all, so finding out about it after the fact was disappointing, I'll tell you. No one even called Theresa, and she was Ginny's best friend and maid of honor."

"I thought you couldn't be engaged while you were code-breakers?" Julia asked.

Miss Dicey's brow drew down. "Not initially, but you put twenty-five thousand women and at least that many men together and something's going to happen. Several of the Charleston girls had steady beaus or fiancés by the time we were dispatched from duty in '45. Most kept it quiet because we weren't the sort to flout rules."

"And yet the rules were relaxed."

"The war came to an end," she said sensibly. "Most of us went home, ready to keep our silence, especially after receiving those notes."

"Only you Charleston gals?" asked Meredith.

Miss Dicey shrugged. "We thought so. No one knew for sure, because we were told not to talk. Threatened to keep silent. So if you're asking did I make contact with other groups from Boston or Princeton or Wellesley, the answer is no. Absolutely not. I made friendships with a few of the other girls, but we Charleston women tended to stay in our own little clutch when it came to privacy matters."

Making it easier to segregate them and control them, Meredith realized. But to what end? "Did your group work together? Were you all working on one significant project?"

"No. We were in various groups in a complex outside of Washington, but a few of us shared rooms. Like sardines in a can, but that was all right. Everyone had soldiers to write to, some seri-ous, some not serious at all, to keep up morale, you know? It was important to keep up morale, and those letters meant something, going back and forth across war-torn seas."

"You have a pretty way with words, Miss Dicey," said Julia.

"That was a help," Miss Dicey told her. "Being able to see words in code, being able to sense the meaning and direction. I knew next to nothing about Japan and Asia, but once I studied the Japanese language for weeks, I began seeing patterns. Understanding messages. I spent the next two years helping our military sink ships, and then seventy-plus years wondering if I was being watched." She reached for her glass of tea but then didn't touch it. "I have no regrets about the former but great reserve about the latter in retrospect. Perhaps I'd have made different decisions about life and love if I hadn't been afraid. Still, it's old news now. Like me."

The hum of voices filtered their way. A solid group of elderly men and women were moving down the hall toward the solarium.

Miss Dicey stood. She took a firm hold of her walker, and it was good to see her upright. Less delicate than she'd seemed before. "We can talk more another day. It's good to talk about this, even if it's been so long."

"You're really okay with it?" asked Julia as Miss Dicey began moving toward the opposite hall, leading away from the approaching group and back to the elevator that would take her up to her room.

"I wondered if I would be," she admitted, and then she nodded. "I am, although it can't come to anything after all this time, I suppose. But it's just plain good to get it out there."

"I'm sorry about your friends," Meredith said. "That had to be so hard."

"It was. I expected it would take a while for Bennington to move on, but he married a widow the next year and had a few children. Folks said that Ginny died of unexplained heart failure in her sleep while Ben was away, but I didn't believe it. Couldn't believe it. Ginny was the picture of health, and she worked out in the gym more often than every other woman there, including some who went on to become naval officers, so the thought of her dying in her sleep never set well. But worse was the thought of her dying alone, because Ginny was the kind of gal who attracted a crowd wherever she went. She was never, ever alone, so to die that way was just wrong."

"She had Jesus." Meredith whispered the words as they accompanied Miss Dicey to the nearby elevator. "If we believe, we're never truly alone, Miss Dicey. The Lord is with us, every day."

"Ginny was a staunch believer." Miss Dicey stared forward as if deep in thought then sidled a look toward Meredith. "You're right, you know. And I know that. Maybe it just made me plain mad to think of her all alone like that when we'd shared a flat with two other gals, so crowded and fun because we knew we were doing a good thing. Each of us sending money home to help families. Well, all but Coco. Her family didn't need money. We had a sisterhood. Not like a convent, mind you." Her eyes twinkled when she met Julia's smile. "We had our share of dates and sharing nylons and clothes because no one had an excess. But that just drew us closer."

The elevator door opened.

Miss Dicey went in. She turned slowly, hit the button, and the doors slid shut.

Julia signed them out as the solarium filled behind them. "She still keeps her distance, even now." She made the observation softly as she and Meredith moved toward the door and out into the parking lot. "Not from fear, from habit. When you've spent all those years being alone, it's got to be a hard habit to break."

"Maybe the confusion of the noise and voices wears on her too," offered Meredith, but then she remembered the look in Miss Dicey's eyes when she talked about her friend Ginny. "No, I think you're right, Julia. I think she tucked herself away out of fear and wasn't able to live free again."

"I know she doesn't have much time left," said Julia as she clicked her fob to unlock the car doors. "But I sure would like to give her some peace of mind in her final days."

Meredith's phone signaled a text. "Carmen says that Maggie Lu is coming for coffee in a few minutes. Let's get their take on the whole thing. I won't pretend I'm not dying for a slice of this." She held up a picture of a scrumptious-looking layer cake for Julia to see then stopped, aghast, as she spotted the rear window of Julia's car.

BACK OFF!

"Someone spray-painted my car?" Julia's mouth dropped open right before her jaw went tight and her face grew stern. "I just had this car cleaned and detailed after an annoyingly long, wet winter. Whoever did this—"

She whipped out her camera and snapped pictures while Meredith called the police. It took a little while for them to get there, but when two of Savannah's finest joined them beneath the newly leafed tree, the first one out of the cruiser met Julia's gaze. "Judge Foley, right? Who you been ticking off, Judge? You left the bench a while back. I haven't heard your name insulted in some time."

"Anton Dillinger." Julia shook the officer's hand. "You helped straighten out your share of miscreants in my time on the bench, but this time I'm afraid it's not court related. I'm investigating a problem." They'd agreed not to let out who they were working for. Meredith didn't want a stock loss on her conscience, especially when there might be nothing happening.

"You ladies have ruffled some feathers." The other officer was older than most beat cops. Like retirement age older, not the norm. "Are you investigating the assisted-living facility?"

Meredith shook her head. "No. Well, actually…" She turned to Julia. "How do we know why this person targeted us, Julia? Because of case number one? Or case number two?" She glanced toward the adult facility.

"There are that many people out to get you ladies?" There was no hiding the grain of amusement in the older officer's voice as he tipped back his hat and gave them a skeptical look.

"At least one, it seems," Meredith said. She indicated the window with a dour expression. "But why? Now that's the question. And you, sir, are not our typical streets of Savannah beat cop." She didn't point out his age.

"I tried retirement," the older officer said as he reached into the cruiser and brought out a canister of wipes. "Didn't suit. I'd rather be working. So maybe we have something in common." He reached out a hand to Julia first, then Meredith.

She accepted the gesture with a quick but light grip. "Meredith Bellefontaine."

"Ron's wife." Did he hold her hand a little longer than necessary? Maybe.

But maybe not. She noted the compassion in his gaze. "Widow now," she said.

"I know. I'm so sorry. I'm Dixon Mulvaney. Your husband and I were together on the force decades ago, and I was away when he passed. I'm truly sorry for your loss, Mrs. Bellefontaine. Ron was a good man, right out of the gate. I was glad he branched out on his own, but we missed him on the force."

"There aren't many of Ron's fellow officers still working," she told him. Most officers took their retirement fairly early these days.

He let go of her hand and lifted one shoulder. "I expect I'm one of the few in that regard. Like I said, retirement didn't work for me." He moved toward the car, where Officer Dillinger had just finished photographing the words. "At least they used washable ink." He proved it with a couple of wipes from the canister.

"Washable ink?" Meredith stared at the smeared words and the red-stained wipes in his hands.

"Like they use at dealerships," he said.

"I never thought of that. I saw words and expected paint and a big job."

"I'm glad it's neither, although the words are something to consider, aren't they?" asked Officer Dillinger.

"Threats are never acceptable," Meredith replied. She thought of the dead flowers stashed in her basement.

"Technically, it's not a threat," Dixon Mulvaney said. "There's no caveat. As in 'back off *or* you die' or 'back off *or* else.'"

"Threat by implication," Julia said.

He nodded. "Agreed." He met Julia's gaze then pulled an electronic notepad from his pocket. "Mrs. Bellefontaine, your address?"

Meredith rattled it off for him.

"Phone number?"

She paused. "You don't want Julia's address? And her number?"

He looked surprised, then amused. Again. "Got that from her registration, ma'am, but thanks for checking. Just need your contact information." He paused a couple of slow beats. "If you don't mind."

She blushed.

Meredith didn't blush often, but her somewhat silly mistake of wondering why he'd focused on her was reason enough to elicit a blush. It was a rookie mistake, one that Julia pounced on when they were back in the car with a clean rear window. "He got to you." She grinned when she said it, waved goodbye to the responding officers, put the car into gear, and drove away.

"Nonsense."

"Hah!" Julia took the curve toward the highway and smirked. "I saw the look. And the blush. And the guy is crazy cute. Maybe he'll give Quin Crowley a run for the money."

"He's a sixtysomething cop who couldn't find enough to do on his own so he came back to the only thing he knew: work. I don't think 'crazy cute' applies to men over sixty. Although it might apply to Quin, but that's between us."

Julia merged into traffic then tapped the wheel. "I got a sense of something else. Something deeper, maybe, that brought him back to the force. Whatever, he was nice. They both were. They walked tall and didn't shrug us off."

"Wearing the uniform with pride is a good thing."

"Yes, but it went beyond that," Julia said. "To stature. And self-awareness. With all those years in children's court, I came to know a lot of the cops and deputies around town. The ones with a sense of humor always seemed to be on top of the job. That ability to distance yourself is huge in occupations like police work and medicine."

"We'll probably never see him again, but I'm glad they responded as soon as they did. And that the perp used that washable ink stuff. I'd never thought of that before, but I was glad it wiped right off, Julia."

"Me too, mostly because Beau really prefers that I not get threatened anymore. He says he had plenty of that while I was on the bench issuing unpopular opinions. But who was targeting us today? Someone who knew we were going to see Miss Dicey?"

"No one knew but Carmen and Miss Dicey. And I'm pretty sure she forgot, because she seemed surprised when we walked in."

"Would someone be listening to her calls at the home?"

Meredith frowned. "To what end?"

"Don't know." Julia pulled into her parking space behind the agency. "Or is it related to Payroll Inc.? Anyone could have followed us to the home, spray-painted the window, then left."

"I didn't see any cameras in the home's parking lot."

Julia frowned. "But they have them at the entrance doors. I wonder if any of them are trained outward. We'll have to check."

Meredith's phone rang just then, and an unfamiliar local number showed up in her display. Brow knit, she swiped it. "Magnolia Investigations, Meredith speaking."

"Mrs. Bellefontaine, it's Officer Mulvaney."

"Yes?" She put him on speaker so Julia could hear both sides of the conversation. "You're on speaker, Officer. So Judge Foley can hear."

"Call me Julia," Julia told him in a bright voice.

Meredith scolded her with a look that her friend ignored.

"We checked the camera feed from the east-facing side of the assisted living facility, but we weren't able to see much. The trees lining the parking lot blocked a lot of the view, even without leaves on most of them, but we did see a portion of a small silver or light gray sedan come into the parking lot about six minutes after you exited your vehicle. Unfortunately that's all the camera caught. The car entered, stayed for about two minutes, then left. No license plate or identifiers were visible. I'm sorry about that. We couldn't even tell if anyone got out of the car. The driver's side was completely blocked."

"Thank you for checking on that," Julia said. "We were just wondering if the facility cameras might have caught anything."

"It's not much, but the time frame fits, and no one else pulled in and out like that. Every other car that pulled in had someone who entered the building."

"You checked the full forty minutes?" asked Meredith, surprised. "That's so nice of you."

"We fast-forwarded between cars, but yes. Just doing the job, ma'am." Something in the way he said it made her think that doing a thorough job was part of Dixon Mulvaney's DNA.

"Well, thank you."

"My pleasure."

He hung up, and Julia smirked at her. "Told you he was nice."

Meredith pocketed her phone once she got out of the passenger seat. "You're right. I don't know if everyone would have bothered checking cameras."

"Dream date," teased Julia, but then she held up her three middle fingers in a pledge symbol. "I will say no more to anyone about this. Promise. Pinkie swear, even."

Meredith rolled her eyes and went inside the agency, but she knew Julia meant it. She wouldn't tease Meredith about personal things like that in front of others. That had always been their way. In front of Beau and Ron, yes.

Now she didn't even do it in front of Beau, Meredith realized. Julia was sensitive to the change in status with Ron gone.

But as she greeted Maggie Lu and Carmen in the cozy, updated kitchen, she realized something else.

Dixon Mulvaney was nice. And attractive. Even if she didn't want to admit it.

Chapter Seventeen

"MISS DICEY WAS A CODEBREAKER in World War II?" Carmen raised both eyebrows as she sliced the sumptuous-looking layer cake.

"She was," Meredith replied. "It was kept secret until she spilled it to Jubal a while back. The whole thing was kept secret until folks finally broke it out in the open with books about the codebreakers, and that shed light on the whole thing. But the problem isn't the codebreaking. It's what happened at the end of their term outside of Washington that Miss Dicey wants us to investigate." She explained the story to Carmen and Maggie Lu while Julia fixed coffee. "In the end," she concluded, "some of the gals from Charleston College were given these threatening notes to maintain their silence. They thought it was the government being overly concerned, but when three of their group died very soon afterwards, Dicey figured the government meant what it said."

"She stayed alone her whole life, just to protect others from what she knew," Julia added. "Never married, lived by herself once her family was gone, and taught music to children."

"Why would they be the only ones threatened?" Carmen asked.

"We don't know that they were, but can you jump on that this afternoon?" Meredith requested. "Because if they were—"

"Then it's not the government posing a threat," figured Carmen as she jotted notes. "The problem with this case is like a few of our others have been. Age is a factor. Finding people who were alive during World War II is getting trickier every day. But there may be some who were children at the time who are familiar with what went on. And public records," she noted as the women tasted the cake. Carmen paused, obviously waiting for their reaction.

"Amazing." Julia licked the crumbs from her fork before taking another bite of the seven-layer cake. "This is exactly the kind of cake I love, Carmen."

"Tender cake, perfect jam, and silky-smooth frosting, all in perfect ratio to one another," agreed Maggie Lu. She set her fork down and leaned in. "I was a babe in arms during the end of the war, and I saw through a child's eyes until I was a teenager, but let me say that listening to the older women talk about those war years was an eyeopener. How women stepped up to do their part and were summarily dismissed at the end because having jobs for men was crucial. Jobs for women were not considered vital, and the folks in power saw no disparity in that. Nothing they wanted to touch, anyway, because losing the male vote would have been catastrophic. And veterans tend to vote. But I can also say that women who spoke up in their own defense were few and far between back then. There were notable ones, but it wasn't until we got to the sixties that women began speaking their minds, having their say, and it wasn't always appreciated then. In my community, women spoke their minds more. Black women had more sense of equality with our men back then, I think."

"United by shared difficulty?" asked Julia, and Maggie Lu nodded.

"In some ways, yes. Women had a lot of small businesses in the black community, and they ran them their own way, so it was different from what their white counterparts were doing. It was still haves and have-nots, but the pieces on the chessboard were starting to move. In Miss Dicey's time, a lot of Southern women were the suffer-in-silence type. I was too, for far too long," she added. Old wrongs and secrets had kept Maggie Lu quiet for decades, which likely helped her understand Miss Dicey's predicament.

"If the government didn't send those threats, then it was someone who knew the women's secret—that they were codebreakers." Julia set her fork down as she spoke, and there was no missing the reluctance in her eyes as she paused eating the delicious cake. "And this person or persons targeted these girls to keep them quiet. Maybe for a reason that has nothing to do with codebreaking. And if they make the women think the government has means to silence them, what's to stop them from believing it's the government's hand at work when one or two die? It's the perfect cover."

Meredith could suddenly see the possibilities. "But who would have criminal intent against these women?"

"Against one woman, possibly," said Carmen. "You target the many but aim for the one."

"We're still talking about a long time ago. That's a pretty tough roadblock right there." Julia gave in and went back to eating cake, waving her fork for punctuation.

"So we follow the paper trail as usual," said Meredith. "See where it leads. See where things happened and who was around."

"I'll get all the online history of these women I can," Carmen promised. "I'm free to stay late, if I need to."

"Tonight's your night with Harmony, isn't it?" asked Meredith.

"She's sick, so she can't hang out with me tonight. Her foster mother was apologetic, but she's right. She needs to be home." Carmen washed and dried a cake cover that had been stored in an upper cupboard for a long time. When it shone brightly, she set it over the remaining cake. "Part of me feels helpless when something like this happens. Like I'm not doing enough to help her."

"I think that means you're falling in love with this little girl," said Julia. "Kind of like I fell in love with a certain teenager who needed a little love and guidance at one time."

Carmen smiled in agreement. "I love hanging out with her, giving her some special attention."

"How long is her mama in prison, Carmen?"

"Almost four more years. If they parole her then. And even so, she might not regain custody right away, if at all."

"And no family for this sweet baby child?" breathed Maggie Lu, but then she held up one hand. "You don't need to answer that, I understand. And her foster family is nice?"

"Very. She's one of three foster kids there, and Katie, the foster mom, is great, but all three kids know it's temporary. That even if someone wanted to adopt them they couldn't, because none of the three are free for adoption."

"Something else to pray about," said Meredith.

"Pastor Ed has a community outreach he started last year," Julia told them. "It's amazing how nicely it's come together, and one thing he's doing is matching up families. Two of the children he's matched weren't free for adoption, but he put his prayer team to work, and within six months, it all worked out."

Her words stirred Meredith, because Pastor Ed Markham was a solid man of God who put his faith into action. As that thought came to her, she realized that was what she'd been missing the past few years at her church.

Faith in action.

She loved putting her hands to a task, and that was part of her discontent, she realized. She was working, yes, but not volunteering in a ministry. Something that had been a mainstay in her life before Ron died.

Everything had changed in that first year of widowhood. As she sat there, listening to her friends talk, she realized that she missed that altruistic work. The giving of her time and hands, with no expectation of payment.

"Are we considering this lunch?" asked Julia. "If we are, I'm okay with that. I've been doing too much sitting lately, and if we're doing supper at the diner, I'm going to get back to work in my office."

"And I'm going to the library because my afternoon shift will be starting soon," Maggie Lu said as she stood. "I love the morning shifts with those baby-friendly programs, but I don't mind the quiet of the afternoon shifts. Mostly older folks and an academic or two. I'll see you at the diner at five thirty, all right?"

Maggie Lu started for the door then paused and looked back. "I want to thank all of you for supporting Charlene's enterprise the way you do. I wasn't sure it was a good idea when she launched a whole new business on her own, but I can see it was fear that goaded me into thinking that way. A fear that came to nothing, just showing how trusting in the Lord's timing is important. I'm dismayed when I forget that sweet truth."

"As am I," Meredith assured her. "Fortunately we can keep one another on track. The way friends do," she added with a smile.

Maggie Lu left, and the women went to their offices.

The sun shone brightly along the south side of the building, bathing the offices in light for hours. When the light disappeared, Meredith checked her phone just as a warning tone indicated a severe thunderstorm watch.

"I hope Beau isn't on the water. Or the golf course." Julia met Carmen and Meredith by the front windows. "That sky looks fierce."

"He wouldn't stay out in the storm, would he?" asked Carmen.

"Well, he tends to consider himself invincible, but he's also smart. Usually." Julia shook her head.

"Did you call him?"

"I did. Straight to voice mail, which means either his phone died or he accidentally hit the Do Not Disturb icon because he's always fiddling with his screen. That's happened more than once, I'm afraid."

A flash of lightning lit up the sky west of them. Cloud-to-cloud and cloud-to-ground.

Their phones all sounded a warning again.

"I love a storm, but standing in front of a big window when a bad one is heading our way isn't the brightest move," Julia said. "If the rain keeps up, I'll pick up Maggie Lu and we can drive to the diner." She turned to Carmen. "Why don't you come have supper with us?" When Carmen looked hesitant, Julia slung an arm around the young woman's shoulders. "My treat. Since the weather's gone rogue and your date with Harmony is canceled, let's do a girls' night."

"I'm in," said Meredith. "We can pretend we won't talk about work, but we know we will, so we can consider supper a conference call with the benefit of food."

"That sounds good, because I've got a couple of names on the codebreaker case for you all to check out tomorrow, if you can fit it in. I know the other case is high priority, but two of these folks live in the Savannah area, and they're not getting any younger. If you know what I mean," Carmen added with a wince.

"And with Wyatt working at Payroll Inc. tomorrow, we'll want to keep our distance. At least until he finds something," noted Meredith.

"I'll fill you in at supper," Carmen told them. "These might not be considered strong threads, but they're threads."

A crash of thunder rattled the windows.

"I'm so glad we got those repairs done when we did," Meredith said as she turned toward her office. "A solid roof and bug-free walls are a comfort in Georgia, and that's a fact."

Lightning lit up the sky again, a brilliant, crackling flash, bright enough to cast shadows below. As it did, the lights went out, the AC paused, and the entire office went quiet.

And dark.

In the sudden silence they heard a sound they'd never heard in the building before.

Like a howl. A cry for help. An inhuman sound, or maybe a human wail. Long. Low. And drawn out.

It was coming from the basement.

Meredith pulled out her cell phone and hit the flashlight icon. So did Julia and Carmen, and together, like the three musketeers they were, they crept their way down the hall.

Chapter Eighteen

MEREDITH CLUTCHED HER PHONE AS if it were weaponized.

She led the way to the stairway and opened the door. Out of habit, she flicked the switch.

Of course nothing happened.

She ignored the harsh beat of her heart. And the soft pounding in her temples, a reaction that happened in times of strife or fear.

She stepped down once. Twice. Three times.

Julia followed closely behind her, the beam from her phone casting odd shadows with every step Meredith took.

"Do you want me to go first?" asked Julia softly. "I've got my gun."

"But then we might get blood on the carpet, and you know what a pain that is to clean," Meredith whispered, only partly in jest.

Then another sound came to them. A scraping sound, soft but insistent, as if someone was digging for something. Or at something.

Meredith turned the final corner.

The noise stopped.

She couldn't tell if it had been coming from the laundry area or the storage room at the near end of the finished basement. When Ron set up his office they'd rented out the lower level to help make mortgage payments. They hadn't had a tenant in years, and the long family room, small utility kitchen, and laundry area weren't updated but were still in great shape. The single bedroom was at the other end of the finished basement, next to the small full bath.

She trained the light around.

Nothing.

Then a slight noise on her left drew her gaze.

Her heart sped up.

Adrenaline pumped into high gear.

She shone her light that way, half hoping she'd see nothing, but when she saw nothing, that meant she had to go deeper into the darkened areas.

She moved forward.

So did Julia and Carmen. Carefully they trained their lights up and down. Back and forth. Just as Meredith was about to creep back the other way, a sound came from behind a closet door near the laundry area.

Don't open the closet! Don't you remember what happens to women who open doors in every horror movie ever made? Run upstairs right now and call that cute cop and get him over here. He's got an even bigger gun than Julia!

She had to work to clamp down her fear. She reached out one tentative hand to gently draw the closet door open.

She trained her light down.

And when she did, her heart melted into a puddle right at her feet. "A mama cat. And a kitten," she breathed softly as an unfamiliar dark-toned calico stared up at them.

"And another on the way," said Carmen as contractions took over the mother cat's body. Within a minute, a second kitten appeared, and the mama cat ignored the women in her quest to care for her growing family.

"Do you recognize her?" breathed Julia. "Is she a neighbor's cat?"

Meredith shook her head. "I don't, but she's a beauty, isn't she? She could be from anywhere, a stray, but how did she get in here?"

"No clue. I promise, I haven't left any doors open despite the beautiful weather," said Carmen. "Not after the snake debacle. Well—" She paused and took a deep breath. "We did have a pile of packages at the back door from today's deliveries, and I propped the screen door open long enough to bring them in. Not for long, but possibly long enough," she admitted.

"I do that all the time," Meredith told her. "That could have been the moment this little beauty was looking for."

"Should we just leave her?" suggested Julia. "I have no experience with birthing animals."

"A box," declared Meredith. "Not too big, and lined with an old bath towel. And we'll need a litter box and litter and food dishes."

"I'll make a run to the store," Julia offered. "I'll check how far the power outage goes, and I'll bring that stuff right back. Does she look all right to you?" she asked Meredith.

"A little stressed, but that's normal enough. We'll let her get on with her motherly duties and get her checked out later. In the meantime, we can see if anyone's missing a very pretty calico."

"Sounds good."

Carmen came back with a stout box as Julia left to get supplies. "This is where the age of online deliveries comes in handy," she said as she lowered the lined box. "I grabbed an old towel from the laundry room closet."

"Better than my clothing," noted Meredith, secretly proud that the cat had sense enough to do what needed to be done, even at the expense of an old hoodie and sweater.

The cat had pawed the garments into her own personal birthing chamber. Carmen lifted one newborn into the box. Meredith lifted the other, and when Mama Cat hopped into the box to care for her babies, Meredith slipped the soiled clothes out of the closet. They slid the box into place and left the door slightly ajar. "We'll let her finish up, and as soon as Julia comes back, we'll set her up with food and water and a litter box."

"You don't mind?" asked Carmen. She slipped her hand into a plastic bag and picked up the clothing then took it straight over to the washing machine. "I'll toss these in here, but we can't run it until the power comes back."

"I'll make a note to start it," said Meredith. "You know, this is like a scene from a James Herriot book." When Carmen looked blank, Meredith made a face. "An English veterinarian, back in the Second World War, who wrote the best stories about being a vet and dealing with farm folks and animals and birthing all kinds of little creatures. Heartwarming stories." She pointed to the closet as they moved upstairs. "Finding her was like a scene out of one of his books."

"I love animal stories. I've never in my life had an animal of any sort, and my landlord doesn't allow pets. When I was fifteen I was in a foster home that had pets, but they made it clear that the dog was their son's and the guinea pig was their daughter's and I could gaze from afar. But when the dog actually liked me better than the son, they sent me back into the system."

"Oh, Carmen." It hurt Meredith's heart to hear such reality. Why take children into care if you couldn't be fair, impartial, and loving? "I'm so sorry."

"I survived. Well," she added honestly, "after getting into no small amount of trouble and Julia finding me and challenging me to be a better version of myself. Her mentorship changed my life."

"And she loves you," added Meredith.

"That goes both ways," Carmen assured her. "If mama kitty is fine for the moment I'm going to gather my information upstairs. I already printed out what I found, so we don't have to view Google Docs on cell phones to share information. But if the diner is out of power, we might have to change our plans."

"Let's give it an hour and see." Power outages weren't unusual, and depending on the spread, they could either be fixed in an hour or out for days. But when the outage map flashed on the local app, it was clear that utility crews would be working into the night to clear broken branches and fix downed wires.

Julia returned about an hour later. "I had to take a scenic drive north to find an open store with power, but mission accomplished," she said as she came in the back door, toting supplies. "The kitty food is still in the car."

"I'll grab that." Carmen went out the back way as Maggie Lu came in the front.

"Back here," called Meredith when she heard Maggie Lu's soft voice drawl, "Hello?"

Maggie Lu arrived in the kitchen as Carmen came through the back door, lugging a fair-sized bag of cat food.

"We have a visitor," Meredith explained as they all moved downstairs.

"GK has come to keep y'all company?" supposed Maggie Lu. She looked perplexed when Meredith shook her head.

"No. An unexpected visitor," said Meredith softly, and as they trained their flashlights slightly away from the closet, she eased open the door.

"Oh my word, such a lovely lady," crooned Maggie Lu. She bent right down and stroked the mama cat's head, and the calico's instant warm purr indicated she wasn't feral. "She just wandered in, looking for birthing facilities, kind of like that long ago trek to Bethlehem. And you have opened the doors of the inn, I see," she teased Meredith and Julia with a soft smile. "Does she have a home, I wonder?"

"She can stay here on a temporary basis, but GK would not take to having a friend, being as how he's not exactly the world's most sociable creature," said Meredith.

"And we just got our cat," said Julia. "But there's no one here on weekends, so I wouldn't want her to stay here for very long."

"Well, this is one to think on, isn't it?" Maggie Lu asked softly as she continued to stroke the cat's head. Meredith filled the new litter pan and Carmen took care of the food and water dishes, and all the while, Maggie Lu whispered sweet nothings to the newest Whitaker Street arrival.

"I think you're smitten," teased Julia when they'd finished setting up the cat's cozy corner of the room.

"I am every bit that," confessed Maggie Lu. "I was telling Charlene that I miss Sydney the third and was thinking of getting a pet to keep me company in the evenings. You know how that is," she said to Meredith with a look of empathy. "Just something else to be breathing the same air as I am." Sydney the third was a friend's cat that Maggie Lu had kept for a while.

"I understand completely," Meredith replied. "But first we must see if she has a home, and I do believe there are four babies here. Now, her little family may be complete or not, but did you think to get flea medication while you were at the store, Julia?"

Julia handed a small vial to Maggie Lu. "Do you want to apply it?"

"I surely do, because I cannot see overrunning the office with little hoppies here, there, and everywhere," Maggie Lu said. She gently applied the drops to the cat's skin and then stood. "There you go, little mama. We'll leave you in peace. Right now, food, water, and the amenities are all cared for, so you just focus on those sweet babies."

The cat meowed as if thanking Maggie Lu.

That was one smart cat, Meredith decided, because the look on Maggie Lu's face made it plain—if no one claimed this beautiful cat, she was bound for a new home on Le Grand Street. And that would bless the cat and the new owner.

"Charlene has texted me that the Downhome Diner is still without power and probably will be throughout the evening," Maggie Lu told them.

"I thought of that while I was driving." Julia tucked the bag of litter out of the way as she spoke. "Let's order sandwiches from Charlene and go to my place. Beau has a meeting with a whole bunch of fishermen, and my neighbor said there's still power, so we can talk in peace and comfort. That way Charlene gets the business, and we can discuss what we've found this afternoon."

"My hair is the current barometer on the heightened humidity and lack of air-conditioning," drawled Meredith, who felt like her hair must have doubled in volume over the last two hours. "This is Southern hair at its finest." She increased her drawl deliberately and fluffed her frizzy hair.

"Volume, volume, and more volume," teased Carmen.

"Conditioner can only do so much," replied Meredith, but she smiled. "After my fair share of summers with these curls, I'm accustomed to the look. But only when we have uncontrollable conditions, like today. And I like that idea," she assured Julia. "Small businesses can't afford shutdowns, so if Carmen can call in an order, we can get it in a few minutes."

"She did say she's got a fryer going on the stovetop, bein' as how that's a gas stove," said Maggie Lu. "She can do fries, if anyone would like them."

"Let's get two orders of her sweet potato fries, and we'll share them," suggested Julia.

They picked up the food twenty minutes later and arrived at Julia's ten minutes after that. The welcome blast of cool air made them all sigh as they walked into her house.

"We may be made to glisten," said Julia as she set several to-go containers on the kitchen counter. "But look at us, deep-breathing this cool air like we were half-starved for oxygen, and it's only March. Ladies, I cannot think of how whiny we'll all be when this happens in June or July."

"I'm too hungry to even think about that, but I do believe that's why we have friends with pools or houses on the water, darling." Meredith winked as she withdrew containers from the bags. "But let's hope that doesn't happen. I may be a Southern gal, but we all know I get mighty tired of heat by August, so we'll take our power outage now. And hope for no more this year."

"I concur, and once we've eaten, I've got some news you're both going to want to hear," said Carmen. "It is news worth sharing."

They ate quickly, and then Carmen took some papers from her tote bag. "There wasn't a lot to find, understandably, because the government put a lid on the work these women did. But having said that, there's no record of any kind of threat against anyone. Just typical military procedure to stay quiet. So then I pulled up family histories on the women in Miss Dicey's group. I focused on the two women who died in that first year, and then the friend who died nearly two years later. Here's what I found." She handed out the papers.

She'd posted a marriage announcement for Virginia, followed by a news article lamenting the young woman's untimely death from natural causes. Then there was a notice for Theresa's unexpected accident the spring of the following year. Carmen had found two newspaper articles about the accident, a fall from a hiking trail into a rocky ravine below.

And finally, a short death notice for the loss of Pansy Warren. It said almost nothing, typical of the time and how folks handled suspected suicides, with as little voice and fanfare as possible.

"There's not much else about them, but there was this and it led me down another trail."

Carmen handed each of them a vintage article about Virginia's husband. It was dated a decade later and noted his rise to esteem on the bench, his thoughtfully written decisions, and his young family. Pictured was a lovely blond wife named Cynthia and three children, Adelaide, Bennington Jr., and Melissa. The older girl looked to be in her early teens.

"This is a beautiful family, and I expect folks were happy to see him move on, because the Converse family was beloved by so many in Georgia and the Carolinas," said Julia. "My mother held them in high esteem when I was young."

"Folks looked on them like our northern counterparts see the Kennedy clan," added Maggie Lu. "So many rising stars, but with tragedy marking its heels alongside, and not just with Bennington's first wife. His aunt and her sister-in-law died in a tragic boating accident a few years before that, and his great-grandfather was killed in a hunting accident earlier in the century. Some said it was pride that killed that old man because he didn't listen to anyone about anything, and he was stubborn as could be. They were having an old-fashioned fox hunt. It had fallen by the wayside after the Civil War, but he was determined to have one on their property. He got into a quarrel with his neighbor over who had the best dog in the hunt. When men are fighting over such things, it's best not to have a gun at the hip, if you know what I mean."

"He was shot?"

"Killed by a bullet, and the judge called it inadvertent. He took a shortcut during the hunt and came up a rise just as a volley of gunfire was aimed toward the foxes coming his way."

"The thought of hunting anything makes me cringe," said Carmen. "Why hunt innocent animals when there are perfectly good grocery stores nearby?"

"Well, dearie, if folks hadn't learned to provide by hunting game back then, we'd have starved from the get-go," said Maggie Lu practically. "We might even be too reliant on those stores these days. I believe folks should know the best way to care for themselves in times of trouble, and that includes hunting or fishing or growing food. Just because they're becoming lost arts doesn't mean we're wise to brush them aside. Skills learned are seldom forgotten, and I could still skin a rabbit if need be. Fortunately, I haven't needed to use that particular talent in some time," she finished.

"So there were trails of controversy and sadness following the Converses, but then Bennington remarries and has a family," noted Meredith as she studied the image.

"And didn't wait any too long, judging by the ages of those children," added Julia.

"I see that." Meredith frowned. "As a widow, I can't understand the push to hurry into remarriage. Then again, I was widowed at an older age. A young man might see it differently."

"Perhaps." Maggie Lu drew her brows together as she examined the Converse family picture. "I'm going to expect that you'll discover this oldest child was Cynthia's before she married Bennington. That child's of an age that makes being his impossible."

Meredith jotted a note onto her small legal pad. "I'll check it out. I was thinking the same thing, Maggie Lu."

"Are there any Converses around the area now?" asked Carmen. "I looked for them but couldn't find any."

"Bennington's daughters moved to the West Coast," Julia said. "I read his profile in the court pages one day while I was waiting for a very pokey public defender, and it said both of his daughters moved to California and Bennington Jr. passed away nearly twenty years ago. Not long after his father died. Of course, the girls would be old women now."

"My age," said Maggie Lu in an amused tone. "Or nearly. And the younger one is closer to your age, I do believe."

"My mistake." Julia flashed a grin. "Not old at all!"

The other women laughed as Julia's phone rang. "It's Wyatt." She stood to take the call but didn't make it very far before she stood absolutely still. "You found it?"

Whatever he repeated to her had Julia's eyes go wide and her mouth drop open.

Maggie Lu took the hint right away. "Carmen, child, let's go see what Julia's got planted outside and give these ladies a little elbow room to chat."

Julia sent them a thumbs-up, and when they'd gone outside, she switched Wyatt to speaker. "Go ahead, Wyatt. We can both hear you now."

"I found it." He sounded half-pragmatic, half-excited. "I haven't said a word to anyone at Payroll Inc. or flagged it at all, and I was careful to tiptoe away from the code without leaving a mark. Let's just say I looked from beyond and decoded so that no one inside the corporation would know I'd stumbled onto their not-so-little cache. They hid it in plain sight, disguised as a nominal state fee. No wonder the auditors missed it. I would have too, if I wasn't hunting for suspicious activity."

"How can you hide money pilfering in plain sight?" asked Meredith. "Either the credits and debits line up or they don't, right?"

"Not anymore," he said. "Not when it's got code. If something's got code, that means it's a bona fide use of money serving, and this code was expertly designed to look like a governmental fee applied to all transactions."

"A fee?"

"Yes, coded to look similar to a state disability or unemployment tax code under a blanket design so that each person receiving a paycheck was paying twenty-six cents per pay period to this slush fund."

"That's a miniscule amount," said Julia, and Wyatt responded with a light laugh that didn't sound all that happy.

"Not when it's multiplied by nearly three-and-a-half million paychecks every two weeks."

Meredith did the mental math. "That's over nine hundred thousand dollars. Biweekly."

"Exactly, and it's nothing that anyone would notice in their paycheck unless they were really examining things, because each state has a few tax-supported slush fund items. But this isn't really going to any state fund. It's being fed into an offshore account with so many bends in the road that I can't see where it ends up. This isn't casual thievery here, ladies. This is grand theft auto at a national scale, and someone is getting very rich on this deal."

"Someone who is very good at computers and coding?" asked Julia. She pulled Mick Cavendish's card out of her wallet and held it up for Meredith to see.

"Yes. And someone who understands that people rarely check the fine print, the tiny details. No one cares about a twenty-six-cent nominal state fee. Dollars raise eyebrows, but pennies are a whole other thing. So yes, someone who is good at computers and programs has engineered this seamlessly. From state to state, it looks absolutely legitimate. But it's fraud, one hundred percent."

"Committed by whom?" breathed Meredith.

"That's the kicker. There's no trace-back on the code. It was done through the interoffice access computer system, so it could be anyone who has ever had access to entering channeling code for the corporation. I will say, the funneling of this, and the work it took to make it appear like a bona fide state deduction for every state in the union, means it can't be someone who walks in as a temp or a short-term hire. This took work, so either someone who has outside access—"

Julia tapped a finger to Mick's business card again.

"Or a long-term employee, because this wasn't a quick course of action."

"Wyatt, I can't thank you enough," breathed Meredith. "And no one knows you found anything. You're sure of that?"

"One hundred percent certain unless your phones are tapped," he told her cheerfully.

The women exchanged quick, worried looks.

He reacted as if he could see their expressions. "I'm not serious, your phones aren't tapped, but do let me reiterate my initial warning. This goes way deeper than what we initially thought, Aunt Julia. And with much greater reward for the thief. No one who's bilking over a million and a half a month is going to think twice about keeping two women quiet. You have to tread carefully."

"Like meet with Carolanne and the board?" pressed Julia.

Wyatt didn't hesitate. "Meet with no one. Don't breathe this to anyone. Pretend you know nothing and give things a few days to unfurl. If the thief thinks we found nothing but is nervous because people are looking, he or she could tip their hand. So keep a cool gumshoe, all right?"

"We're good at that," Julia assured him. "I love you, kid."

"Love you too. Be safe. And be silent. Mostly."

"We will," Meredith promised him, then Julia disconnected the call.

"Now that we've found it, what on earth are we going to do about it?"

"For the moment, we're going to have supper and bring those sweet gals in from the heat. But then tomorrow, come over to my house early," Meredith said. "We can talk without danger of anyone hearing us."

Julia called the ladies back in, and the rest of the evening was outwardly calm. But in Meredith's head the question of who created that code spun in various directions. By the time she put her head on a pillow a few hours later, she was no closer to figuring it out. And that made for a restless night's sleep.

Chapter Nineteen

1945
Arlington, Virginia

The summer morning should have gleamed with hope. The war was over, troops would be streaming home, and everything would return to normal. But what was normal? Dicey wondered as she slipped over to the apartment Coco Lee shared with Pansy Warren and two non-Charleston women. Those two women had gone out for breakfast, leaving Coco, Pansy, and Dicey a narrow window of time to talk.

Coco opened the door when Dicey came up the steps, and Dicey slipped inside.

Coco and Pansy had been friends since childhood, and a more unlikely pair didn't walk the planet in Dicey's opinion. Coco's brash nature was softened by Pansy's more tentative manner. Sometimes. In return, Pansy was inclined to follow Coco's lead on things. As unlikely as it seemed on the surface, it worked for them.

Dicey slipped her note out of her pocket. "Did you two get notes like this?"

Pansy nodded, and her worried expression said a lot.

Coco made a sound of disgust. "I took my sewing scissors to mine," she declared in a hot voice. "That's what I thought of the whole thing. I did a job, and I did it to the best of my ability. I appreciate that we don't want to be feeding a future enemy our methods, but I won't be bullied by some invisible jerk who has nothing better to do than threaten women. Definitely a man," she'd accused in a low and angry undertone. "Most assuredly threatened by the rise of women, so look for a scrawny worm of a man. With glasses," she added, as if wearing glasses was a derisive addition.

"You didn't think we might want the note as evidence?" Dicey asked.

"One has no need for evidence if one is going to absolutely, positively ignore the situation, which is exactly what I'm doing. I am done with men lording things over me or taking charge. I'm an educated woman, and I'll do what I please, when I please."

Dicey would love a bigger portion of Coco Lee's resolve, but while Coco wasn't exactly a Yankee, her mother did hale from northern Pennsylvania, which meant she'd never be a Southern woman. Not really. At the moment, Dicey envied the other woman's panache.

"Pansy, what about you?" Dicey kept her voice low. The walls of this thrown-together housing weren't thick, and it wasn't hard to hear even normal conversations through them, if one was inclined to listen.

"I put it away."

"Throwing it away would be a better choice," scolded Coco. "You can't let this idiot hold a threat over you, Pans. You know how negative stuff messes with your head. But that's because you let it. Throw the thing away, or give it to Dicey. Or burn it. In any case, it's not in anyone's best interests to dwell on this stuff."

"Do I dare give away a government order?" Pansy wrung her hands and looked from Dicey to Coco and back.

"No letterhead, which means it's not official," Coco shot back. "If nothing else, military rules level a measure of believability to things. If this were a mandate from higher-ups, it would be on standard military issue paper with a letterhead."

Dicey couldn't help but disagree. "I don't think the military likes to put thinly disguised threats on letterhead. As a rule," she added. "Pansy, do you want me to take yours for you?"

Pansy looked undecided, then she bent down and took a folded piece of paper from the lining of her shoe.

"Great hiding place," Dicey said sarcastically.

"Better than my brassiere," Pansy confessed. "I'd have an easier time handing it over as evidence out of my shoe, if you know what I mean."

"I absolutely do," Dicey assured her. She carefully opened the folded note. "Same writing, same words."

"Same nonsense," stated Coco. "My guess is we rattled some lame duck's hold on power, and he's overreacting. Something I never do."

She was right about that. Coco had maintained her cool throughout the college years and as a codebreaker. She was *one tough cookie, and Dicey would have loved a cupful of Coco's courage. Unfortunately, Dicey was more like Pansy at times. But not about this, she vowed to herself.* "You're both leaving tomorrow?"

"Heading home, and then on with life," Coco said. "Having an endless supply of available military men buying me dinner has been nice, but I'm ready for some old-fashioned shrimp-and-grits and real sweet tea. The kind you only find back home. And for a house." *She eyed the thin-walled apartment with a frown.* "This did all right for a while, but I'm ready to go south. At least until life calls me elsewhere."

"I couldn't agree more," *replied Dicey. She put the folded notes into her pocket.* "We'll stay in touch, right?"

Pansy paled at the thought. "We've been told not to talk."

"But we're friends, Pansy." *Coco shot her a look of impatience.* "There's no rule saying we can't be friends."

"But what if this person thinks we're talking about our assignment?" *Pansy didn't hide the worry in her voice.* "How would they know we aren't? And what do they mean by silencing us exactly? There's nothing about that that sounds good, Coco."

"Oh, Pans." *Frustration drew Coco's brows down.* "How I wish you could just let things roll off your shoulders. It's not healthy to let anyone or anything have control over you."

"And yet a healthy dose of fear does keep prey from stumbling into predators' traps," *Pansy reminded her. She motioned toward the window.* "Brenda and Thea are coming back."

"My cue to leave." Dicey gave them both a quick hug. "Whatever else life brings us, it's been a pleasure serving with you both."

Coco snorted. "Serving would have meant the same pay grade and respect the men got, and not being referred to as maintenance workers and pencil sharpeners, but I know what you mean. It's been a job and a lark, all in one. Godspeed, Dicey."

"And to you."

She hurried down the outside steps as the two other women came her way. She gave them a quick, friendly wave. She didn't know them well. They tended to keep to themselves when the Charleston girls came around, but they waved back today. Maybe happy to be going home, like so many others.

Ginny Redding brought her note to Dicey later that afternoon. She slipped it to Dicey with a furtive movement, as though afraid she was being watched, and Dicey couldn't fault her for it. "I'll keep these in a safe space," Dicey whispered. "How did you find yours, Ginny?"

"It was slipped underneath my satchel while I was sketching a landscape from the hill." Ginny's paintings had been her hobby for years. "There were folks all around, saying their goodbyes. The climbing roses were so pretty, crawling along that old farm fence, as if time went on pause for just a little bit. It was a picture-perfect day, so to find this threat didn't just cast a shadow." Ginny shuddered. "It ruined the moment and my work, because I couldn't get beyond the fact that I was sitting right there, with my back to the satchel, when the person tucked it into place. To know he was that close and I was unaware was unnerving. Still is," she admitted. "I can't wait to get home and put all of this behind me."

"But doesn't that seem odd to you, that we have to pretend we weren't codebreakers?" asked Dicey.

Ginny shook her head. "When my brother returned from the front, he said there were a lot of things he wouldn't talk about," she acknowledged. "But there were others he couldn't discuss because they wanted to keep a lid on some operations. I don't think that's abnormal. But delivering worrisome notes to people isn't normal. I want answers, and I want them now. But how do we track this down without talking? Do we simply accept the threat as part of the program? I'm not comfortable with that."

"Nothing about this whole thing can be construed as comfortable," agreed Dicey, "But now—" She flashed a bright smile to comfort Ginny. "Our future awaits. Back home and in a few short weeks, a wedding for you!"

"And so much to be done between now and then." Ginny hugged Dicey quickly. "We'll go to the train together tomorrow, all right?"

"Yes."

Sleep refused to come that night.

So much going on, so many changes, so much to look forward to, now besmirched by the notes.

Even more worrisome was the clever stealth involved. The predator walked freely among them. Whoever it was had managed to blend in. Did that mean it was someone they saw *every day? Or was the anticipation of peacetime making them less aware of their surroundings?*

That was partially it, Dicey realized. Amazing how a declaration of peace made her relax her guard. Maybe she shouldn't have done that, but it was too late now.

When sleep did come, it came broken, and she woke up feeling worn.

The whole thing would amount to nothing. She tried to convince herself of that as Ginny climbed into the back seat of a cab with her.

It had to.

The codebreakers were going in diverse directions, to unique lives. There was no reason to threaten anyone.

So when she received a note saying Ginny had died in her sleep less than twelve weeks after her Labor Day wedding, Dicey was pretty sure her heart froze solid in her chest, because whoever this was...

And for whatever horrible, twisted reason...

They meant what they said.

If you talked, they would find you. Silence you.

Forever.

Chapter Twenty

MEREDITH MET JULIA AT THE door the next morning. "Coffee's fresh and strong and I need it, because it wasn't exactly an easy sleep kind of night, even with the AC coming back on."

"I know. Fortunately Beau sleeps with earplugs these days. Frog-song keeps him awake, so he was blissfully unaware of my restlessness. A million and a half per month." Julia's raised eyebrows highlighted the enormous figure. "And who knows how long it's been going on?"

"I wonder if Wyatt can find a code initiation date," said Meredith while Julia filled a mug. "Everything in computers is dated, isn't it? Especially the things folks don't want anyone to find."

"That's a good point." Julia jotted the question down in her electronic notebook.

"And the fact that it could be an outsider doesn't make just Mick Cavendish a possibility. It makes any hacker who may have gained access before a hole was closed a possibility. Now that we know it was disguised as a bona fide payout, we know that someone took advantage of access."

"Maybe repeatedly. I'm adding extra sugar to my coffee." Julia stirred a third spoonful into her mug. "I need a kick-boost this morning."

"Can't fault you for that." Meredith lifted her mug in solidarity.

"From what Wyatt said," Julia mused once she'd sipped her coffee, "it sounds like whoever did this had time to do it from either inside or outside the corporation. But you can't do this in the open, can you? Go in and alter or add code with no one noticing?"

"Another question for Wyatt," Meredith said. "When you're funneling this kind of money, wouldn't there be an automatic kickback notice that things had been changed?" GK had come into the kitchen, no doubt to snoop for food. He spotted Julia and promptly turned tail and stalked out of the room.

"That cat does not like his normal messed with."

"He's got a no-tolerance profile," Meredith admitted, then brought the topic back to embezzlement. "I get a notice on a backup account if I simply change my password. There must be some kind of auto-alert in a money-centric system like Payroll Inc. Who would get the alert? Payroll or accounts or audits—"

"Or Carolanne or the CFO," added Julia.

"Unless the thief knows how to block that automatic notification." Julia added that question to her list. "Let's add the CFO to our list of possibilities too. He was grumpy enough at that mandated supper disguised as a party."

"And Mary Murphy."

Julia winced. "Do you think an assistant could have access to that kind of code? Really? I hate to think that Mary could be involved. I've scanned her desk each time we've been to the offices, and that woman does a pile of work every day."

"For all we know, Mary could be a hacker like Mick, especially if it's a self-taught thing. That's all I'm saying. I don't want it to be her either, but we can't dismiss the possibility."

"I know." Julia frowned as she jotted it down.

"What about the actual data entry people?"

Julia tapped her stylus on her tablet. "There's got to be multiple levels, right? They have thousands of employees. I'll ask Wyatt how that works, but I expect it's a top brass–only kind of access." She called Wyatt and put him on speaker. "Hey, we've got a few questions for you."

"I figured you would. I'm surprised it took you until seven forty. Restless night, Aunt Jules?"

"Not the first and won't be the last," she told him. She went through their questions, and Wyatt's responses cleared up some of the picture.

"Only a very few people will have any kind of access to channeling funds," he told them. "A bigger number can see where funds go but have no ability to adjust that. A few executives, internal auditors, and the CFO. People with access to directing money flow are few and far between out of necessity. They may allow an auditor or accounts manager in for a specified time then lock down the access with a change of password. I'd be amazed if there are more than a handful of people who can get into this in an official capacity on a regular basis."

"So we need to know who those people are."

"Xavier Rahm, Carolanne, and Audie Phillips top the list."

"We haven't met Audie Phillips." Meredith frowned. "I saw his name on the list of executives, but I haven't seen him at anything. Including the office."

"He's out on long-term sick leave after having triple bypass."

"Were you able to see when this new channel of funds was put in place, Wyatt? We didn't think to ask that last night."

"Nearly a year ago."

"So someone has bilked about eighteen million dollars so far?"

The amount fairly staggered Meredith, but Wyatt dealt with megasums on a daily basis. "Correct. And if that someone is smart, they'll be getting nervous about now. My guess is they turn tail and run and catch the soonest international flight out of Atlanta, unless they can't for some reason. Or unless they assume they're that good and the theft is that well-hidden. And honestly, they are and it is."

"We'd have never figured this out without you."

Meredith chimed in. "You're the best, Wyatt. Thank you!"

"Give me a shout if you have follow-up questions. And those three names I gave you might not be all the suspects. It wasn't as if the files kept a list of people with access, but those would be the top-line typicals. And your hacker buddy, of course."

Meredith kind of hated adding Mick to the list, because he seemed like a good guy, but there was no downplaying his look of frustration when he met with that woman outside the coffee shop. At the very same time he was supposed to be going home to his wife and infant daughter.

"We'll let you know what we find out, but we're taking the bread-baking approach right now," Meredith told him.

"Bread-baking?"

"Mix the ingredients and let it ferment. Then see who or what rises to the top as the yeast does its thing."

"There you go. Talk to you later."

They disconnected the call.

Julia stabbed a finger at the list she'd made. "I'm going to be very disappointed in Xavier Rahm if he's taken this opportunity to go back to those old roots of double-dealing. Nobody needs that much money. He's already making millions a year. Why steal more?"

"The 'never enough' rule of humanity," Meredith replied. "No matter what we have, it seems like we should have or want more. Never satisfied."

"Well, that just means we're spoiled." Julia scowled at the list.

"I can't disagree. Honestly, I think being grounded in my faith is the only thing that has kept me from that with so many rich people around me all my life. Maybe that's part of why I'm not thrilled with my church anymore, because those acts of service and sacrifice helped me keep my feet on the ground. If that's no longer a part of the church, I feel like my faith is in name only. And I want more than that."

"That's exactly how I felt when we found New Beginnings," said Julia. "Like I'd found a place where everyone worked together. It wasn't because they were looking for a pathway to heaven. God's got that covered through His amazing Son. They just wanted to keep their hands busy for the common good." She lifted one shoulder. "It seemed good to feel that way and be surrounded by others who felt the same."

Meredith understood exactly what Julia was saying, but she tabled the discussion for the moment. Something to think about—and pray about. But right now they needed to figure out who was bilking great sums of money in miniscule increments from Payroll Inc.'s paycheck service. "You don't want it to be Xavier or Mary, and I don't want it to be Mick, because he's a fun, up-front guy. At least he seems to be."

"Up-front guys don't have disturbing clandestine meetings with women on corners," Julia reminded her. "He's charming, but he stays on my list."

"Well, Carolanne hired us, so I'm casting an absentee ballot for this Audie Phillips guy. He had access, and it was the stress of stealing that gave him his bad heart."

Julia laughed and nearly choked on her coffee. "You officially made that up."

"Total scapegoat mentality," Meredith agreed cheerfully. "But we'll figure this out. It's the waiting that's tough, although we can go see Audie Phillips. He's postsurgery enough to warrant a visit."

"And we might hate the man on the spot." That seemed to make Julia happy, but when they got to Audie Phillips's home for a scheduled appointment nearly five hours later, the house was empty.

"He said one o'clock, correct?"

Julia nodded. "He did."

"So where is he?" wondered Meredith. "Do you think he's sick? Or in trouble?"

Never one to hold back, Julia rounded the house to peer into a window. "No lights. No TV. No bodies," she announced with satisfaction.

"And no note or text for us. Or voice mail." Meredith popped open the mailbox, just in case Audie Phillips left a note. He didn't. "Our Mr. Phillips might be on that international flight like Wyatt suggested."

Julia moved back along the side of the house, put her face to a window, and looked into another room. "No bodies here either."

"Reason to celebrate," began Meredith, but she stopped talking when a police cruiser rolled into the driveway. It pulled right up behind Julia's car and stopped there. No lights. No siren. A stealthy move. That made it more worrisome.

Two officers stepped out of the cruiser, two officers who looked annoyingly familiar. "You two again. Did you bug Julia's car?" asked Meredith. She was only half kidding.

"No need." Dixon Mulvaney tipped up the visor of his cap. "The neighbors here get funny when folks start peering into windows they've got no business peering into."

Julia came around the pristine front garden. "Officers! How nice to see you! How can we help you?" She gave them a wide-eyed look of such innocence that any self-respecting officer should realize they meant no harm. Unless Phillips was stealing millions of dollars. In which case he'd consider their interference quite harmful.

Come to think of it, a police escort might be a real good idea.

Julia's expression didn't fool Dixon Mulvaney. He lifted one brow then sighed, but the sigh said enough. He wasn't buying Julia's innocent expression.

The younger cop scolded them, arms akimbo. "You can't go around snooping into people's homes. Judge Foley, surely you know that, even if your friend is unaware."

Meredith, unaware?

After helping her husband on cases for decades?

Right about now Meredith was tempted to give Anton Dillinger some "unaware" that might cool his jets, but Dixon Mulvaney beat her to it.

"Mrs. Bellefontaine probably knows as much about the law and limits of the law as our finest detectives, Anton. Her husband skated a thin line, but skated it well, and she was right there with him, I expect."

His defense was nice. And compassionate. And unexpected. So unexpected that melancholy threatened to steamroll her and she had to fight it down. "We had a one o'clock appointment with Mr. Phillips."

"You did?" Dixon's raised brow—the right one—showed the proper amount of skepticism. "You know that's what everyone says when they're caught snooping around an empty house."

"It's not supposed to be empty, he's supposed to be here, meeting with us," Julia told him firmly. And a bit tartly too, sounding like the magistrate she'd been for a whole lot of years.

Meredith held out her phone, put it on speaker, and hit voice mail. A man's voice that she assumed to be Audie Phillips confirmed a one o'clock appointment with them. "I called this morning, he agreed to meet, and we showed up." She shrugged. "Considering his heart issues, Julia wanted to make sure he wasn't in need of medical assistance."

"Exactly." Julia stood beside Meredith and faced the two officers. "But I will say that I'm grateful for your dedication to our community, gentlemen. After all those years on the bench, I know that having the people and the police working hand in hand is crucial to a strong society."

Dixon drew his brows together. "Accurate fluff, ma'am, but still fluff. Now that you know that Mr. Phillips isn't home, it's probably best to leave and go about your day. Don't you think?" He said it nicely but in a tone of voice that meant business. "You might want to leave him your business card or something. We'll wait."

He'd wait?

Those two words hiked Meredith's pulse again, but not in a good way this time. "You think we need supervision?"

He rocked back on his heels. "I think it's probably not a bad idea, Mrs. Bellefontaine. At times," he added, and there was that crooked grin again, as if he knew her. He was right—she did sometimes push the line of the law. But just a smidgeon.

At that moment a hefty SUV pulled into the driveway and dashed her thoughts on Dixon Mulvaney.

The woman driving seemed unnerved by the sight of the unanticipated gathering on her front sidewalk, but then the garage door rolled open and she drove straight in. She climbed out one side, and a short, balding man climbed out the other.

He came forward somewhat grudgingly. "You're still here." He gave Julia and Meredith a look that could have been called the stink eye.

"These ladies said they had an appointment with you, Mr. Phillips."

"They did, and I wasn't here," he grumped. "Which would tell any reasonable woman that she should turn around and go home. But over the years my awareness of Southern women has taught me a great deal." He scowled their way. "They don't take hints easily."

"Your manner of speech says Boston?" guessed Julia. "Where I expect those soft-spoken women do take hints."

He grunted, then almost laughed. "No, they're worse. There's a reason the term Boston fishwife became well known, and that's a fact. I used to think Southern women were more genteel, but that Yankee influence seems to be having its way down here of late, probably from those escaping New York taxes." He yawned, then seemed embarrassed by the action. "You might as well follow me."

The yawn inspired Meredith's sympathy. "In truth, Mr. Phillips, if you're unwell, we can certainly come back another day. It's gotten chilly now since that cold front moved in. We don't want to worsen your medical condition."

He eyed her a little more carefully now, and then he smiled. It wasn't a big smile, but it was a smile. "No, come in. Shawna's got tea in the fridge. The AC felt great yesterday, but I'm ready to turn the heat back on today. Sixty degrees isn't warm. Not when seventy-five felt so good. I'll answer some questions, but not too many, all right?"

"Fine," Julia assured him.

He waved off the officers. "Thank you, gentlemen, for protecting life and limb, but I expect I can hold my own with these two."

Anton nodded.

Dixon raised that brow again, openly skeptical. "They're feisty, Audie. Keep your guard up."

"I've learned the truth of those words, Dixon." Audie Phillips winked at Officer Mulvaney. "Good to see you back on the job."

"Glad to be here."

Curiosity tugged at Meredith.

Why had he gone off the job?

Was it to retire, like he'd intimated before? Or was there another reason?

Not her business. But as he walked away, she gave him a backward glance over her shoulder.

He did the same thing. At the very same moment.

Their eyes met. Not for long, but long enough to make her wonder what it was about Dixon Mulvaney that made her take that second look. And why had he looked back?

Chapter Twenty-One

"So you gals are working for Carolanne?" Audie asked once they'd taken seats in a comfortable, magazine-friendly living room with a view of a stunning golf course.

"I like a person who gets right to the point, but why do you say that, Mr. Phillips?" Julia used her noncommittal judge voice to rebut the question.

"Because I called her and asked her straight out the minute I heard from you," he told her bluntly. "This is what happens when a woman takes the helm. Not because of the woman, necessarily," he hastily added before Julia had a chance to lambaste him. "But there are some men in the company who don't have any confidence in a woman handling the major tasks. They respected Rusty, but they see Carolanne as a flake. A smart flake, but that's neither here nor there. She fought the push to go public, which was foolish on her part because the company's business and valuation both soared, but Carolanne doesn't like sharing control. Unfortunately for her, there are several on the board who have long memories."

"I'd think the men would respect that, wouldn't they?" Meredith posed the question as Audie's wife joined them with a lovely pitcher of tea and four bright-toned plastic glasses.

She immediately poured four glasses, even though Julia held her hand up to stop her.

It was instantly clear that there was no stopping Mrs. Phillips.

Ever the lady, Julia accepted the glass with a courteous smile.

"I know I should leave you three to talk amongst yourselves," drawled Audie's wife, "but I have found that complete honesty between a husband and wife is of the utmost importance in a good marriage, and I'm sure you women agree." She reached out a hand to Audie.

"I concur about ninety-five percent of the time." Julia smiled broadly. "But Beau Foley knows that there are some things he should downplay, especially when he's out fishing in a storm and how I look when I'm in at-home casual attire. There are certain rules of marriage that must be fudged. At least in our house."

"A little downplaying is often in a man's best interests," Audie agreed. "Ladies, this is my wife Shawna. Shawna, you're welcome to stay, although we might be boring."

"You're never boring, darling." She made moon eyes at him, and Audie smiled back.

"We actually stopped by Carolanne's house this morning when she said she wasn't going into the office until later," Audie told the women. "She was there with one of the twins. Holly or Hadley."

"Holly," noted Shawna. "The odd one. Not that we saw her, but I heard her in the kitchen, scolding the cook."

"We assumed it was her," added Audie.

"She said Holly is living at home," said Julia. "I met Hadley at the dinner party Carolanne hosted last week. A lovely young woman, and to raise identical twins? How fun that must have been."

"I've never seen two girls more different in my life," declared Shawna. "Hadley works as a speech therapist at the Caldwell School."

The Caldwell School was a private facility for the upper crust.

"A lovely profession," said Meredith. "I haven't talked to the girls since my boys were in high school."

"The girls were really cute back then, but I don't think Holly was ever happy," said Shawna. "She pretended to be, but I'm certain that was to please her mother in public. Of course they had those girls come to every company function, like a pair of princess dolls, and if Holly wasn't sulking in a corner, she was on her cell phone, ignoring people. Even before it was common for kids to have cell phones, and I won't tell you what I think of all that," finished Shawna in a tone that made it quite clear what she thought of all that.

"When Rusty passed away I told Audie he should cast his net upon the waters and look for something else. I was sure we were in for some rough times at Payroll Inc., but then it didn't get as bad as I thought. I respectfully apologize, darling." She smiled at him again.

Audie patted her hand. "Things settled down after a while, once Carolanne realized she had to play by board rules. And that calmed those waters, didn't it?"

"It did," Shawna said. "Audie thought of retiring with his heart scare—"

Meredith understood what a wake-up call that was, to have a life-sustaining organ go awry.

"But modern medicine prevailed, and he's good to go now. That's why we were late. The doctor's office was grossly overcrowded and probably overbooked, but Audie's cleared to go back to work by the end of next week."

"And I'm excited to be going," he said. "Shawna's taken good care of me, but I'm ready to be back in my office. As soon as we get back from our little south-of-the-border jaunt," he added.

Meredith's ears perked up. South of the border jaunt? She forced herself not to exchange looks with Julia.

"I need to be back on staff," Audie continued. "My heart condition put a lot on Xavier's plate, and that's not fair to him. Although he's not afraid of hard work and a little extra power."

Meredith took note of that last comment, but then Audie leaned forward. "I know there's scuttlebutt around Payroll Inc., an attitude of distrust, but we've had two firms come in and give us a clean bill of health. How could anyone get something by those two massive auditing companies? They couldn't." He seemed quite confident about his mistaken impression. Maybe too confident?

"Their stamp of approval was enough for me," he continued, "but Carolanne explained how she brought you two in to look from a different perspective to help quiet the grumbling. I think it's a waste of time and money, no offense, but if there's nothing to be found, the dissatisfied personnel should either shut up or move on. A strong company can't stand with all that internal bickering. And I've said that to Shawna many times."

"He has." She beamed at him. "We raised our kids that way, and they're lovely adults now. I don't like my son's girlfriend, but that's a topic for another day."

Meredith took a long draw on her tea then set the glass down and stood. "This was wonderful," she said. "Mr. Phillips, it's good to see you in full recovery mode, and I'm happy to have met you. I don't think we'll have too much more to do once you're back at work, but we didn't want to leave you out of the loop."

"My hope is that your positive report—" He paused quickly and hardened his gaze. "It will be a positive report, I presume."

Julia stood too. "Presumptions are tricky things, aren't they? Sometimes right, often wrong, and Shawna, thank you for your gracious hospitality. It was most appreciated."

Meredith hadn't missed Audie's quick about-face. He'd watched their reactions carefully, and Julia's open-ended comment didn't make him happy.

And that said a whole lot to Meredith. "We can show ourselves out. Thank you again for taking the time to meet with us." Meredith moved toward the front door. When they pulled away in Julia's car, she waited until the Phillips house was out of sight, then turned to Julia. "He made it clear that he expects us to give the company a clean bill of health."

"And he's flying out of the country," noted Julia. "Which could mean he's certain we haven't found his steady trickle of ill-begotten funds."

"Or he's ready to have a few days of fun after six weeks of fear," said Meredith. "Either way, we add him to the suspect list, because even with his whole Boston persona, there's a dash of my-way-or-the-highway in that man. And that's nothing we can take lightly."

Meredith's phone rang. She saw the office number and answered. "Hey, Carmen. What's up?"

"You know how you asked me to check into Miss Dicey's class-mates who died?"

"You found something?" Meredith put Carmen on speakerphone.

"Bennington Converse."

"Ginny's husband."

"That woman he married after his wife died? She was a widow with a baby girl."

"A lot of widows back then," observed Meredith.

"Well, you have to be married to be a widow, correct? And this gal had never been married before."

"A lot of out-of-wedlock babies back then too," said Julia. "It's an unfortunate truth."

"Also true, but how about an out-of-wedlock birth that just happens to have Converse DNA?"

"Say what?" Meredith shot Julia a look of disbelief.

"I'm looking at a DNA website...."

"You hacked it?"

"No, Magnolia Investigations paid for a proper subscription, but you'll be amazed when you see who you're related to, now that I have access to files. The Bellefontaine and Hall families have quite a rich past."

They sure did, but there wasn't time to talk about all that now. "Carmen, you brilliant girl!"

"Anyway, the oldest daughter that we saw in that picture, whose family is now on the West Coast, wasn't just Converse's adopted daughter. She was his biological daughter. Which meant his second wife was pregnant with his child when poor Ginny died."

The timing was far too significant to be coincidental. Wasn't it?

"But what about Theresa? And Pansy?"

"I'm checking into them, but that's a huge red flag from any wifely standpoint, ladies. He was conveniently out of town when she passed away from some kind of heart failure in her sleep—"

"Unknown causes resembling a pillow to the face or an overdose applied by someone else." Julia didn't mask the disgust in her tone. "And he got away with it."

"I'll keep checking," promised Carmen. "I also got your text about Carolanne's daughters. There's not much out there. Hadley's been lauded for academic accomplishments, but I think their parents drew a firm screen down on them to limit access, and the girls have maintained that. It's unusual, but not leaving a digital footprint is more suspicious than having a dicey one, because you have to go out of your way to keep names off the web. Oops, there's the other phone. Gotta go!"

She hung up, and Meredith shifted in her seat to face Julia more directly. "Which daughter was at the dinner?"

"Hadley," said Julia. "She was lovely and seemed to interact well."

"Or Holly pretending to be Hadley."

Julia looked puzzled as she took the expressway entrance ramp. "This isn't *The Parent Trap*. These gals are grown-ups. And if Holly has issues, would Carolanne have her come to the dinner? She introduced herself as Hadley. So is the speech therapist in line for a corporate position? Because that's a stretch."

"Carolanne said Holly was living with her. So why would Hadley be at the dinner and not Holly?"

"Maybe Hadley is more comfortable with people."

"It's possible. Presenting the heir apparent, perhaps?"

"It's a big leap from speech therapy to running a major corporation that you've never worked in, and the board would never approve it. But that sixteen percent ownership does give Carolanne clout. Then again, maybe she just wants some family support when she hosts a function," Julia suggested. "It's got to be hard to put on your game face and do it alone. You saw how rattled she gets."

"So true." Meredith used to give dinner parties for friends and clients. It meant a lot to her when an event went well. She'd stopped doing it after Ron died and hadn't been inspired to do it again. If Carolanne wanted some support on hand, Meredith understood completely. "We've got some time, don't we?"

Julia nodded.

"Let's swing by Mick Cavendish's office."

"And see if he offers up evidence by way of reaction to questions?"

"Surprise attacks are always best," noted Meredith cheerfully. She pulled down the visor, checked her hair, and sighed. "I was hoping the cooler temps would tame my hair, but no. I look like a cross between Goldilocks and Shirley Temple. Humidity is the enemy of a smooth do when you've got hair like mine."

"But it means winter's over, and I'm okay with that," said Julia as she took the exit toward Mick Cavendish's part of town.

"Says the woman with perfect hair."

Julia laughed. "When I was little I wanted a head full of curls like my sister, but as I got older, I realized just how easy it is to take care of this." She fluffed the right side of her hair meaningfully. "Compared to that." She hooked her thumb toward Meredith's curls. "It amazes me how your hair changes in the humidity. As if it soaks up the water."

"I'm sure there's a scientific equation behind it, but even the priciest conditioner has little effect by midday, so why waste the money? And"—Meredith shrugged as Julia found a parking spot in a small lot up the road from Mick Cavendish's office address—"after all these years, I should be used to it."

"I think our surprise interlude with a couple of Savannah's finest officers is actually making you think of your hair. And isn't that an interesting turn of events? That Quin isn't the only fellow that inspires your blush?" teased Julia.

Meredith wasn't about to admit that, even to Julia. "Let's consider that a 'nothing to see here' conversation and move on," she said firmly.

"Absolutely," Julia agreed. But her grin suggested otherwise as they fell into step on the sidewalk. "I'll be like those monkeys. See nothing, hear nothing, speak nothing. But it's nice to know you still blush, my friend. And oh my, what have we got here?" She paused in front of a pretty duplex home with a brand-new FOR SALE sign in front of it.

Nothing on the house or lawn suggested a business inside, so was Mick Cavendish flying under the radar? Was this even his address? "The Cavendishes are moving?" Meredith snapped a picture of the sign before she headed up the steps. "Let's see where they're going, hmm?" She was about to ring the bell then remembered there might be a sleeping infant inside. She knocked instead. And when no one answered, she texted Mick.

AT YOUR FRONT DOOR WITH A QUICK QUESTION. DIDN'T WANT TO WAKE BABY.

A few seconds later a return text came through. BE RIGHT THERE.

And he was. In less than a minute, Mick Cavendish opened the front door. He put a finger to his lips and indicated the house with a jut of his chin. "My wife just left for work, and Maya is asleep. I might burst into tears if we wake her. And it won't be a pretty sight." He stepped out onto the covered porch. "Welcome to my world."

"You're moving?" Julia motioned toward the sign.

"Not by choice, but the landlord is selling the house, so yes. We planned to move next year, but the new owner might have other ideas, so we're actively looking, which takes time, and time is the last thing I have right now. We've talked about getting a nanny for the afternoons so I can work, but I hate the thought of being downstairs in my office when Maya needs something and having someone else do it. Although it's probably going to be the new reality, because a part-time nanny is way cheaper than a full-time nanny and a rented office."

"Protecting the bottom line is clutch in any business," agreed Meredith. "Mick, Julia and I don't pretend to be numbers or computer experts, so I wanted to ask you a question. If someone wanted to misdirect payroll funds from individual paychecks, could they do that? And if they could, how would they do it?"

Her question raised absolutely no red flags in his reaction. He stroked his chin for a moment before answering. "Anything is possible. Money can be directed down any lane, just like any commodity. In some ways money is easier, because we're talking digital transfer. So the actual money isn't flowing through the channels— it's being directed. It's the gaining access to the payroll flex that's the hard part. It would be difficult for anyone, inside or outside the corporation. You're talking a legitimately time-consuming effort because there isn't a blanket way to do something like this. Not that I'm aware of, and I'm pretty aware."

"How would someone do something like that?" wondered Julia.

"Access." He said it point-blank. "Someone would have to let you into the system. Once in, it's not as hard, if you know what you're looking for. A line of code that repeats from area to area, redesignated for each municipality's rules."

"That sounds quite impossible to me," said Meredith frankly.

"It's not impossible, but it's not something a guy like me can access from outside. This is different from finding holes and taking advantage of them. This is accessibility intrusion, and there are so many doors one would have to get through to gain that kind of contact, it would have to be someone above suspicion with plenty of time. Or at least too powerful to point a finger at, lest you lose your job."

"So only an insider?"

"Not something you could do. Really?" Julia arched one of her absolutely perfect brows as if slightly skeptical and complimentary, all at once.

He laughed. "No. I know what you're getting at—if I can take over all of their computers and deliver an ugly clown, I should be able to get into the payroll systems, but that's a whole other thing. Hacking into the system isn't the same as hacking into their payroll clients and diverting funds. Now, outside funds would be different," he said. "Standard funds, bank accounts, etc. But not the payroll flow funds. That's more of an art form than a hack, and it would take dedicated effort. If I were guilty of that, I'd throw you offtrack with that answer, grab my baby and run, but since I'm not"—he flashed that sincere smile again—"I'm being straight up. You can check the landlord's listing too. Jill and I weren't anticipating a move this year with the baby so small, but things all work out. Business is booming, so that's good, because Savannah prices aren't exactly middle-class friendly. There are a lot of businesses out there, and a lot of programming gaps. So working from home is the plan for the future."

Meredith believed him. But she still had to ask the question. "Mick, when you left the coffee shop after our first meeting, you met up with a woman."

"You saw that." His gaze showed regret.

She kept her face serene. "Yes."

"My sister. Stepsister, actually. She's been having a tough time in rehab, and I'm always nervous when she calls. There's something about having a baby that makes you cautious, you know?"

"So true." Meredith had had to be careful not to smother the boys with caution when Ron was working tough cases twenty years back.

Mick continued his explanation. "Stephie got into the drug scene years ago, and it's been a roller coaster ever since. I think she's solid this time, but she's slipped before. I don't give her money, but I do give her gift cards for the grocery store. She doesn't want help from my mom and her dad. She wants them to think she's making it on her own, but like I said, Savannah isn't a cost-effective city, and marginalized people like Stephie have a hard time making ends meet. We worry that if we make things too comfortable for her, she'll fall back into the drug scene. Discretionary income is a dangerous thing in an addict's hands."

"I'm sorry." Meredith meant the words sincerely. "I didn't mean to pry, but I wanted to be on your side. After doing this kind of thing in some way for nearly forty years, I'm pretty good at discernment.

Thank you, Mick." She reached out and shook his hand. "A pleasure doing business with you."

"Same here."

When they got close to the car, Julia sighed. "Carmen could have been another Stephie."

"Except you stepped in," said Meredith. "You gave her advice and hope and support. And love."

"And she took it," said Julia. "So many don't. Can't. Won't. The lure is too great. Luckily she hadn't gotten into drugs, but it could have been the next step from petty larceny. It often is."

"And now look at her, amazingly smart, strong, funny, and what a help she is to us. She's marvelous, Jules. You made a huge difference in Wyatt's life and Carmen's. That's a pretty solid street cred if ever there was one."

Julia bumped shoulders with Meredith before rounding the car. "I love hearing you use terms like street cred. You're so sick, Mere."

"I'll never figure out the new way of using words that have bad connotations to fit good aspects, but since it's not my job, I don't care. Let's head to the office, see what Carmen's got, and figure out the next move. But let's not fill Carmen in on Wyatt's discovery," she added. "The fewer people that know about that, the safer we are, because Wyatt is right. People kill for far less than the money we're talking. We'll keep her on the quest for Miss Dicey's information. That keeps her safe and sound, and maybe we'll get some answers for our aged friend."

"I'd like that," said Julia. "The thought of a life half-lived doesn't just bother me. It makes me fighting mad because things could have been so different for Miss Dicey, if only she hadn't lived in fear. If we can clear that up for her before she passes from this earth, I'll be happy."

Chapter Twenty-Two

1947
River View
Savannah, Georgia

"Oh, Miss Dicey, it's so good to see you!" Ten-year-old Pansy Covington Warren dashed across the music room floor and threw her arms around Dicey's middle. Her school chum's namesake was an absolute dear, much like the older Pansy Dicey used to know so well, only far more outgoing. *"I've missed you so much. I didn't even care to go to the mountains this year, it's such a bore, but Mother insisted and so we went."*

"Vacationing with well-meaning parents being such a hardship in life," drawled her mother, Karen Covington Warren. *"Pansy, darling, you are a card."*

Pansy rolled her eyes and took her seat at the student piano. Dicey motioned to the finger-limbering exercises, and Pansy dove in with exaggerated gusto. Clearly a message to her mother that she'd been away from her beloved music lessons for far too long. *"I'll see your mother to the door.*

When you're done with your warm-up, why don't you look over that new piece you'll find on the piano? I picked it especially for you. The music fairly leaps off the page, Pansy."

"As she leaps through life," whispered her mother on the way to the broad front door. "It is good to be back home, although her drama could be curtailed," she noted with a wry look toward the music room. "Still, it was enough to keep us out of the way for a while after losing her beloved auntie. I still can't believe she's gone."

"Nor can I." The loss of a sweet soul like Pansy Warren was both a challenge and a threat. Another codebreaker gone, the third in two years, but Pansy had died from natural causes. Still, her passing brought up old feelings Dicey had worked hard to bury or at least deal with. Ginny gone. Theresa gone. And now Pansy. "Mama said she was taken ill suddenly and there was nothing that could be done."

Karen raised both brows. "That's what Mother Warren would like all to hear and believe, but Pansy was never the same person once she came back home from Washington."

Dicey frowned. "She was one of the kindest people I knew there, with a keen mind for learning." Pansy had possessed a marvelous insight into people and codes, and often used her studied knowledge of the enemy commanders to break their messages, a unique trait among the women.

"Kind and shadowed," Karen stated calmly, having no idea what her words were doing to Dicey's pulse. "Always looking over her shoulder this last year or two, as if waiting for something to happen. I only saw her a few times a year.

She'd become more reclusive after PawPaw died. In fact we dubbed her our very own Emily Dickinson, reclusive to her dormered room, but despite Mother Warren's efforts to draw her out, to reengage her with life, Pansy seemed to just withdraw further and further into her shell. And then we lost her."

Dicey couldn't believe what she was hearing. "She wasn't taken by tuberculosis?"

"By hanging," Karen whispered. "On a day when everyone was away. They came back to find her gone by her own hand. Do not share this," Karen warned. "Dale's mother would have my head for being truthful about this. Pansy was a delicate, kind soul. We loved her dearly, but she drew away from everyone and stayed pretty much to herself. She'd gone off to school with such a heart for changing the world, and then was broken when she learned of Ginny's passing, and then the loss of Theresa. I understand they were dear friends at school and work, and Pansy just never recovered from the grief."

Dicey's heart didn't just speed up.

It pounded like a freight train in her chest, the huge sort that rumbled past the nest of depots in Atlanta. "She took her own life?"

Tears filled Karen's eyes. She nodded and pressed a hankie to her face.

"Are you sure?" Dicey didn't want to ask the question. She didn't want to press the issue. She really wasn't even sure she wanted to know. "Is Mrs. Warren certain it was by her own hand?"

"Well, how else?" breathed Karen, but she must have read the concern in Dicey's face because she inhaled sharply. "You think she could have been killed?"

Saints alive, Dicey couldn't be talking of this. Not here. Not now. Not ever. And with a child in the next room, and a dear woman here, in the doorway, who could repeat whatever Dicey might say. "Of course not. That's silly, isn't it?"

But Karen's expression was one of horror. "Why would someone hurt Pansy? There's no reason. None at all. Is there?"

At that moment Dicey hated herself.

She hated herself for being weak and for the lie she was about to tell. "No. You said she was overtaken by sadness, and that's a cruel master for anyone. I'm sure you're right. Forgive me. It's the shock, Karen. The shock makes it seem quite unbelievable."

"There is great truth in those words." Karen's eyes had rimmed with tears, and once one fell, others followed. "If we'd known the depth of her sorrow, we could have helped. We could have drawn her out, dragged her back into life. But we were busy, and we all went on, letting her slip away until it was too late. I don't rightly know how to forgive myself or all of us, really, for letting that happen."

What if that wasn't what happened?

What if this family was mantled with guilt when it was truly a case of one person taking the life of another? How could one tell?

They couldn't, of course.

Unless Dicey or one of the other women went to the law and shared everything they knew...everything they'd been told not to share.

Oh, her heart.

She'd prayed. She'd prayed good and hard and long for God's direction, and she'd gotten no reply. If Holy Scripture was right, that the truth would set one free, did it take into account the threats against these women? Had those threats now been carried out against three of her college colleagues?

"Dicey, I'm sorry. I shouldn't have said a word about this." Karen looked concerned for her, instead of the other way around. "It's the shock of it all and being told to keep it quiet wearing on me, but I should have been stronger. Kept it to myself. My mother-in-law's feelings shouldn't be disregarded in this case."

"It's a shock," Dicey repeated. "I'll pray for your family, Karen. The sorrow of a young life lost goes deep."

"I can't even imagine." Karen's gaze lifted to the dancing notes coming from the music room beyond Dicey. "To lose Pansy or her brother would wreck me, so I understand the misery Mother Warren faces daily. And I will say no more. To anyone," she said, then added, *"but I'm glad to have spoken up finally. There's something heinous and wrong about keeping everything bottled up inside, and while I shouldn't have burdened you, it was a release for me. Please forgive me for using you."*

"There is nothing to forgive." Dicey never meant anything more sincerely. "I am shocked and saddened, but how much worse it is for all of you, Pansy's dear family."

Karen blinked, nodded, then gave Dicey a fierce hug. "You're a true friend, Dicey. I'll be back in an hour."

"Yes."

She quietly closed the front door after Karen left. She turned for the music room, paused to take a breath—a deep one—and crossed the grand foyer to the room beyond.

The music called to her. It always had, and this tune, light, playful, and quick with dancing notes, would be a signature piece for little Pansy. She was of a unique talent, and Dicey had no doubt she could become a celebrated musician, but for today all she wanted to do was get through her lessons and then hide.

Kind of like she'd been doing for the last couple of years.

Chapter Twenty-Three

"So the judge was having an affair before he married Ginny." Julia's expression of disgust left no doubt about her feelings. "And Ginny conveniently died in her sleep—"

"Leaving him her share of her grandfather's fortune," noted Meredith.

"And free to marry the mother of his child and carry on, unfettered by a murder inquiry that should have happened."

"You think he might have killed her?" Carmen refilled everyone's coffee mugs but gave Maggie Lu a tall, cold glass of sweet tea instead.

"He had motive but no opportunity," stated Meredith.

"Unless Theresa figured it out." Julia tapped a finger on Theresa's name. "What if Theresa knew what happened, or surmised what happened, and Bennington took her life to keep her quiet?"

"Would he risk that?" asked Meredith.

"It's amazing what folks will do when pressed to the wall," said Maggie Lu. "To save face, to save money, to save a reputation. And if one has killed once, it is probably even easier to step over that line again. Heinous crimes against the innocent often went unpunished. Bennington Converse was a renowned scholar, but he was also street-smart. You can see that in his rulings. And rich enough to have bought silence when he needed it."

"You think he could have led two lives?"

"Basically one once the bodies were buried," said Maggie Lu practically. "Money and prestige bought a lot of silence back then. So could Bennington have done this? Yes. But why Theresa?"

"She was Ginny's closest friend before and after their time in Washington. And her maid of honor. Probably a confidante. If Ginny shared her concerns—" Meredith left that open.

"Or it could be that Theresa didn't buy into the 'died of natural causes' decision." Julia tapped a pencil on the table, thinking.

"So she had to be silenced," offered Carmen.

Meredith had been studying the scratch-pad timeline she'd set up. She took a hefty sip of her coffee then faced the other women. "What if he set this all up?"

Three frowns met her gaze.

"What if Bennington sent those notes to the women?"

"You mean he planned to kill Ginny and so he sets things up to look like someone was threatening the whole group?"

Elbows propped, Meredith put her chin in her hands. "Either that or just to keep them quietly apart. If he throws everyone off by sending threatening notes, then when Ginny dies, suspicion is pulled away from him because they were all told to keep quiet. And no one was contacted about Ginny's funeral. That's odd, isn't it? Why was none of their Charleston class informed?"

"Yes, Dicey said she was surprised none of them were informed. Most of the women lived within a few hours of Ginny, close enough to attend a friend's funeral. And not long after, Theresa dies in an accident up in the hills. Conveniently with no witnesses to say what actually happened."

"Ruled accidental, no foul play involved," said Carmen. She slipped a copy of the report out of the pile.

"So we're supposing the sheriff was in on it too?" Julia frowned. "That's too big a stretch for me. Or we're supposing that Bennington was that good, and that's also a stretch. It's very rare that no one sees, hears, or suspects anything twice. And to have two dear friends die within a year is suspicious, isn't it?"

"Not if grief is a factor." Maggie Lu's soft voice added a measure of sense. "Distraught over losing her friend, hiking in an unknown area, slips and falls." She pulled some papers out of her purse and unfolded them. "Rebecca and I took a little time to check the microfilm files once we straightened out the returned book debacle. She's been home these past few days with a nasty cold. She blamed allergies, but when her antihistamines weren't helping, she went back home to bed, poor thing. But she was there long enough to help me track this down."

The short article from the Savannah newspaper cited how the loss of Theresa Becket left her brother Eric as the sole heir to the beautiful, high-class Becket & Mansfield Hotel on College Street in Macon. And that was it.

"I expect the distance minimized her death here."

"Miss Dicey said that none of the women were informed in time to pay their respects."

Julia muttered something under her breath, then folded her hands. "The thought that an esteemed magistrate might have gotten away with murder galls me," she told them through clenched teeth. "And then he went on to become one of the state's most respected judicial figures, all the while hiding his nefarious past. I don't care that he's lying cold in his grave, I'm ready to dig him up and make him pay for what he's done."

"Except this is all circumstantial," Meredith pointed out. "So maybe we shouldn't exhume his body quite yet."

"And that's important to remember," said Maggie Lu. "There is evil in the world, but even though this is an awful tragedy, I like to look at the benefit of what those women did back then. Gathering together for the good of mankind, for the good of our country and the world, even though their presence and efforts were downplayed when government officials laid claim to their success. They helped win a war, and that's nothing to shrug off. That's an accomplishment, for certain."

"We have come a long way," Meredith agreed. "I wonder if there's any way to prove this."

"A conveniently written confession would be nice," said Carmen. "Barring that, it's a lot of dead ends. No pun intended." She brightened. "On a happier note, Mama Kitty is doing very well downstairs and those kittens are *muy adorable! Mas preciosa!*"

"I am so happy to hear that." Maggie Lu's eyes lit up. "Spring and new life just go hand in hand, don't they? The promise of Easter looms bright despite the shadows around Miss Dicey's past."

Her words touched Meredith's heart. They couldn't very well go to that sweet centenarian and fill her with thoughts of a horrific pair of unproven murders. And then there was Pansy Warren, right here in Savannah. Was her death related to these other two? Or a sad coincidence?

"Ladies, I must take leave of this clue-gathering session because Clarissa is meeting me at Charlene's condo and she is bringing my sweet baby boy along for some GeeGee time. I'm going to spend a few hours with that blessed baby before Charlene leaves the diner in Maribelle's and Rhonda's capable hands after the early rush so we can all have supper together and dote on little Jake Philip Beasley." She withdrew her phone and took a moment to pull up her digital photos. "Here's our little darling Jake Philip right after being fed yesterday. That smile says it all."

"Oh, Maggie Lu, he is precious." Meredith handed the phone to Carmen.

"A beautiful boy. And a family name to be proud of," said Carmen.

"His daddy and his great-uncle, two good men. And life goes on." Maggie Lu reached up and patted her hair, making sure it was in place, an old-fashioned trait that Meredith loved. "I'll see y'all presently."

Head high, she walked out the front door. The soft metallic click indicated its closing.

Meredith looked down at the copies of old pages. Pictures of the judge, sitting proudly, with his wife and children. Carmen had printed several of them and set them out in chronological order, and as time went on, an interesting dynamic became clear. All three children, the two daughters and the son, gravitated away from their mother, flanking their father's right side, while their mother took a very pronounced spot at his left.

Meredith studied the images, side by side. She swallowed hard and looked up, first at Julia, then Carmen. Then she pointed a finger, not at Bennington, but his very self-assured and beautiful wife and said, "I think we might be suspecting the wrong Converse, ladies.

We're so used to expecting men to be culprits that we're not looking at the other obvious choice. Cynthia Converse, clearing the way for her lover to become not only her husband, but the father to their love child. And when Theresa sensed something was wrong, she took care of her too."

Carmen's eyes went wide. "I never thought of that."

"Because it's unthinkable, which makes it even more likely that she got away with it for that very reason," Meredith supposed. "Jules. What do you think?"

Julia had stood right up. She studied the pictures before she raised her gaze to Meredith and Carmen. "I wouldn't have imagined it."

"Nor I, except for the pictures."

"And do you see what I see in the notes?" asked Carmen. "That funny dot, almost a circle, over every lowercase *i*. Men don't do that, do they?"

Julia withdrew the few notes they had from the file. "No. And it's subtle because of the fountain pen, but it's there if you look closely. Almost as if someone was trying not to do it."

"Carmen." Meredith glanced at her watch. "I've got a phone meeting at four, but can you find out if we have any access to Cynthia and Bennington's children or grandchildren in this area? Or even cousins. Anyone who might have memories of the Converses that might shed some light on all of this."

"I'll get right on it."

Julia slung her purse up and over her arm. "Old Judge Weingardt knew Bennington personally. I'm going to stop by the Laurelwood Home and see him. His legs may have given out, but his mind is sharp as a tack, according to my mother. She stops by the home regularly."

"She's got a good heart that she passed on to her daughter," said Carmen as she moved toward her office space at the front of the building.

"And she's nosy." Julia waved goodbye as she headed for the back door. "Another trait she passed on. And not a bad one for an investigator to have." She exited the building but returned less than two minutes later, and none too quietly either. When Meredith hurried back to the kitchen to see what was going on, Julia smacked her purse flat on top of the granite-topped island and folded her arms. "Four flat tires."

Meredith's mouth dropped open. "No."

"Oh yes, and when I get my hands on whoever did this, I'm going to—"

"Julia, this is unbelievable."

Julia's expression seemed to find it quite believable and maddening.

"The person must be caught on camera." Ron had installed a monitoring system to make sure the Whitaker Street property was well protected, but when Meredith pulled up the camera feed inside the house, there were no images. A blank screen appeared, with absolutely nothing on it.

"Someone's tampered with the camera?" Meredith stared at the imageless readout and then the system connection. She hurried outside, barely noticing the cooling temperatures and the rising wind. She stared up at the camera and scowled. "Tape."

"Tape?"

"Someone got up there and put duct tape across the lens, see? But it's dark tape, so unless you're looking for it—"

"Or checking the feed, which we never do."

Julia was right. There hadn't been a reason to check the camera's images in a long time.

"But someone would see them tampering with the camera," said Julia. "Wouldn't they?"

"I think the creeper vine that gives us such great privacy would thwart that now that's it's leafed out," said Meredith. She pointed up, through the blossoming trees. "Unless old Mr. Dawson happened to be in his attic, and that's not likely. That's about the only angle that might have a chance once things are growing again. Julia, I'm sorry." Guilt swamped her.

Not because she had done anything to bring this on, but the thought that partnering with Meredith caused her dear friend fear or pain was unnerving.

Julia scoffed. "Nonsense, this means we're making someone nervous. Which means we're close, Mere. Really close."

"Well, I'd like to be close with working cars and no threats of murder," said Meredith in a tight voice, but she had to admit that Julia was right. They must be breathing down someone's neck, but whose? "Who could have done this?" She kept her voice low because Carmen was on the phone up front and had no idea what had happened in their parking area.

"Not Audie," said Julia. "We might as well check him off the list because there's no way he could have accessed that camera. Whoever did that probably did it at night, don't you think?"

That made sense.

"And we only just met Audie today, so I don't think he's on the list. Whoever did this didn't mess with the camera in broad daylight."

"And we've crossed off Mick," said Meredith. "For good reason."

"Which leaves Mary Murphy and Xavier Rahm. What if I don't want it to be either of them?" asked Julia.

"Well, I don't think you get your wish this time, my friend." Meredith slung an arm around Julia's shoulders. "Call the police, let's make out a report, and then we can get your car fixed. I'll go tell Carmen what's happened."

"It's a good thing you charged Carolanne a boatload of money for this investigation," said Julia as she punched in 911. "We'll need it to pay for these tires. They aren't cheap."

"We'll add it to her bill," Meredith corrected her. "And maybe a fee for pain and suffering. Not to mention camera tampering."

A few minutes later a police car cruised to a stop on the Howard Street side of their building. It parked just behind Julia's damaged car. And then—

Wouldn't you know it?

Two familiar figures climbed out of the car.

Meredith tugged a hoodie off the back of a kitchen stool and hurried outside with Julia, and when Dixon Mulvaney tipped back the brim of his cap and smiled, she smiled back.

"And so we meet again, ladies? This is becoming a habit," he said with a look of amusement to his partner.

"There's generally a reason for that, sir," said the younger cop. He may have darted a glance toward Meredith, but she was too busy directing them to the business at hand to be sure.

"Gentlemen, we're talking a crime here," she said in the most professional tone she could muster while Dixon bent to look at Julia's tires.

"Yep. Flat. All four of 'em."

She bit back a big sigh. "We know that, but we need a police report."

"Is your camera working, Mrs. Bellefontaine?" asked the younger officer. He pointed toward the back door and the sabotaged security system.

"Someone taped it, Anton," Julia informed him.

Dixon's smile disappeared instantly. "Someone taped your lens?"

Meredith nodded, and when he drew his brows together and strode up the back steps, she hurried right after him. "Four slashed tires aren't a big deal, but a piece of tape is?"

"Tampering with a security system takes planning. Then you have to carry out the action, get access, get up there, and sneak away without being caught or seen. Anyone can take two minutes to slash tires with the right tool." He stared at the camera, the back door, then her.

And for the first time since talking to Wyatt about this case and hearing his caution, fear crept up her spine. "You're talking premeditation."

"And follow-through, and I don't like it." His brows knit tighter as he worked his jaw. "I don't like it at all." He nodded toward the door. "Can we talk inside?"

"Of course." Julia led the way in. Dixon stepped back and let Meredith precede him. Then he and Officer Dillinger followed them into the back entry and the kitchen.

The women turned and Dixon scrubbed a hand to his chin for drawn-out seconds before he addressed them. He seemed to choose his words with care. "You're not required to tell us anything, but I'm going to assume that you're working on something to do with a local major payroll company, and I'm making that assumption because you were at Audie's place earlier." He spoke in a firm, direct voice. No nonsense, and no teasing smiles now. "I have nothing but respect for the work you ladies do, but I am very concerned about that taped camera. The perp may have taped it to slash tires, sure. But they may have taped it to do more violent things, and I can't stress enough that you need to be careful. Not because you're women, but because when a person feels cornered, they're likely to overreact. And if it's big money we're talking about, or power, that reaction can include violence. Nothing is worth that, ladies."

Oh, the look on his face, as if he knew that personally.

"We'll write this up and leave you a copy of the report. That way you can make an insurance claim if needed, but I'm adding my personal caution to all of this. Be careful."

He met Julia's gaze and then Meredith's, and there was no disguising the concern in his expression. "I'm going to take some pictures of the tape, then remove it," he told them. "And I'm bagging it as evidence." He pulled a pair of disposable gloves out of his pocket. "Tape is a great fingerprint-gathering device, so maybe we'll get lucky and find out who did this before they go further."

Meredith nodded but her mind was considering their two remaining possibilities, Mary and Xavier.

The thought of Xavier climbing up to tape their camera seemed unlikely.

But she didn't want the image of Mary Murphy doing it to seem right either. Besides, wouldn't they both be at work now? So was it a different person who had stabbed Julia's tires?

She decided that as soon as the officers left, they'd check to see if Mary and Xavier had been at work all afternoon.

"Be careful. Please."

Julia nodded. "We will be, officers. Do you need a step stool to reach the camera? There's one in that closet to the right of the door."

"That will do fine."

The officers went back outside with the stepstool. While Dixon removed the tape, Anton took pictures of the tires, the parking area, and the gate.

They left a few minutes later, and when they did, Julia turned to face Meredith. "Are you scared?"

"Well, I wasn't until Dixon Mulvaney looked worried for our life and limb," she said, exasperated. "He's right, of course. Taping the cameras was planned and left us vulnerable. We'll have to check our home security as well."

"Beau will do it when he gets back," Julia said. "He said since he couldn't golf like he wanted last year, he's going to soak up all the time on the greens he can get this year."

"Can't blame him for that. Should we swoop into Payroll Inc. to see who's at work today? Or play it cool and casual and wait until tomorrow while we go home and check our security cameras?"

"Swoop now while I'm mad enough to take anyone down." Julia was clearly in her take-no-prisoners mode. "Even a big guy like

Xavier Rahm, who, by the way, has plenty of money to hire a thug to do a mean thing like slash tires."

"Would any of the neighbors have street cams that might have caught it?" Meredith asked.

"Depending on how the person came down the road, maybe. But there are plenty of delivery trucks and parked cars on Howard Street this time of day, blocking the view, and it's pretty much garages and storage for folks whose houses face Barnard or Whitaker. We can ask, of course. But the vines and shrubs that provide privacy also shield the back entry from visuals, just like ours."

"Something we might want to consider changing."

Julia grabbed her jacket. "Let's head over to visit Carolanne. I'll tell Carmen we're taking your car. She said she'd watch for the tow truck while she hunts for information on Sweet Cynthia."

Meredith grabbed her bag and keys, her mind spinning.

Mary Murphy didn't have the cash to pay someone to wreck Julia's tires, but she would have the funds if she was bilking money from Payroll Inc.

She'd claimed she liked and respected Julia, but the cops had made a very good point. When people were threatened, they could go above and beyond what they might have ever imagined to avoid capture or loss of power. Even nice people like Mary Murphy.

Chapter Twenty-Four

MEREDITH PULLED INTO PAYROLL INC.'s parking lot.

Xavier had a parking spot marked RESERVED FOR CFO, so Meredith tucked her car behind his. If he made a run for it, it wouldn't be in this car. And if she got a ticket, she'd add it to Carolanne's bill.

"I love your panache," Julia told her as they exited the car. "You were born for this job, Mere."

"I learned from the best," she said. It felt good to say that about Ron, because he had excelled at his job. But it also felt good to be taking the reins of her life again. She pulled the outside door open for Julia then followed her in. They went straight to the elevator leading to the executive floor, got in, and headed up. When the doors slid open, there was Mary Murphy, down the hall to their left, eyes down, hard at work. Could she have been across town in the last couple of hours, slashing tires, and now be back here, diligently working at her desk?

"No way could she have gotten across the city, parked, taped cameras, slashed tires, driven back here, and be calmly working. Right?" Julia murmured the question as they stepped out of the plush elevator.

"It's possible but logistically unlikely unless everything went her way and every light was green. Of course if the cameras were done at a different time—"

Julia frowned. "I prefer my scenario," she whispered just as Mary looked up and spotted them moving her way. She got up quickly, and no trace of guilt marred her welcoming smile. "Judge Foley, Mrs. Bellefontaine, so nice to see you both! I don't think Mrs. Van Valken was expecting you—"

"She isn't," Meredith agreed quickly. "We headed this way just to check on a few things. Is Mr. Rahm in his office, Mary?"

"He's just gotten back, but I know he's on a scheduled Zoom meeting at the moment. It's supposed to go on for about an hour."

"Is Carolanne also in that meeting?"

"Yes. I'm so sorry." Mary seemed genuinely contrite that they'd arrived unexpectedly with no one to talk to, but they had the information they needed. She appeared to have been here, hard at work, and the brown paper bag and half-eaten dish of apple slices that had oxidized slightly indicated she'd lunched at her desk. That added to her dedicated employee image.

Julia's phone buzzed a text. She read it and grabbed hold of Meredith's arm while she started backing toward the elevator. "Thank you, Mary, no worries. Gotta go." And before Meredith knew it, they were back in front of the elevator with Julia stabbing the Down button multiple times, as if that would increase the elevator's pace.

"What's wrong?" Meredith kept her smile in place and whispered the words through the side of her mouth like a really bad pantomime. "What's happened?"

"I'll show you outside," Julia whispered back. "Cameras, remember?"

Meredith remembered, all right. They stepped into the elevator, all smiles, and exited on the lobby floor the same way, but when they got outside and into Meredith's car, Julia handed her cell phone over. "This is what's wrong."

A picture of a note appeared. A note that simply said *Back off or else.*

No specific threat. No names mentioned. Meredith turned, puzzled. "Who got this note? Carmen?"

Julia shook her head, and her chin quivered before she mentioned Wyatt's daughter's name. "Maddie. The wraparound program took the kids to the playground behind the school this afternoon. Anna Beth has a scheduled staff meeting at her school once a week, so the girls stay at school until she picks them up. Maddie came in from the playground and found it in her backpack." She hiccupped on a tiny sob then swallowed hard and clenched her fists. "If Xavier Rahm thinks he can get away with scaring little children and two not-so-old ladies, the man's got another think coming. I am absolutely beyond furious that anyone would bring children into this. It's galling."

"They knew how to hit home," Meredith said. "There's no better way to stop or pause an investigation than by showing people their most vulnerable spot, and in this case, it's Wyatt's children." She started the car. "Let's get over to the playground and find out if they caught anything on camera."

Julia clasped her hands tightly. "Maybe it's a good thing they got to my car, because there's no way I could drive right now, I'm that mad. What kind of man—"

"Jules, it couldn't be Xavier."

Julia stopped talking and stared at her.

"He could have sabotaged your car and gotten back to work in time. Or planted the note. But in the little time that the girls have been out of classes and in the after-school program, there's no way he could have zigzagged across the city, done both, and be on his scheduled Zoom meeting. Right?"

"So then who is it?" Julia flattened her hands against her designer pants and scowled. "We've used up our list."

"We sure did, but what are we overlooking?" mused Meredith as she cruised across two lanes of commuter traffic like it was nothing, another skill she'd learned from Ron. Every now and then he told her she drove like a New Yorker, and that Southern boy meant it as an absolute compliment. "Unless, like Wyatt said, there are two people involved. Remember how he told us that if two people were involved it became much harder to find things without a whistleblower?"

"And yet Wyatt found the leak."

"Maybe because he was actually *looking* for a leak, not looking to balance books."

"Two people." Julia pulled out her notebook and began scribbling quickly. "But who?"

That was the question. It took over twenty minutes to get to Wyatt's house. Anna Beth had taken Maddie and Kennedy to get chicken nuggets for supper, leaving Wyatt free to talk to Julia and Meredith without hiking the girls' anxieties.

"Wyatt, I'm so sorry." Julia pulled her beloved nephew into a big hug. "I can't believe this happened."

Wyatt didn't seem nearly as unnerved. "It's unusual because I'm generally looked at as part of the corporation. Slipping into Payroll Inc. trained the spotlight on me instead of putting our firm in the crosshairs, but it's not as bad as you think, Aunt Julia."

"Putting threatening notes into a little girl's backpack while she's swinging on a playground isn't bad?" In a cartoon setting, steam would have puffed from Julia's ears right about now. Meredith had never seen her friend so angry.

"Not when it gives you this." Wyatt lifted his phone, opened an app, and there, slipping into the Dogwood Lane Elementary School, was Carolanne's daughter. One of them.

Julia gasped.

So did Meredith. And then she whirled around to Julia. "We wondered if there were two people working this."

"Hadley and Holly?" asked Julia. "That old trick of a jury not being able to tell who was doing what because they're identical and have the same DNA?"

"Those are the twin daughters, correct?" asked Wyatt.

"Yes, supposedly as different as night and day but maybe not so different after all," said Julia.

A call from Carmen came through right then. Meredith took it and walked into the next room. "Hey, Carmen. What's up?"

"A couple of things before I close up. The car has been towed, and they'll contact Julia directly. And I got an interesting hit on Miss Dicey's story from one of the decoders she worked with during the war. A woman named Coco Lee Duboisier published some obscure essays about being a decoder, and it seems she was alive when an author was writing a tell-all book about the codebreaking.

I told the author you'd be in touch if she was willing to talk, and she said she'd be happy to talk with you. I gave her your number so she'd recognize it when it comes into her phone."

"Carmen, that's great work. I'll call her as soon as I'm free. Well done, my friend."

"Thank you." Carmen's voice upticked. "Harmony is feeling better, so I get to play big sister tonight, and that's a nice change from slashed tires."

"It is indeed. Have fun." She didn't tell Carmen what had happened with Wyatt's daughter. They'd fill her in later. Right now they needed to figure out Hadley and/or Holly's role in this whole money-grabbing scheme. Why would two rich girls conspire to bilk money from their very generous mother's company?

"Should we call the police, Wyatt?"

Wyatt hesitated. "You need someone on board with this, Aunt Julia. If these two slashed tires, taped your cameras, and are now leaving threatening notes, they could be dangerous. But we have absolutely zero evidence of them having any kind of access to the payroll funding accounts."

"Someone could have let them in. Someone else, signing in for them. And—" Meredith could have smacked herself for being this blind. "There is only one person in that building who would do that."

"Carolanne," breathed Julia.

"Yes, but why?" Meredith tried to wrap her head around the reasoning and failed. "Why would a rich woman misdirect money from her own company? And get her daughters involved? Do you think she went a little crazy when Rusty died? I've heard that can happen to people when grief hits hard."

"I'm more likely to expect it was greed that hit hard," returned Wyatt practically. "Everyone knows that she was against going public, against sharing the company, even though it made them a fortune overall and increased the corporation's standings. But then Rusty died, there was a huge down surge during last year's market troubles, and maybe the combination spooked her. Loss of husband, loss of power, loss of valuation."

"But she's rich. I mean like crazy rich." Meredith couldn't understand it. "Why need more?"

Wyatt frowned. "She might not be as rich as we think she is, but even if that's true, some people always need more. For some folks, it's never enough, and from what I know about Mrs. Van Valken, she fits that profile. That and the problems with one of the twins."

"Audie and Shawna Phillips both mentioned problems with Holly," Meredith said. "They seemed to think Hadley was the good twin and Holly was her evil opposite. Not in those words, per se. And Holly's living at home, according to Carolanne."

"Although I only met Hadley at the dinner," said Julia. "Why wouldn't both girls be there if Holly's living there? Or was it Holly pretending to be Hadley?"

"And we come right back to *The Parent Trap* switch." Meredith had loved that old movie as a child. "But why?"

"Rich people are skilled at keeping their dirty laundry out of the news. If there are problems with Holly, I can assure you that the CEO of a major money corporation doesn't want it known to the general public," Wyatt said. "It may not be fair, but people tend to assume that if you can't handle your own children, you have no business handling their money."

"They had to change the girls' schools when they were younger." Meredith hadn't given the girls' early history a lot of thought concerning the money leak, but maybe family problems went deeper than Carolanne let anyone believe. "Carolanne said that the Lovey Anderson Day School didn't suit the girls' explorative personalities. When they moved the girls to an exclusive boarding school, it only lasted one year. They brought them back here, and they finished school at the Fulbright Academy. My boys had moved on to college by then and we lost track of one another, so I hadn't seen the girls until Rusty's funeral. They were just brokenhearted, all of them."

"Do we know where Hadley lives?" asked Julia.

Meredith shook her head but held up her phone. "No one really gets to hide anymore, do they? And we do know that she works at the Caldwell School as a speech therapist."

"I say we approach Hadley," said Julia. "She's either involved or she isn't, but there's no harm in talking to her."

"And the school's got a parking lot," noted Wyatt. "It might be better to approach her in the open."

Wise words. "Tomorrow morning. We'll be in the Caldwell parking lot bright and early. With coffee."

"Wyatt, are you sure Maddie and Kennedy are all right?" Julia's concern for Wyatt's beautiful daughters showed on her face. "I don't want anything I'm doing to mess them up. Nothing is worth that."

Wyatt hugged her tight. "They're fine, and like I said, I'm usually not the tagman. When the firm takes a case, it's a team effort. That way we spread the animosity much more equitably." He let her go and took a step back. "You figure out who's doing what, and I'll take the girls to and from school until you do. And do not forget what I said," he reminded them sternly. "People do horrible things for money. Some parents are capable of doing awful things to protect their children, especially in homes where the kid can do no wrong and it's always someone else's fault."

The wrong crowd.

"Carolanne said that to me once," Meredith told him. "How she changed schools for the girls to keep them from being in the wrong crowd."

"When their kid actually *is* the wrong crowd," said Wyatt. "Culpability is excused far too often these days."

"We've got some research to do before we intercept Hadley tomorrow." Julia moved toward the door. "Tell the girls Nana loves them."

"They know it, but I'll tell them again. They love you too."

They crossed the yard quickly. "Let's go to your place," suggested Meredith once they were in the car. "I want to see what we can track down about Carolanne's twins. I can't imagine the shock of learning my kid or kids is crooked, but if Carolanne has been covering up for one or both of them all this time, she probably knows it. Don't you think?"

Julia pulled her seat belt into place with a decided click. "She not only knows it, I think she's part of it, Mere. A big part of it. I think she hired us never thinking we'd find a thing, because we're inexperienced. I think we were *her* red herring to the board, and now that we brought Wyatt on board, we're forcing her hand. I think Rusty's widow is playing the black widow part to the max."

"I hate the logic of that." Meredith kept her eyes on the road once she'd backed out of Wyatt's driveway. "But you could be right.

Maybe I've been blind to that possibility because I saw how her grief matched mine. There's no way either of those girls got into money channeling without someone's help. Or unless their mother did it herself. That's a terrible thing to believe about someone you thought you knew."

"She may have been the person you believed her to be back then," Julia said. "But folks change. I've seen it happen again and again. From the sounds of it, Carolanne changed for the worse."

They picked up takeout from a local restaurant, grabbed drinks from the fridge, and had dueling screens set up minutes later on Julia's countertop island. "You want Hadley or Holly?" asked Meredith.

"Holly," Julia declared. "Juvenile court got me a lot of practice with miscreant youth."

Meredith began researching Hadley. "I'm going straight to social media after I call that author. Let's see how careful the girls are about who sees their sites." She put in a call to the author who had talked to Coco Duboisier, and when no one picked up, she left a message on the woman's voice mail. Then she set to work tracking Hadley Van Valken's internet presence and found almost nothing.

Hadley had all the proper guards and locks in place on the single social media site Meredith ventured into under her name. She showed no other presence on the other sites Meredith checked, but when she put in a simple internet search with Hadley's name, numerous accomplishments showed up. "Our Hadley is extremely well thought of in educational circles," Meredith announced as she set her salad dish aside. "Salutatorian of her Fulbright class, high honors in college, several academic awards, and was selected to teach at Caldwell before she'd even completed her full accreditation because of her grade status and abilities noted during her unpaid internship."

"Well, while she's dotting i's and crossing t's, her sister is a major mess-up."

Meredith cringed. "How bad?"

"I went deep," Julia told her. "My guess is we may have juvenile records that are sealed, but from age eighteen on, Holly's had multiple infractions with not only the local police but a parole officer she punched in the face and the county sheriff's department. She's got a sporadic record of police interventions, separated by spaces of time which suggest she was put into rehabilitation programs either by her own choice or court order. At least twice it was by court order. I'm not sure about the other times. But she's not afraid to jabber about the world's atrocities on her two social media accounts, which are under a different name."

"How do you know they're hers?" asked Meredith.

Julia shot her a guilty look. "I friended a friend and they have very interesting exchanges. So even though Holly has one level of protection on her site where she labeled herself 'Don't Try This At Home,' I can see her responses on her friend's feed. And they're very interesting."

"You friended someone on her feed?"

Julia pushed her glasses up farther on her nose. "I used an alias. And made it look like I was new in town, looking for the best places to hang out and have a real good time."

"It troubles me to think how easily young people lure other young people into things these days."

"Strength in numbers." Julia tapped a few keys. Then she paused her fingers. "Uh-oh."

"Uh-oh what?"

She made a face. "Two days ago this girl, Tiffany, wanted to meet up this weekend, but Holly said, 'No can do. Heading out of town for a while. Maldives.'"

"Maldives has no extradition treaty with the US," Meredith said.

"And we know there's a bankroll of misdirected money somewhere, waiting to be accessed."

"They're about to run."

"So it would seem. Do we dare wait until tomorrow to talk to Hadley?"

"We have to," Meredith conceded. "We have no idea where she lives, and she's careful enough not to leave a strong internet footprint. But let's set up a meeting with Carolanne for right after we talk to Hadley. If Hadley tells her we've approached her, they might all run instantly. I'm going to text Carolanne that we've got some good news for her, and we'd like to meet with her tomorrow to finish things up."

"String her along with our own red herring," Julia grumbled. "I'm insulted to think we were hired as shills, but it makes me happy that we got the job done with Wyatt's help."

"She got to you, big-time," observed Meredith, but Carolanne's ploy stung her too. Would they be in time to find out if they were right and stop the Van Valkins' flight?

"Never could take easily to highfalutin types, and I've got less tolerance for them now. Especially now that I figure she's sabotaging her own company for personal selfish means."

"What if we're wrong?" asked Meredith. She'd been searching Carolanne's online profiles, and other than aligning herself with every possible influential and upscale business and government official in the state of Georgia, no one knew a thing about Carolanne Van Valken. Except from the business periodicals that lauded the success of Payroll Inc., launched by an intelligent and ambitious young couple over three decades before.

"Then I'll be the first to apologize, but we're not," Julia replied. "My gut's been rumbling on this from the beginning. I should have trusted my instincts, but then we wouldn't have taken the job. This way we might be able to catch her before she flees. Did you send the text?"

"I did, and just got her answer. We'll meet her at eight thirty at her house. She says she's staying home for a video conference before she goes into the office."

"A video conference from a plane," remarked Julia.

"Encroaching thunderstorms are on our side," Meredith told her. "A strong cold front running into warm air from the Gulf is supposed to set us up for some tough weather beginning overnight. The airport is already advising people to expect major delays tomorrow morning."

"Well, let's bless those mysterious ways of the Lord," Julia responded. She stretched and yawned. "I'm done in."

"Me too. I'll be here at seven, all right? We'll go straight to Caldwell, see if we can grab a few minutes with Twin Number One and then move on to Carolanne and Twin Number Two. Any word on your car?"

"They texted that they'd have it ready for pickup in the morning."

"Good." She still felt guilty that Julia's car was targeted but glad they hadn't slashed all three vehicles. And then she wondered why they hadn't. Had something interrupted the onslaught? "I'll be here at seven."

"We'll swing by to pick up our coffee order from the app on my phone. If I've got to look decent by seven in the morning, my coffee better be ready for pickup by seven-oh-five."

"I can't fault your reasoning," agreed Meredith. She reached out and gave her good friend a hug. "See you first thing."

"I'll be ready."

Chapter Twenty-Five

MEREDITH'S PHONE RANG ABOUT THIRTY seconds after they picked up their coffee orders the next morning. "Cat Caufield," she told Julia when she spotted the display. "I called her on a hunch."

She hit the Bluetooth connection and answered. "Cat, thank you for calling early. You never let things dawdle. I've got you on speaker so Julia can hear you too."

"Julia!" Cat Caufield's exuberance was always a pleasure to hear, and the fact that their old college chum had built one of the largest real estate businesses in lower Georgia made Cat a go-to person whenever they had a real estate question. "I love that you're the kind of businesswoman who takes early calls, because I'm an up-with-the-chickens sort of gal myself. What can I do for y'all? You buyin'? Sellin'? Or solvin' crimes, my friends? Because it's a very interestin' time for you to send me an inquiry about the Van Valken estate. Almost like you know more than anyone should know."

"Cat, no one can manufacture an instant drawl as well as you," said Meredith with a laugh. "You are pure South as needed or straight-talk-no-drawl as required. Neat trick."

"Well, your text has me curious because I closed the sale on the Van Valken estate about fourteen hours ago. But it was a silent sale, so how did y'all hear about it? Nothing will be officially transferred for three days, but the CEO of MacIntyre Tires will soon be the official owner of that amazing piece of property. It sold at a cool price tag that can't be revealed, but a good million below market value. The MacIntyres got a steal, and Carolanne can buy her kid's freedom at least a couple more times." Cat didn't hide the disdain in her voice. "For my money, I'd have just disciplined Holly when she was a little brat. Big brats are far more difficult to handle and much too costly for my peace of mind. But then that's me."

"So she's had to bail Holly out of trouble in the past?" asked Julia, as if she didn't know.

"Too many times to count," Cat replied. "And under a lot of assumed names. I'd feel bad for gossiping, but it's not gossip if it's just the flat-out truth, like when you see a freight train approaching a broken bridge and you predict the final outcome, but the conductor is sure everything will turn out fine."

Carolanne secretly sold her house. Meredith's palms grew damp against the steering wheel. Obviously it was flight time.

"Did Carolanne say where she was moving to?" she asked Cat as she took the turn toward the Caldwell School. She had to work to keep her voice matter-of-fact. "Is she downsizing?"

"She's moving in with Hadley. She paid off the mortgage on the house on Turnbull. That's where Hadley lives now. She bought it two years back, and if Russell hadn't tied up her inheritance in a trust she can't access until she's thirty-one, she could have just paid cash. It's a sweet older home, Mere, the kind you'd love, and Carolanne said she's ready to spend less time keeping house and more time loving life."

Meredith exchanged looks with Julia and then addressed Cat. "Cat, thank you. I owe you coffee and dinner for this one."

"Naw, you gals owe me nothing but time, and I'll take that supper offer. Too many days and nights working, and at our age, there's a limit to what you need to leave your children and how much money you can spend. Supper with two good friends sounds wonderful. Glad to help. Talk later. I've got a few things to do outside before the storm hits and before the workday officially begins."

As soon as the call disconnected, Meredith spoke up. "She paid off that house for Hadley because she's leaving with Holly. That house on Turnbull was Rusty's grandmother's house. It's a family place and must have some special meaning for Hadley."

"And once again Carolanne positively reinforces the negative behavior of one child while barely giving a nod to the positive behavior of the other. Although a six-hundred-thousand-dollar house is a nice parting gift, I suppose." Julia had searched the web for the Turnbull address and held up the pic for Meredith to see.

Cat was right. The old house had been remodeled in recent years but they'd kept the timeless beauty of the home and the vintage setting. "Access to the water. Hadley was a rower, wasn't she?"

"All through college. Well." Julia drew a deep breath as they turned in to the school parking lot. "Let's talk with the good twin. See what she knows. My guess would be she's on the upside of this downward trend, but the one thing I discovered on the bench was that you could never be too sure. Instinct is good, but evidence is better."

Meredith swung into a nonreserved parking spot at Caldwell at seven twenty-nine and Hadley Van Valken pulled into a space in the next row about six minutes later.

Julia slipped out of her side of the car and moved toward the single set of steps leading to the beautifully restored series of brick buildings.

Meredith headed straight for Hadley. "Hadley?" She waved and yoo-hooed in fine Southern woman fashion. "It's Mrs. Bellefontaine, a friend of your mom. You used to hang around with my boys when you were little." She indicated a little-kid size with her right hand. "Carter and Chase. Remember?"

Hadley's expression went from startled to puzzled as she tried to make sense of Meredith's purpose. "Vaguely."

"They were in different schools, so you guys only got together when you were small," Meredith gushed. "My husband and I were friends of your parents back when they started Payroll Inc."

"Ah." Hadley seemed at ease with that statement. "My mother's circle of friends changed as the company soared. But I do remember your younger son. He was always ready to include me in games."

"And he hasn't changed a bit," Meredith assured her as Julia came their way. "He's a professor at Emory, and his students love him. I'm not surprised that you both ended up in education. A servant's heart, you know."

"What a nice thing to say." Hadley gave Julia a curious look but tapped her watch. It wasn't an ostentatious five-figure watch like her mother wore. It was a simple timepiece, the kind you find at a neighborhood drugstore. "But I have a first session student, so I must get inside. Nice seeing you again."

"I need to ask you a couple of questions, Hadley, and I wouldn't have caught you out like this, in a parking lot, but I didn't know how to reach you." Meredith hoped her words would pause Hadley, and they did. "It's your sister. I'm afraid she might be in deep trouble."

Anger darkened Hadley's features before she controlled it, but it was enough to show her displeasure. "I'm not at liberty to talk about Holly. I really must—" She started to go left, but Julia stood firm, blocking her way, and her first words paused Hadley again.

"Your mother sold her house." Julia didn't pull any punches. She stood in the rising wind and still looked like she could be on the cover of a Southern ladies' magazine. "Silent sale, closed yesterday. We have reason to believe she's about to leave the country and take Holly with her, but she did pay off the house you're living in, so it's not like she totally forgot you."

Hadley stared at Julia, and her throat convulsed slightly. Her chin shook.

But then she firmed it, and Meredith suspected she'd had to stifle her emotions about her mother and sister on a fairly regular basis. "They're in trouble," Meredith told her in a soft voice. A few cars began trickling into the school's parking lot, and people hurried up the stairs to beat the rain. "I think your mother's going to make a major mistake by trying to flee the country. But if we're right, she's already made some significant mistakes. If you know anything that would help us stop her, we'd be grateful." The wind whipped around Meredith's hair, and the warm scent of humid rain came their way.

"I can tell you this." Hadley didn't cry, but she looked like she wanted to, and that broke Meredith's heart. "I've lived like this all my life. Every choice, every decision, every holiday, was based on making Holly happy, but nothing ever made my sister happy. And that hasn't changed. Is she spoiled? Or mentally ill? I don't know." Hadley's frank expression put another crunch on Meredith's emotions. "All I know is that I went unnoticed. But then"—she ticked off her fingers as she listed a litany of complaints—"I wasn't starting fires, trashing my mother's camellia gardens, pretending to be my twin sister while wreaking havoc with our classmates, or exchanging favors to score drugs. My college tuition didn't cost a fraction of the pricey rehab facilities my sister has called home too many times to count, none of which have done any good. So if my mother is running away to save Holly's hide again, I say go. Go in peace, and leave me alone. Because I honestly don't care if I ever see either of them again. And now, if you'll excuse me."

She slipped around Julia and moved toward the steps, but she paused and turned just shy of the curb. "My father tried. He tried so hard, but even with his money and influence and charisma, there was no separating or dealing with whatever kind of enabling relationship my sister has with my mother. Sometimes I think his death was an escape, because no matter what he did, it kept getting worse. And then he was gone." For a few seconds, sorrow claimed her pretty features. "He should have been stronger. I knew that. He knew that. And I think in the end it killed him that he wasn't strong enough to stop the madness. He loved me. I never doubted that for a minute, but a strong father would have stood up for me. Protected me. At some point in time, a strong father would have put me first. And that never happened. Not once. So whatever scheme my mother and sister have going, it's only one of many over the years. And maybe this time one or both of them will have to pay the price."

She turned again and this time didn't look back.

A big fat raindrop landed on Meredith's cheek. "Duck and cover!"

She hit the unlock icon quickly, and they got to the car just as the heavens opened. She started the engine and popped the car into gear then headed for the Islands Expressway, but there was nothing fast about the morning commute today. As they waited in clogged northbound lanes, Julia tried Carolanne's number. When Carolanne finally answered on the fourth try, Julia dove right in. "Carolanne, it's Julia. We're on our way, but we've met with some traffic. I didn't want you to worry if we're a few minutes late."

"And most mornings that would be fine, but I'm in an absolute time crunch today," Carolanne replied in an almost breathless voice. "I've got to get Holly to an appointment. She spent the night at a friend's house, so I've got to drive there, grab her, and make the appointment. I'm so sorry we can't meet in person. Feel free to send me a wrap-up of your findings via email. Mary will print them up and file them accordingly, and thank you both for trying. I'm just so glad you found nothing. That supports the work of the other two firms and should appease our board. I'll forward your payment out straightaway."

"Except we did find something, Carolanne." Meredith said it in a voice dripping with sympathy, feigning sorrow at having to deliver bad news. "Julia and I are quite taken aback by it, but also impressed at the ingenuity, because whoever started bleeding small increments of money from paychecks over a year ago was fiendishly clever." The traffic in their lane began to ease, and Meredith was finally able to move forward. Not fast, yet, but they were no longer stuck, so that was a relief.

She aimed toward the exit ramp and kept talking. "It's such a blessing to have someone with Wyatt's skills on board with us. When you have a true forensic auditor at your beck and call, well—" She paused and whooshed out a breath for effect. "You can imagine what a help he is. I promise we won't take much of your time. We've narrowed down the list of potential codebreakers, and if you can give us your input, we should be able to let the feds step in and finish the rest."

"The feds?" Carolanne's voice went from Southern alto to high soprano instantly. "You mean like the FBI?"

"Exactly." Meredith flicked on her signal to take the exit for Johnny Mercer Blvd. "This is their jurisdiction because it crosses state lines. All of them," she declared in a voice that held admiration. "Including Hawaii and Alaska, which is quite impressive. Whoever set this up was skilled in the simplicities of subterfuge, something Ron taught me long ago. It's not about the amount," she stressed as she cruised toward Wilmington Island Road. There was lighter traffic in this direction, and the commuter travel going off the island had tapered too. "On this caper, the exponential effect goes straight to the millions. Someone saw a way to get rich and seized it. We're just about to pull into your drive," she added as the entrance to the lavish estate came into view. "And—"

The connection went dead, and they didn't pull into the driveway.

They couldn't, because Carolanne's high-priced luxury SUV was barreling down the drive at a high rate of speed. She barely hit the brakes when she got to the road, and careened around the corner like the lead car at Talladega.

Tires squealing, Carolanne tore up the road, back the way they'd come, heading toward the Islands Expressway.

"Did you see Holly in the car?" asked Meredith as she swung a quick U-turn.

"No. She was either hiding, or Carolanne was being honest and she didn't come home last night. Do you think she's thwarting her mother's getaway?"

"From what everyone's said, I think she's doing what she's always done," Meredith replied as she narrowly missed an oversized mailbox. "Putting herself first. And Carolanne's still determined to save her precious darling."

Julia muttered something under her breath as Meredith put the pedal to the metal, but Carolanne's high-end torqued engine outstripped her quickly as she tooled up Wilmington Island Road. As the white 4×4 drove out of sight, Julia set her phone to speaker mode, hit 911, and alerted the police that they were following a person of interest in what could be a major federal crime.

"Are you in pursuit of this vehicle, ma'am?" asked the dispatcher.

"Yes," Julia said, one hand gripping the passenger door handle as Meredith navigated a curve. The turn brought the approaching storm into full view, and spring storms were nothing to challenge in the South. Today, there was little choice in the matter. "She could be heading for Route 80."

"Ma'am, it is advised for you to discontinue pursuit at this time and let the authorities handle it. Chatham County sheriffs will be responding."

But would they find Carolanne in time? Get to her? Stop her? They might. But they might not. Meredith was determined to keep her in sight.

Julia covered up the sensitive microphone on the phone. "Are you giving up the chase?" she asked as Meredith passed a slow-moving Mercedes.

"No way. We've got room to maneuver. So I intend to maneuver."

"She just cut someone off," Julia exclaimed as the dark sky they'd left in Savannah found them, full force.

"Watch and see which direction she goes," Meredith said. "I've got to pay attention to the road."

"On it!" declared Julia. She withdrew a small pair of binoculars from her bag. "Every self-respecting gumshoe needs a pair of these babies," she muttered as she trained them up ahead. "Going toward the city, Mere."

"Along with a lot of other people." The traffic heading into Savannah had thinned, but Carolanne wasn't driving like a normal person. She was driving like a woman running for her life, and maybe that was what it felt like to her. "I'm backing off a little. We don't want to cause an accident."

"I agree. Have I mentioned yet that I don't like your friend?"

Meredith winced. "Now and again."

"But I can't say I haven't enjoyed this case, because we totally get to see justice done to someone who tried to play us big-time. In case you haven't noticed, I don't like being played."

Meredith dropped back and merged into the flow of traffic. "I'm giving her a false sense of security," she said. "Do you still see her?"

"Sure do. Looks like she's taking the Truman."

A diversion? Or a destination?

Meredith had no idea, but she wasn't about to let Carolanne lose her. She increased her speed, followed the exit onto the southbound Truman Parkway at Victory Square, and noticed something odd as Carolanne proceeded down the highway.

The rain was a downpour. Anyone driving anything, even a high-priced SUV like Carolanne's, would apply the brakes as they curved or changed lanes to avoid hitting other vehicles.

Carolanne's taillights glowed red, but there was no additional intensity to indicate braking. And when she seemed to swerve left, then recover too much to the right, Meredith's observation turned to one thing and one thing only: Carolanne's brakes were failing.

"She's got no brakes, Jules." Meredith's heart was in her throat.

"Who? Carolanne?" Julia peered into the slashing wind and rain.

"Call her on my phone so the Bluetooth picks it up," Meredith directed as she increased her speed more than she should for the conditions. "Tell her to shift down. To use her drive shift to go to a lower gear. And then tell her to aim for the Montgomery exit. The bushes there will help decrease her speed naturally."

Julia called from Meredith's phone.

The call rang twice and went straight to voice mail.

Meredith gripped the wheel tighter. "Try her again." She flashed her lights as she drew closer, hoping Carolanne would get the message and pick up the phone. "Let's hope she answers this time."

Whether it was the flashing headlights or the second call, this time Carolanne picked up. There was true desperation in her voice. "I can't stop, Meredith! I can't stop! I think she's trying to kill me!"

Who is trying to kill her? Meredith shoved that thought aside for the moment because right now her focus was on saving Carolanne's life.

"Carolanne, listen to me." Meredith used the toughest voice she could muster. And the loudest. "Pump your brakes as hard as you can. Push down with all your might. If that doesn't slow you down, then downshift to the lowest gear. That will help slow you down."

"I don't know what you're talking about! This car isn't a manual! There's no gearshift. I—"

Julia stepped into the conversation so Meredith could focus on driving. "All cars downshift, Carolanne, even automatics. I know you're scared, but you need to do this and do it now. Put it in the lowest gear," she directed firmly. "That will help. There's a wide swath of thick bushes at the Montgomery exit. Pull on your parking brake to help you slow down even more, then aim for that exit and those bushes."

"I can't!" Even while saying that, she must have downshifted, because the car seemed to slow as Meredith drew closer.

"You did great," Julia told her. "Now the parking brake."

"The emergency one?"

"Yes. Put it on. The exit is coming up on our right."

It was, but there were two slower moving cars and a delivery van in that lane. Carolanne would either hit them or need to shoot in front of them, and Meredith wasn't sure she had enough room. But at this moment there really wasn't much choice.

She laid on the horn aggressively to warn the other drivers while she moved ahead to flank Carolanne on the left.

"Bushes, Carolanne! While we're on this upgrade. Go now!" Julia barked the command and just as she did, Carolanne's SUV shot across the right lane and toward the incline of bushes and trees.

Meredith backed off her speed then merged into the lane behind the delivery van. She braked quick and hard, then followed Carolanne's car across the grass, praying for a good outcome. Carolanne might be dishonest and misguided, but she didn't deserve to die.

Or be murdered. That thought sobered Meredith.

Could one of the girls have done this?

Not Hadley.

No matter what else happened, Meredith didn't want the good twin to be involved, but that left Holly. Or was there someone else they didn't know about?

The crunch of metal to tree bark and bushes ended in a cloud of white steam from Carolanne's engine.

Meredith screeched to a stop on the wet grass. She and Julia hopped out and ran through the driving rain as two sheriff's deputies and a Savannah police car raced their way. Meredith got to Carolanne's door and yanked it open, ready to pull her out then stopped.

So did Julia.

Carolanne wasn't badly hurt. That was obvious.

But she was on her phone, telling someone to run. "Get out, now!" she screamed into the phone. "Go somewhere. Hide! You have to—"

Meredith swiped the phone from Carolanne's hand. She was tempted to test her softball arm and pitch it into the swale leading to the lake, but she stopped herself because it probably held evidence.

Instead she handed it to Julia, who tucked it into her pocket for safe-keeping from the storm.

"You're still trying to save her." Right now Meredith didn't care that she was getting wet despite the rain slicker. She didn't care one whit. She'd dry off later. She leaned down and stared into Carolanne's pale eyes. Eyes that *were* a little bit scary, like Julia said the week before. "You risked it all to save one child at the expense of the other, and you're still trying to get her off the hook, even after she tried to kill you."

"She didn't. I shouldn't have said that. Holly loves me! She needs me! She—"

The sheriffs were hurrying their way. Lights flashing and sirens wailing, an ambulance and a rescue wagon rushed toward the scene.

"Are you all right, ma'am?" A deputy moved forward with firm steps. "What happened?"

Julia faced him. "What happened is that this is Carolanne Van Valken, and she's going to be wanted for a multimillion-dollar theft that crossed state lines as soon as the feds see the evidence my nephew is presenting to them and the Payroll Incorporated board right now. She crashed her car while trying to flee to the Maldives with her daughter. The daughter damaged the brake lines to kill her mother, so you can see there is little honor among thieves, even rich ones. Don't leave her unguarded for a minute," Julia told the sheriff. "And don't believe anything she says, because she's a consummate liar. Oh, and there's this." She reached into her pocket and withdrew the cell phone. The deputy slipped it into a zippered plastic bag before putting it into his own pocket. "She was talking to her fugitive daughter, warning her to run when we approached the car while her very nice other daughter is helping children with speech difficulties at a local school." Julia aimed a parting look at Carolanne, and Meredith got a glimpse of what criminals in her courtroom must have faced. It wasn't pretty.

But it was thoroughly justified.

Julia leaned in. "You will bear the full weight of the investigation you started, Carolanne. And I'll be glad to testify for the prosecution. If I were you, I'd take whatever plea deal they offer, put your sociopathic daughter in a lockdown facility, and thank God you didn't die today. Because if you don't do that, your daughter's going to cause even more harm than she's already done, and that will be entirely your fault."

Julia didn't walk away.

She stalked. Meredith understood her anger. To see Carolanne still trying to protect Holly, even after a possible murder attempt, shook her too.

She slipped their business card to both sheriffs. "I'm sure the warrant for her arrest will be forthcoming. Her daughter was the last phone call on the phone. Her name is Holly Van Valken, she's got a record with the department, she's a definite flight risk, and she's accustomed to getting away with anything she's ever done. This time it was almost murder." She turned to seek the shelter of her car.

Dixon Mulvaney was standing there, arms folded. He looked at her then lifted a brow. "Mrs. Bellefontaine, you look chilled and soaked and thoroughly put out, and I expect you and your partner could use a good cup of coffee about now. What do you say to me and my partner buying you a cup of coffee and meeting you at the precinct so we can get your statements? In my book, good coffee makes everything better."

She looked at him, and when his cheek gave a tweak of understanding, she knew she had to say yes. "Usually I'm elated when we solve a case," she told him as they sloshed their way through the unmown grass to her car. "This time I just want to punch someone, so yes, Officer Mulvaney—"

"Dix," he said, and something in his calm, even voice sounded good. It felt good too. "Call me Dix, and we'll meet you back at the station in ten minutes, give or take. All right?"

And then he did it. One of those little kindnesses that said so much about the man.

Instead of trotting back to his cruiser that was angled off the road about sixty feet away, he paused and opened her car door for her, even though the rain and wind beat against them. He held it open while she got settled in with her seat belt on. "All set?" he asked, with the door leaned shut, and when she said yes, he gave a quick nod. "See you in a few."

Only then did he shut the door and trot to the shelter of his cruiser.

Chapter Twenty-Six

"*Have you never had a true love, Aunt Dicey?*"

Dicey palmed Allison's curls and scolded the impulsive twelve-year-old girl with a wry look.

"*Because you're so pretty and all. That's why I'm asking,*" *Allison continued. A head full of red-gold ringlets, banded back, and a sprinkling of freckles highlighted Allison's Celtic roots that came from both sides of her family tree.*

"*Allison, Aunt Dicey's life is her own to share or not,*" *scolded Jubal Early Jones, the girl's father. "It's not our place to pry, but you're absolutely correct." He was reading the newspaper, and he lowered it just enough to let his eyes twinkle at Dicey. "She and your Grandmom are beautiful ladies. Two of Savannah's finest. The Oglethorpe genes run strong through their veins.*"

"*Well, then there's Mom,*" *Allison reminded him as her mother came into the room. "You always said you found the sweetest and the best and were kind of amazed she even gave you the time of day.*"

Jubal laughed then grabbed his wife's hand and gave it a quick kiss. "True on all counts. And she's presented me with two amazing children."

"And one more to come." Allison grew moony-eyed, but her brother Jared snorted.

"Babies smell, and they take up everybody's time. I've got soccer and baseball tournaments all summer. How will I get there?"

"I may be a few years older than your grandmother," Dicey told Jared, "but I'm quite capable of driving youngsters from place to place. And cheering you on. Mom will need some time once the baby's here."

"Can we get ice cream?"

Dicey laughed. "Exorbitant amounts, my friend."

"I'm in!" Eleven-year-old Jared gave her a gentle high five. For him a surprise little brother or sister was a nuisance.

"You don't mind, Aunt Dicey?" Jubal asked when Jared had dashed outside to join a pickup baseball game with an assortment of neighborhood kids who found River View's broad yard to be the best playground of all.

"Not at all, and that car of mine needs to see more action." Dicey had been doing a crossword puzzle. When Jubal spoke again, she quietly set it aside.

"Why did you never marry?" He folded the paper and gazed across the cluttered morning table. They were staying at River View while their home was being exterminated. A nasty mess of carpenter ants had been having a field day for far too long, and it was time to make them feel most unwelcome. "You must have had chances. I can't believe the men of Savannah were that blind or stupid not to see what a prize they had in you."

She'd set the puzzle down.

Now she put the pen alongside it. Then she raised her gaze to his. "There were opportunities, but the war took its toll, Jubal. Not just on the numbers of men, but the outlook of men who'd been to war. And there was a time of shadow after the war. Not for everyone, perhaps, but for me, and for others, where it wasn't clear what might bring retribution or what might waylay us if we did too much or spoke out of turn."

"Spoke about what?" he asked softly. There was no denying the concern in his voice. "Why would that cause trouble? Was there trouble for you, Aunt Dicey? Trouble for the Oglethorpes?"

She wanted to tell him.

She wanted to tell someone.

Was Jubal the one she could open up to? He was a thoughtful man. A little dramatic at times, but his mama was a bit of a drama queen herself, so Jubal came by it honestly. And he was a good man. A family man.

Would you really open up about this now, with so much at stake? her conscience warned. A wife, two children, one on the way. Why would you risk anything here?

So many years.

Years of silence, and those Charleston codebreakers who had gone home to Jesus far too young. A couple of others had since perished from normal causes, so maybe it was all right to talk about it. To tell Jubal the stories. To share what she knew. Maybe—

His wife had followed Allison to the front room. Now she bustled back, her rounded profile a testament to their love and affection and perhaps a bit of mistiming, because they'd both professed that Jared was their last child. That wasn't the case any longer. A new life would soon join the family, and seeing Tessa bend down, kiss Jubal's cheek, then touch a protective hand over the baby in her womb, Dicey choked back the words she longed to say.

Jubal might be a good person to talk to. His flair for drama didn't negate a strong and reasonable mind. But what if it was too soon? What if—heaven forbid!—the threat persisted?

And something happened to this marvelous family?

She couldn't live with that. She pressed her lips together and shook her head. "No, the Oglethorpes were blessed throughout. As was I." She took a final drink of her sweet tea. "I've been blessed to teach some of the finest young musical minds Savannah has had to offer for nearly forty years. I had a solid legacy from my parents, and enough Oglethorpe real estate investment work to keep me busy until the grave. Or until you young folks take it over. There is still much to do in running a business like ours. And on that note, I'll complete my puzzle later. There's some newfangled computerized system going into your grandfather's office, and I need to be present."

"Your office now, Aunt. It has been for over twenty years," Jubal reminded her. "You've done a fine job keeping every-thing afloat. God blessed you with that keen business intel-lect that's kept investments growing."

"They go up, they go down," she said softly. Wealth wasn't her mainstay. Nor the lack of it. It was this. Family. Faith. Friends. They deserved all the protection she could give them.

She stood and looked at him for long, drawn seconds. "But yours is the true wealth, my boy. You and Tessa and these children that I love so dearly. Family monies come and go with the times, but the true blessing is right here in this house. And I'm grateful to be a part of it."

"A feeling we share, Aunt Dicey." Then Jubal did some-thing he rarely did anymore. He stood up and gave her a big, gentle hug. "We love you."

"And I, you." She smiled at Tessa over Jubal's shoulder, knowing she was doing the right thing. This family was pre-cious to her and so many others, and she didn't want anything she might say to threaten that.

And so, once more, she stayed quiet.

Chapter Twenty-Seven

"ARE YOU ALL RIGHT? FOR SURE?" Carmen met Julia and Meredith at the back door. She took charge of their wet slickers while they shucked off their soaked shoes. "We'll set those out in the sun to dry when the storm passes," she said. "I can't believe what you said on the phone. You have to tell me all about it, but wait for Maggie Lu. She's on her way over from the library."

"We'd have picked her up if we'd known," said Meredith, but the jangle of the front door announced a new arrival. A moment later, Maggie Lu came down the hall. She was carrying wet boots, the kind that slip over shoes. Old-fashioned and quite practical, perfect for their dear friend.

"Iced tea and a fresh pot of coffee." She smiled approval at Carmen. "That gives me time to dash downstairs and have a look-see on Miss Kitty and her sweet family. But first, there's this," she said in her quiet voice as she set a plastic-wrapped glass cake pan on the island. "Rebecca sent this delightful cake that was a gift to her from one of her neighbors. With her sugar problems, she can't be eating something like this. Which means we get to share it."

The crumb cake was filled with pastry cream and topped with some sort of streusel, and Meredith couldn't deny how happy she was to see it and her friends. Warm and dry were blessings too.

"Wyatt is on his way." Julia raised her phone as evidence while Maggie Lu slipped downstairs. "He just texted. He should be here in fifteen minutes, and he's got the other half of the story."

"So we wait and hear it all together, if that's all right." Carmen poured steaming mugs of coffee and set a pitcher of iced tea on the island. "Do we want to meet here or in the conference room?"

They'd remodeled Ron's former office into a small conference room, but Meredith took a seat on a stool. "I'm fine here. There's something so right about gathering in a kitchen, isn't there? And it doesn't matter where that kitchen is."

"My *mami* used to call some folks *amigas de cocina*, 'kitchen friends,'" said Carmen. "I knew that meant they were special friends. Her besties."

Maggie Lu came back up the stairs, and her radiance indicated all was well in the lower level of the office, which meant that if no one spoke up for the pretty calico, she'd most likely be moving to Le Grand Street for a permanent location. "When Miss Carmen told me about your misadventure, what that poor woman was doing and what her child was willing to do, my heart just went *kerplunk* in my chest," she told them. Compassion and sympathy filled her expression. "A misguided parent is an awful thing for a child, no matter what their financial circumstances may be. Sometimes saving them from consequences is the very worst thing we can do."

"I saw quite a bit of it in my courtroom," said Julia. She took a seat on one of the island stools and brushed a damp tendril of hair from her face. "A large share of the cases I heard were either overly indulgent parents whose kids could do no wrong or sorely neglected youngsters with lack of parenting. Both situations ended with negative results for the kids and the parents."

Meredith grabbed her sweater from the back of a chair and slipped it on. "I'm still getting over the fact that she hired us to throw folks off and stage her getaway, and we ended up finding what she was doing."

"But do we know why?" asked Carmen. "She's already rich. Why steal?"

"Power and greed are strong motivators," Julia told her. "Wyatt said she sang like a caged canary when they got her daughter down to the station, and Holly started talking smack about Carolanne and how awful she was."

"Oh. Ouch." Carmen made a face. "Talk about biting the hand that feeds you." She straightened in her chair. "I have a bit of news I can share before Wyatt gets here."

"You do?" Meredith wouldn't mind hearing something that had nothing to do with Carolanne for a moment. "What's up?"

"Well." Carmen took out the cake server and began to slice generous wedges of the custard-filled butter crumb cake. "It seems the *San Francisco Daily Record* ran a series of mental health reports in conjunction with a mental health awareness campaign put on by the university's Behavioral Science department three years ago, and look who was their fourth interview." She slid a printout across the island as Maggie Lu finished pouring herself a glass of iced tea.

Meredith read the opening paragraph then stopped, surprised. "This is Ben Converse's out-of-wedlock daughter."

"It sure is, and Adelaide is now a renowned psychologist in the California wine country. She agreed to do the interview now that both of her parents have passed away."

"'Cast Aside.'" Meredith read the headline then the title of the article. "'How Living with a Narcissistic Mother Brought One Woman to a Life of Empathy and Compassion.'"

"Meredith." Julia leaned over to peer at the article. "Do you think Cynthia really could have killed Ginny?"

It had been supposition a few days before. This revelation from Adelaide's life with Cynthia made it seem much more possible. "And Theresa when she dug too deep?" Meredith skimmed the article then raised her gaze to Julia's. "Julia, that would explain why no one else was hurt. If Pansy was a sensitive soul that just couldn't handle life any longer—"

"Like Miss Dicey said," added Julia.

"Then maybe this explains what happened to Ginny and Theresa. The mother of Bennington's love child gets the wife out of the way by killing her—"

"While Bennington was in DC on business, leaving the door open for them to marry."

"And then Theresa meets with a tragic accident within the next year, leaving so many questions."

"While Bennington has two more children with Cynthia after legally adopting her firstborn."

"Who was his biological daughter," added Carmen.

Maggie Lu sat on a stool and fanned herself vigorously. "This has all the makings of an afternoon soap opera, doesn't it? Death and secret babies and staged accidents with an evil woman at the center."

"Except it's not fiction," Julia said. "If we're right, this woman got away with murder and got the husband, the kids, and the kitchen sink."

"But she was never happy, no matter what she did. It was never enough," Carmen said. "Read the last three paragraphs."

Meredith and Maggie Lu both read the final paragraphs then passed the newspaper to Julia. After a moment Julia looked up. "She sent her children away?" Indignation charged her tone.

"One by one," said Maggie Lu. "They were in her way, the daughter says. They cost money and took time and attention away from her because Bennington doted on his children. So she made their lives quietly miserable to keep her hold on Bennington."

"What in the world is wrong with these people?" exclaimed Meredith. "This isn't simple selfishness. It's evil."

"And we've already had our share of that this week," said Julia. She turned toward Meredith. "Miss Dicey spent years in hiding, afraid of speaking out, afraid of getting attached. If only she'd known what was behind the notes..."

"That they were to cover up Cynthia's intent to get rid of Ginny and leave the door open for her and Bennington."

"We know it now," said Julia. "And even if we can't prove it, we can show Miss Dicey."

"I think this little bit of added information will get you to share what you know with the Atlanta Police Cold Case commission first," said Carmen. "It seems not everyone believed Theresa's death was an accident, and her parents put a twenty-thousand-dollar reward in trust, for any information leading to the truth. No one has removed the trust, and it's quadrupled in size."

No matter what else happened, Miss Dicey deserved the chance to receive that reward. Her final forthrightness had brought them to this conclusion. The sound of Wyatt's car door had Meredith slip the new information about Cynthia Converse aside. "Carmen, you did great. We'll follow up on this right away, and I expect the police will be able to connect the dots now. And if Miss Dicey gets that award, I expect it will go straight to the music conservatory to bring River View up to code. That will be a huge worry off her mind."

Wyatt came in just then.

He spotted Julia's and Meredith's still-damp hair and folded his arms. "I heard you saved Carolanne's life today."

"We certainly helped, if only to give the prosecution its day in court." Julia patted the stool beside her, but Wyatt shook his head.

"I'd love coffee, but I'll stand. Too much nervous energy right now to sit. Let me just say this has been the best and quickest forensic case I've ever done. And by far the most exciting ending because the Payroll Inc. board was not only shocked, they went somewhat ballistic to find out that Carolanne had siphoned all that money from their clients. They'll be making quick restitution and are combing files to make sure they haven't missed anything. And they're doubling the agreed-upon fee they were contracted to pay you two," he added. "Without your investigation, she might have gotten away with it. She wasn't running away this weekend out of fear. This was the target date all along, and you two stopped her."

"With your help," said Julia.

"Yes, but you knew to call in the help and to stay low profile. The board is extremely grateful. And so is the prosecution. I was on the phone with the feds, and they wanted you to know they'll be in touch. They also said to thank you."

"But why?" Meredith couldn't wrap her head around Carolanne's reasoning. "Why did Carolanne do it?"

"Two reasons," Wyatt said. "Once they got Carolanne down to the federal office building, the sheriffs brought Holly around. She spewed a whole lot of hate toward her mother. I think that pushed Carolanne to talk, that maybe she finally realized the depth of Holly's problems. It seems Carolanne was against Payroll Inc. going public because she felt that having the control of the company taken out of family hands was a bad decision. Russell did it anyway. He knew he was sick, and he didn't want to risk all they'd done. He knew how she was with Holly. It seems he left Xavier Rahm a note explaining that.

"In her head, if she could just get Holly away from all the negative influences in this country, her beautiful daughter would turn her life around. She'd have restitution for the sale of her company to investors, and she'd have Holly."

"But not Hadley." The reality of that grieved Meredith. And yet, despite all of this, Hadley seemed all right.

"Well, Hadley will benefit well, because Carolanne and Holly will have to rescind their association with Payroll Incorporated, and Hadley will have full control of their stock portfolio. She loses her family but wins financially. Not that she ever had much of a family to begin with." Wyatt checked his watch and moved toward the door. "Gotta go. It's almost time to grab the girls and take them for ice cream. A daddy/daughters date."

"Just like it should be." Julia said the words softly.

"And if it isn't that way"—Wyatt's eyes twinkled Julia's way perhaps not unlike the boy he'd once been—"a fellow is blessed to have the best aunt and grandma in the world step in and make sure he feels all the love he could ever possibly need."

His words made Julia misty eyed. He laughed at that, sent them a thumbs-up, and hurried out the back door.

"You did well, Julia." Maggie Lu followed Wyatt's departure with quiet approval. "He was blessed to have you, and you were blessed to have him. That's how it should be with family. And now I'm going to pass out this cake, because it looks and smells fine! So fine!" She lifted the cake plates Carmen had arranged and set them around the island. Then she raised her glass of tea into the air. "To family, which should always be above fortune."

They raised their mugs in agreement because no matter what life sent their way, faith and family should always rank first.

Chapter Twenty-Eight

2001
Savannah, Georgia

"My first two married, and little Cecily is now a teen-ager." Jubal was frying catfish in a big cast aluminum kettle out behind his house because Tessa was smart enough to refuse admittance to the fish or the grease. "Aunt Dicey, it was a beautiful wedding, wasn't it? And so many fine folks gathering to wish Jared and Marcy a happy day."

"It was beautiful, and an absolute pleasure to see how wonderful your youngsters have turned out, Jubal," she replied. "While some would look at the downturns in our business and lament the changing economy, I just look at the blessing of these faces and I'm at peace. As much as I can be, anyway."

Jubal set the last of the catfish on a newspaper-covered pan. Moments later, Tessa hurried through the back door, lifted the pan, and carried it inside for the large group of people who gathered together for a Southern Sunday meal. "Aunt Dicey, every now and again you get that look in your eye." He pulled up a chair alongside her and leaned forward.

"A sad look, like a little girl lost, and every time I see it, I wonder about it. You're nearing eighty, Aunt Dicey."

"Staring it square in the eye this year," she admitted.

"So what makes that look appear?" he wondered. "If it's none of my business, you can just say so and I won't say another thing about it, but if there's a way of helping, I'd like to do it."

Eighty years old this year.

That meant she'd been sitting on these secrets for over five decades. That was a long time to stay mum about things that probably made no difference anymore. Would he think her foolish?

She saw herself that way from time to time, or maybe cowardly was the better term. "I had a special job back in the war, Jubal."

His right eyebrow shifted up. She didn't have to say which war. So many of her generation and his were by-products of World War II.

"There were twelve of us who were in my class at Charleston. Women," she told him. She could see family moving about inside, filling plates. Laughing. Loving. "Smart, savvy puzzle solvers. Codebreakers."

He'd been sitting kind of hunched over, listening politely, right up until then.

His back went ramrod straight, and those bushy white brows shot up. "Aunt Dicey, you were a codebreaker?"

She flinched, because in all her days no one had openly addressed her wartime tasks like this. "Yes."

"*The dickens you say!*" *Brows still up, he gave her a look of surprise, half-grudging, half-respectful.* "*You broke Nazi code and never breathed a word about it to anyone? Why not? I'd have been shouting it from the rooftops,*" *he extolled, and she could see him doing that very thing.*

"*And Japanese too,*" *she said, then shrugged.* "*I couldn't tell anyone. We were told not to,*" *she explained, but then she half choked on the next words.* "*We were threatened, and so we stayed quiet. Then three of the girls turned up dead. Their deaths sent a cold, hard message to the rest of us: hold your tongue.*"

His mouth dropped open, and he stared at her in disbelief.

Allison had come to the door to call them in. He waved a hand her way. "*We'll be in presently, darlin'. Grab Daddy his notebook, won't you? And a pen.*"

"*I sure will.*" *She came through the door a few moments later and dropped off a large pad of paper and a pen.* "*Here you go. You sure you don't want to eat first? Fish is always better when it's piping hot.*"

"*In just a few,*" *he assured her with that gorgeous smile of his.* "*By and by.*"

She left them, and Jubal picked up the pen. "*You said women died?*"

It grieved her to have to admit this now, but she nodded. "*Several. And was it because they talked? I don't know. But twenty-five percent of the women involved facing an early death doesn't seem like just a coincidence. Some have passed on as old ladies, but those first three were troubling. And Jubal, I didn't dare say anything, not a word, because what if they came after me? After my family? Whoever was involved had no heart. No soul. And clearly no conscience."*

"Why would they do it?" He was jotting down quick notes. "Can you give me names and dates?"

She did.

It was as if now that she'd removed the lid, everything she'd held back for so long came pouring out. Names. Dates. Places. There wasn't a one of them she'd forgotten or messed up, they were that engraved on her being. "But what can you do with this?" she asked him once he'd filled two pages. "What can be done at this late date, Jubal? Nothing, I fear, and that's because I never had the courage to raise a ruckus about it before. It was simply easier to hide myself away at River View and be a piano teacher."

He pondered the pages of information in his hand. Then he faced her straight on. "Maybe nothing. I'm not the problem solver you are, Aunt Dicey, but maybe we can put it all out there for the world to see and let them decide what should be done. Let the collective see if they can figure this out."

She drew her brows together. "I don't understand."

"A book."

She stared at him. "You want me to write a book?"

He nodded. "With me. We can collaborate, we can put things down, we can even fictionalize it if you'd prefer, but it would be your story, Aunt Dicey."

A story of cowardice? A story of shame, brought down on the historic Oglethorpe name? Why would anyone think that was a good idea?

She began to argue, but Jubal put a gentle hand on her arm. "This isn't about you not coming forward. It's about someone threatening American patriots, women who took up the charge they were given to bring down terrorists and tyrants. Women who stood their ground and then were denied the kudos they should have enjoyed so that government officials could reap the credit for the codebreaking. What if—" He hunched forward so that only she could hear should someone come out back. "What if Hoover himself was behind silencing your group? And other groups? From the little that's out about codebreakers, there were pockets of them all over. What if they were all muscled into silence?"

She couldn't believe that.

And yet...

Someone was behind the silencing. Someone had orchestrated the notes and the threats and the fears, and maybe even those deaths. But the head of a government agency?

The thought of that put stark shivers down her spine. Not from cowardice this time but from anger that anyone might abuse their position of power. She put her hand over Jubal's. "Are you of great enough courage to do this with me?"

"I am. I'm only sorry that you've had to live all this time in the shadows of fear. Whatever happened back then should be brought into the open. And if you can give me every detail you can remember," he encouraged her, "we'll see if between us we can make sense of the puzzle and create a story that all of America will want to hear. We'll find out who, if anyone, hurt your friends."

A veil of peace came over her for the first time since she heard of Ginny's demise. A veil that offered the possibility of truth, at long last.

It might not matter to many in the end. Jubal often had a pie-in-the-sky mindset that had to be brought back to earth, but he was a good, solid man of principle and she was grateful to have him by her side. And to finally have the light of day shining on all her questions and doubts.

Would the truth set her free?

Maybe. Maybe not.

But if nothing else, it should be told, and maybe she and Jubal would be the ones to do it.

Chapter Twenty-Nine

DICEY OGLETHORPE STARED AT MEREDITH and Julia in disbelief two weeks later. The St. Patrick's Day celebrations had brought the city great joy this year. With March winding down, it was time to move ahead, but first they wanted to share all they knew with Miss Dicey and Jubal. "Bennington's second wife killed Ginny and Theresa?"

Jubal was sitting at her side. Meredith and Julia had approached him first because they didn't want to push the elderly woman too far.

They needn't have worried. As Meredith slid a picture of Cynthia Converse over to Miss Dicey, Dicey didn't gasp. She growled. "Thea."

"Thea?" Meredith lifted both brows in confusion. "You knew her?"

Miss Dicey shook her head. "I knew who she was. She was staying with Pansy and Coco for the final few months of our time in Northern Virginia. She never hung out with any of us. I saw her rarely, but Coco always said she had an eye for the men, and of course Bennington came to Washington on business now and again and would see Ginny. They'd been quietly engaged for some time, and Ginny often said he was getting anxious to, how shall we say?"

Discomfiture filled her face. "Get on with things? But Ginny held him off until they were married because it was the right thing to do. It seems he found comfort elsewhere."

"I'm afraid you're right, but he didn't give Ginny up," Meredith said. "So maybe he truly loved her. And when Ginny died, Cynthia was smart enough to lie low for several months. She had the baby and didn't say a word until they 'accidentally'"—she made air quotes with her fingers—"ran into each other at a fair where Bennington was speaking. He realized the baby was his and began quietly courting her. The police figure that once Cynthia realized that Theresa was suspicious, she took care of her too. A car that was seen on the scenic road not long after Theresa's probable time of death has been linked back to Cynthia. It belonged to her mother and had been garaged for months after her mother passed away, so it was the perfect vehicle to use."

"Without any corroboration, they couldn't go further," added Julia, "but once we gave them the information from Coco Duboisier and Cynthia's oldest daughter, they were able to put it all together."

"All these years later."

"Sometimes the passage of time allows more things to see the light," said Meredith gently. "Coco wasn't ready to tell her story until she retired, and Adelaide had to deal with her childhood anger before she was ready to address her mother's evil. And that's exactly how she framed it, Miss Dicey." Sympathy thickened Meredith's voice at the thought of Adelaide and her siblings being set aside, mere tokens on a board that had little to do with motherly love. "She said her mother seemed to have no conscience. She lived for herself and herself alone but wanted the image of the doting, wonderful judge's wife and perfect mother. And that's what she got, for a lot of years."

"Unbelievable." Jubal held Miss Dicey's hand. "Aunt Dicey, you've managed to amaze me yet again. At age one hundred and one, you've not only broken code. You've helped solve a crime. That's going into my book. Even if I have to self-publish, I'm going to let everyone know what an amazing and wonderful person you are. And always have been."

"Well, then there's this." Meredith motioned for Julia to hand over the check from the trust account. "Theresa's parents put twenty thousand dollars into a trust as a reward for information about their daughter's death, but with no proof of foul play, no one could claim the reward. It has grown substantially, Miss Dicey, and the trust is being paid to you."

Miss Dicey's hand shook as she eyed the very generous figure before her. "This is impossible."

"It's quite possible and all yours," Julia said.

"Are you certain?" Miss Dicey peered at them over her glasses. "Quite certain?"

"One hundred percent," Meredith assured her, and when she did, Miss Dicey turned to Jubal.

"I have no need of this," she said. "And you don't have a big need of it either, but if we take half for your great-grandchildren's educational fund and half for the costs of restoring River View for the music association, then I see us turning something evil into something of great good. Would that be all right with you, Jubal?"

Jubal kept her hand in his and nodded. "It will be fine, but honestly, Aunt Dicey, you've done for me and mine all my life. We know that restoring River View will take massive funding. I say we donate all the funds to the music association's needs with our family's blessing. If you don't mind, I would like a plaque made, reminding folks of the Oglethorpe name as they come through the entrance. That's enough recognition right there. All my life you taught me that blessings weren't measured in dollars and cents but in love. And you were right."

He leaned over and hugged her gently.

She tried to hug him back, but strength failed her.

Meredith swept a hand to her moist eyes.

Julia did the same. Then they both stood. "We're heading out," said Julia. "And wishing you both the very best."

"Thank you." Jubal stood also. He gripped Julia's hand then Meredith's, and there was nothing of the showman in his honest gaze. Today he was a simple man, showing gratitude. "Thank you both. Very much."

"You are most welcome," Julia said.

The gratitude shining in Miss Dicey's eyes warmed Meredith through and through as they said goodbye.

They crossed the solarium, signed out, and went outside to a fresh new day.

Savannah buzzed with tourists, and shops were teeming with customers.

And one old woman was able to put the past to rest at long last.

Julia hooked a thumb toward the north. "Coffee?"

"You buying?"

Julia laughed. They'd just received the double payout as promised from Payroll Incorporated, including an extra stipend for four new tires. "Sure am."

Meredith laughed too then looped arms with her beloved friend. "Then I'm in. And hey, I'd like to try out the services over at New Beginnings on Sunday. Would that cramp your style?"

"To have my best friend and partner and amazing colleague pray with me?" Julia rolled her eyes. "You can cramp my style that way anytime. If you park around the corner, it's easier to get out," she added. "Folks tend to get stuck talking in the parking lot, planning this, that, or the other thing."

The thought of people gathering together, planning things after a church service, didn't sound just good. It sounded wonderful. Meredith clicked her key fob to unlock the car doors and smiled. "I think the parking lot sounds absolutely perfect. My cup of tea, dear friend. My cup of tea."

Dear Reader,

I had so much fun writing this story, revisiting my friends Julia and Meredith and the gang in Savannah. It's a pleasure to watch these characters develop from story to story, to see the growth but also the ability to change, because we all know that while change isn't always welcome, it's quite often good for us.

So why do we fight it tooth and nail?

And what does tooth and nail even mean???? ☺

Our ladies began this new venture at a crossroads of life. One widowed, one retired, neither one ready to be put to pasture, and I love the chutzpah that takes. To grab the reins and do something different, something independent, to go boldly forward into uncharted territory takes courage, and I love writing women of courage. Meredith, Julia, Carmen, and Maggie Lu are no exception. They listen. That's a rare art, isn't it? And while they like to chat over food, they're just as likely to forget to eat in the busyness of solving the day's problems…but they'll make up for it later and they never forget their coffee!

This book was particularly fun because we get to see the art of forensic accounting, the pitfall of greed, and the far-ranging effect of a narcissist. I have a CPA son in Texas, and when I asked him the best way to hide corporate money, his reply "in plain sight" was crucial and I used it in this story. Lessons of the past inspire both good and bad in the present, so let's pray that history lessons are taught forever. History engages the mind. The insight of the past can guide our plans into the future and avoid a pitfall or two. Not all, of course.

Where's the fun in that? Pitfalls build character.

But using the past to detect the problems in the present is a wonderful skill, one our ladies have sharpened nicely.

Thank you so much for reading *Patterns of Deception*! I hope you enjoyed this newest story and the entire wonderful Savannah Secrets series. Huge thanks to Susan Downs, Ellen Tarver, and the wonderful editors of Guideposts, because without their guidance and expertise, none of this would be possible and I'm so glad it is!

Signed,
Ruthy

About the Author

USA TODAY BESTSELLING AUTHOR RUTH Logan Herne is currently holed up on a pumpkin farm in Western New York with a couple of mini donkeys, three dogs, three cats, one husband, a bunch of grown kids, and a marvelous slew of grandchildren who aren't old enough yet to realize she's not as funny as she thinks she is, but they'll realize that soon enough. Author of nearly sixty novels and novellas, Ruthy is having the time of her life and still has trouble believing that she's getting paid to do a job she'd do for free, if needed…but she does like getting paid! Mostly she likes hearing from readers like you. You can email Ruthy at loganherne@gmail.com (and yes, she answers her own email!) friend her on Facebook, visit her website ruthloganherne.com, or come visit her on Thursdays in the Yankee Belle Café, where she and four other authors chat about the everyday life of being an author, mother, wife, sister, grandmother, etc. We even discuss some of our favorite recipes! We'd love to see you there!

The Truth Behind the Fiction

DECIPHERING CODE IS NOTHING NEW! Throughout history people have been vying for power through all kinds of means, including coded messages via foot messengers in the days of Julius Caesar. Codes were meant to confound enemies, and there are still unbroken codes that may be ridiculously complex or simply ridiculous, a historic coder's way to vex future generations.

The World War II codebreakers were a clever grouping of thousands of women plucked from the ranks of schoolteachers and secretaries, picked for their abilities to undo puzzles, their math skills, and their single status. The government certainly didn't want a lot of loose talk from romantic liaisons to get into the wrong hands, and we all know how women talk! (Insert author's groan here....) The reality of these women's contributions has recently become known; they are in a centuries-old line of codebreakers but probably represent the biggest conglomerate of codebreakers history has ever known. And that brings us to RSA encryption, deliberately designed to be undecipherable to protect the internet, showing that coding and code breaking has followed us throughout history.

But coding isn't always about letters, numbers, placement, and patterns. Sometimes it's simple deception to throw others off the trail and take them down a dead-end path, hence the "red herring" of mysteries and crime. If the pursuer takes the wrong road, the person being pursued has time to flee. A good investigator looks beyond the obvious to find her answers. Nowadays we have spy satellites circling the planet, we have listening devices embedded into systems, and ubiquitous cell phones capture history at almost alarming levels, but nothing beats the intricacy of the human mind, sorting and deciphering not just the facts but the human behind the facts—because the human element is the most fascinating mystery of all.

CUSTARD-FILLED CRUMB CAKE

This amazingly delicious confection has been personally developed, because while Rebecca's neighbor made it to share, she is a woman who is not to be trusted in the recipe-sharing department, if you know what I mean. Crucial ingredients and/or measurements have been known to be altered, so Carmen and Maggie Lu put their heads together and came up with an even better version, although neither woman thought that possible. And here it is!

Ingredients for the cake:

½ cup shortening

¾ cup sugar

1 teaspoon vanilla

3 eggs

2 cups flour

1 teaspoon baking soda

1 teaspoon baking
   powder

1 cup sour cream

Directions:

Line a 9×13-inch pan with a sheet or two of heavy-duty aluminum foil so you can remove the cake from pan easily when done. Grease and flour (or spray and flour) foil.

Mix first four ingredients together until light and fluffy. Sift flour, baking soda, and baking powder together. Alternate adding the flour mixture and the sour cream to the butter mixture, starting and ending with the flour mixture. Stir until each one is almost completely combined before adding the next. Spread batter into pan. Cover with streusel topping. Bake at 350 for about 30 minutes, depending on oven temps. A convection oven bakes it more quickly. Cake is done when a toothpick inserted into center comes out clean or with a few moist crumbs.

Ingredients for Streusel Topping:

1½ cups flour	½ teaspoon cinnamon
⅔ cup white sugar	¾ cup butter, softened
⅓ cup brown sugar	

Directions:

Mix flour, sugars, and cinnamon. (This is a lightly spiced streusel for this particular cake. Maggie Lu knows that most streusels have more brown sugar and cinnamon than this one, but she begs your indulgence because she's been Southern and cooking for a very long time.)

Cut in butter until it's well blended. Carmen uses a pastry blender, but Maggie Lu's been using two knives and crisscrossing them from the time she lived close by the Bessett plantation and she sees no call to fancy things up now. Once mixed into pea-sized pieces, sprinkle over top of cake, then bake as directed.

Old Fashioned Custard Ingredients:

3 tablespoons butter, melted

1¼ cups sugar

½ cup cornstarch minus one
    tablespoon

3 cups milk

3 egg yolks

2 teaspoons of vanilla

Directions:

Melt butter in 3-quart pan. Remove from heat. Mix sugar and cornstarch together. Stir into butter. Whisk in milk and egg yolks. Return to heat at medium to medium-high and heat to boiling, stirring regularly. When mixture boils, set it off heat, whisk in 2 teaspoons of vanilla, cover with plastic wrap (to avoid skin on pudding), and chill completely.

When cool, loosen cake from pan. Using a long bread knife (serrated works best), cut cake in half, separating top from bottom, leaving two thin layers. Set top aside. Pile delicious cold custard onto bottom layer. Then put top layer in place. Take a few long strips of plastic wrap and wrap around sides of cake to keep custard in place while chilling. Cover lightly with plastic wrap and chill.

Serve when thoroughly chilled, with whipped cream or without. It really doesn't need it, but whipped cream adds a measure of fancy that we all appreciate!

This recipe was originally inspired by an old-time cake the author's father used to buy at Sibley's Bakery for Easter morning in Western New York. Recreated specifically for the enjoyment of everyone who loves good food!

Read on for a sneak peek of another exciting book
in the Savannah Secrets series!

The Waving Girl

BY GABRIELLE MEYER

August 1, 1931

My Dear Cousin Lavinia,

Your heartfelt letter, dated July 25, arrived only a few moments ago. Thank you for your kind words regarding our retirement, and thank you even more for inquiring about my life on Elba Island. I miss it more than I thought I would. The fifty years I lived there seem only a dream now as my brother George and I settle into our new home in the Bona Bella neighborhood, just outside of Savannah. I tend to my flowers and George putters around the property, mending broken shutters and fixing a leaking roof, but we are both trying to find our new purpose. Our entire lives were spent tending lighthouses, first at our father's knee and then as we took over at Elba Island. It doesn't seem real that our work is done, but, like all things, there is a season.

It will do my heart good to speak of my life on Elba Island with you, but first, I must tell you that contrary to what you have heard in the newspapers (I'm still amazed and humbled you've heard about me all the way in New York City), my life on the island was quiet and simple. Yes, there were moments of excitement, but they were few and far between. I am honored by the attention I have received from the reporters and the city officials, but I do not deserve any of the accolades. They embarrass me more than you will know. I wish to live a quiet, peaceful life, yet people continue to treat me like a celebrity— all but George, of course. (To him, I will always be his little sister, though I'm now sixty-three years old.) I miss the privacy of the island, but more than that, I miss the purpose I found in waving at all the ships that arrived and departed from the Port of Savannah for the past forty-four years.

No matter the hour, nor the weather, I did not miss a single ship. That much of the story you have heard is true. I was never too ill to extend the arm of hospitality. There were nights, if I did not awake on my own, my faithful dogs would wake me to greet the ships. I would light a lantern and wave them in or out. And oh, how they responded. Foghorns, whistles, and the shouts and cheers from the men on deck would make me feel connected to the great big world, if only for a few moments, and help me to forget how very lonely I was.

You ask why I began to wave at the ships and eventually became known as the Waving Girl, but the truth might very well shock you. Only my brother George knows the real reason, though he will take that story to his grave. To this day,

George will not discuss a word of it. In my utter grief and devastation, I turned to the one place I could pour out my heart, and that was my diary. When I left the lighthouse, George told me I must burn the diary I kept since I was a girl of nineteen, when the waving began. I wanted to leave the past on the island, so I did as he asked, but now I feel as if I have lost a part of my very own soul. It was the only tangible link I had to those days so long ago, and now it is gone. I have felt myself grieving over them more now than I did when they occurred. This grief has compelled me to share the story with you, knowing I can trust you implicitly. The only thing I ask, dear Lavinia, is that you burn these letters after you read them. I do not wish to bring shame or embarrassment upon my family name—nor do I wish to hurt anyone who is connected to the tragedy. Promise me this, and I shall share the whole tale with you. It is a tale of love, loss, and one girl's undying hope.

For now, I will say this one thing, which encapsulates the whole story: I once knew a sailor who was searching for a home. By waving, I hoped to make him, and the thousands of others who wandered the world, feel as if they had found a place to belong in Savannah, Georgia.

I hope and pray my desire was fulfilled.

Yours affectionately,

Florence

April in Savannah was Julia Foley's favorite time of year. Bright pink azaleas and fragrant blue hyacinths bloomed outside the Downhome Diner as she pushed open the restaurant's heavy door, greeted by the smell of fresh coffee and warm blueberry pie. The winter chill was long gone, yet the heat and humidity of summer had not yet visited their fair city. Tourists were filling the crowded streets and wandering through the famous squares, but the rush of spring break visitors had subsided and the peak summer travel had not yet begun.

It was as close to perfection as Savannah could offer.

"Julia!" Meredith Bellefontaine, Julia's dearest friend and partner at Magnolia Investigations, waved from a corner booth where she sat with their friend Maggie Lu. "You're just in time. Clarissa was about to leave with the baby."

Clarissa, Maggie Lu's granddaughter, stood near the booth, an infant car seat swinging in the crook of her elbow. She grinned at Julia and turned the car seat so Julia could have a look at little Jacob Philip. He was only four months old, but his bright brown eyes didn't miss a thing as he stared at Julia.

"Isn't he something?" Maggie Lu asked, shaking her head. "I thank the good Lord I have lived to see my great-grandson come into this world. A real blessing," she said as she squeezed Clarissa's hand. "And he couldn't have a better mama."

"Thank you, Gran," Clarissa said, bending down to kiss her grandmother on the cheek. "But I have to run. I promised Jake's daddy we'd be home before he starts his shift at the precinct."

"It was good to see you," Julia said to Clarissa. "And little Jake."

"Bye, Mama!" Clarissa called to her mother, Charlene, the owner of the Downhome Diner, who was standing behind the long counter, pouring a cup of coffee for one of the customers. "I'll see you for supper."

"Oh, let me come and say goodbye to my grandbaby," Charlene said, setting the coffeepot on the warming plate and scurrying around the counter to kiss Jake goodbye. She also gave Clarissa a quick kiss, and they all waved as she left the diner.

"My, my, my," Maggie Lu said as she pulled her cup of coffee into her hands. "That little boy has captured my heart."

Meredith moved aside so Julia could join them in the booth. They were both still smiling after seeing Jake. "He's a doll," Meredith agreed.

Julia settled into the booth and put her purse beside her. "Sorry I'm late. The meeting at church ran longer than I expected. I'm organizing the youth group trip to the convention in Atlanta at the end of the month, and we've had a few issues with finances." A miscalculation in the books revealed they didn't have all the funds necessary to take thirty-three teenagers by bus and put them up in the hotel for a weekend. "We were brainstorming some fundraising ideas."

"No worries," Meredith said as she took a sip of her coffee. Her short blond hair was curled, as usual, and her pretty blue eyes were shining. "Maggie Lu and I were just catching up—and enjoying that great-grandbaby of hers."

Maggie Lu's eyes glowed as she smiled at Julia. "I know you gals are busy. I sure appreciate finding time to just sit and visit with one another."

Julia loved her time with Meredith and Maggie Lu. Since retiring from her position as a judge in the Chatham County Juvenile Court, she had been running Magnolia Investigations with Meredith, and volunteering with the youth group at New Beginnings Church. She helped plan events, schedule volunteers and chaperones, and organize fundraisers. The work she did for both gave her a sense of purpose, but most importantly, it gave her more time and flexibility to spend with her husband, Beau, than she'd had while serving as a judge. Beau had recently retired as an anesthesiologist, and they were both settling into their new normal. For the most part, Julia and Meredith could set their own hours and enjoy an occasional leisurely meal with their friends at their favorite restaurant in the historic district of Savannah.

The Downhome Diner was a mixture of Southern charm and a fifties retro feel. Warm yellow walls, red vinyl booths and stools, pictures of historic Savannah on the walls, and the best Southern comfort food in town.

"Oh goodness," Meredith said under her breath. "Here comes Beatrice Enterline."

Julia groaned and had to force herself not to let her feelings show on her face. Despite Beatrice's overzealous behavior, she usually meant well.

"Hello, darlings," Beatrice drawled as she breezed into the diner and lifted a perfectly manicured hand to wave at them. "I thought I'd find y'all here." The outfit Beatrice wore today was as loud as the woman herself. At her age, ruffles and bows should have been left far behind, but for some reason, Beatrice felt the need to affect a Southern belle persona, even though she was a transplant to the South. Her pink sundress had a stiff underskirt, creating a hoopskirt look. It was a cross between Scarlett O'Hara and a fifties teenybopper.

"Hello, Beatrice," Meredith said, her patience for the director of the Savannah Historical Society far more refined than Julia's. "Won't you join us?"

"Oh, I wouldn't want to impose," Beatrice said. "I just came to tell y'all the most excitin' news."

Julia pressed her lips together, trying to think of a time Beatrice hadn't imposed upon them.

"What do you have to share, Beatrice?" Maggie Lu asked good-naturedly, always eager to hear the latest bit of news about her beloved Savannah. She knew more about Savannah and its history than anyone else in Julia's acquaintance. Her expertise had been used to help solve mysteries several times in the past year since they'd opened their agency.

"Well, since you asked." Beatrice pushed into the booth next to Maggie Lu, her wide skirts sticking out all around her. She leaned forward, her hazel eyes flashing with excitement. "Regina Terrance just arrived in town! Can you imagine?"

"Regina Terrance?" Julia frowned. The name sounded vaguely familiar, but she couldn't place her. "Why do I know that name?"

"She's just the most amazing author on the planet!" Beatrice rolled her eyes playfully. "She's a *New York Times* bestselling author of half a dozen books, including her breakout narrative nonfiction, *The Bridge to Forgiveness*—it was turned into that movie, do you remember?" She didn't let anyone answer, though Julia did remember the movie. She and Beau had gone to see it in the theater. It was the true story of a prisoner of war who was severely tortured during World War II and had returned to forgive his captors years later. "Ms. Terrance specializes in bringing lesser-known history to light,"

Beatrice continued. "She's the author of the latest tell-all about Florence Martus, the Waving Girl of Savannah."

Julia tried not to groan again. "I've heard rumors there was a scandalous book coming out about the Waving Girl, but I didn't believe it."

"Same here," Meredith said, her voice reflecting her own misgivings. "I've heard it's full of never-before-told stories of Florence's life, though I've also heard most of them aren't true."

"When did this book come out?" Maggie Lu asked, a frown on her face. "This is the first I've heard of it."

"Just this week." Beatrice grinned. "And it's already gaining so much attention, Ms. Terrance will be in Savannah for a few weeks to film a documentary! Can you imagine? I wonder if she'll want to interview me for the film. I am the director of the Savannah Historical Society, after all." Beatrice ran her hand over her dark, pixie-styled haircut. "I'll have to see my hairdresser."

"What else will she be doing in town?" Julia asked.

"I'm not sure." Beatrice shrugged. "But she's holding a press conference later this afternoon at the Bohemian Hotel, and I plan to be there." She pushed herself out of the booth and rearranged her skirts. "Well, I should be off. There's so much I need to do before I mosey on over to the hotel to introduce myself." She wiggled her long fingers again. "Ta-ta for now."

And just as quickly as she arrived, Beatrice was gone.

"Perhaps we should start meeting at a different restaurant," Julia said, turning her coffee cup up on her saucer and smiling at Charlene as she came over with a coffeepot. "That woman always seems to know when we're here."

Charlene grinned as she set her hand on Julia's shoulder and filled her cup with steaming hot coffee. "Maybe she drives around town looking for your car."

"Maybe I should buy a new car." Julia knew her irritation at Beatrice was a bit petty, but the woman was Julia's complete opposite in every way. It was hard for Julia to take her seriously. "Why doesn't she just call the office and leave a message?"

"It wouldn't be nearly as much fun for her to share the latest gossip with us through a message at the office," Meredith said with a chuckle. "She's harmless, Jules."

"I know." Julia took the first sip of coffee and savored the flavor. "But I could handle a little bit less of her attention."

"Now, what was she talking about?" Maggie Lu asked, her eyebrows still scooped in consternation. "Is someone maligning the name of our sweet Waving Girl?"

"I'm not sure," Meredith said. "I've only heard rumors. I haven't read the book myself, but a few people have said it's full of scandals, all revolving around Florence."

"What kind of scandals?" Julia asked. She was familiar with Florence Martus's life, as much as anyone else in Savannah—but there was so little known about her. She had led a quiet life on Elba Island, waving at ships coming into and leaving the Port of Savannah for over four decades, but had died sometime around World War II. People had speculated about her reason for waving for years, but the stories were all legends. No one knew the real reason. Florence had only said she was a lonely girl, trying to bring joy to others when she started.

"The book tells of a torrid love affair, a family murder, and espionage," Meredith said. "And it has gained a lot of publicity already, especially because it's written by Regina Terrance. Her track record of revealing hidden secrets from important people in history has made her very famous."

"Well, I won't be reading it," Maggie Lu said with a decisive nod. "Any book that suggests Florence Martus was involved in those horrible things isn't worth reading."

Julia glanced at Meredith, wondering if any of the rumors could be true. The partners had been involved in several investigations that had revealed hidden secrets from unlikely suspects. Could Florence be guilty of the things the book suggested?

Unfortunately, there was little that surprised Julia anymore.

"I suppose," she said to the ladies, "only time will tell." She smiled at Maggie Lu. "Let's hear what's new in your life."

As Julia settled herself in for a nice, long visit, she couldn't shake the unease she felt about Florence Martus and the new book. Something didn't feel right, and she was curious to know why.

A Note from the Editors

WE HOPE YOU ENJOY THE Savannah Secrets series, created by the Books and Inspirational Media Division of Guideposts, a nonprofit organization that touches millions of lives every day through products and services that inspire, encourage, help you grow in your faith, and celebrate God's love in every aspect of your daily life.

Thank you for making a difference with your purchase of this book, which helps fund our many outreach programs to military personnel, prisons, hospitals, nursing homes, and educational institutions. To learn more, visit GuidepostsFoundation.org.

We also maintain many useful and uplifting online resources. Visit Guideposts.org to read true stories of hope and inspiration, access OurPrayer network, sign up for free newsletters, download free e-books, join our Facebook community, and follow our stimulating blogs.

To learn about other Guideposts publications, including the best-selling devotional *Daily Guideposts*, go to ShopGuideposts.org, call (800) 932-2145, or write to Guideposts, PO Box 5815, Harlan, Iowa 51593.